advance praise for **CRIMSON ORGY**

"An authentically seedy, almost charming tale of zero-budget horror moviemaking morphs cleverly into a genuine splatterfest in Williams' unnervingly enjoyable debut... wholly convincing, escalating crises and all... horror film buffs should be delighted and chilled in equal measure."
—*Publishers Weekly*

"First-time novelists are told to write what they know and it so happens that a talented tyro named Austin Williams is an expert on 1960s gore films, from the anything-for-a-buck producers and $50-a-day-plus-car-fare actors to the sleazy storylines and gruesome special effects. *Crimson Orgy* is the rare book that you seem to be watching rather than reading, because it's so visual that it will remind you of those bloody horror films that played at the drive-in forty years ago, only with more intelligence and intentional humor."
—Danny Peary, author of *Cult Movies* and *Guide for the Film Fanatic*

"Real good stuff and a fascinating look at the exploitation film industry... the tension builds as we move toward the conclusion... it's a book that will leave you twitching uncomfortably when you finish."
—Don D'Ammassa, author of *Narcissus* and *Dead of Winter*

"Austin Williams' novel is not merely a sleazy grindhouse movie replayed; *Crimson Orgy* uses the lowest of the low budget cinema as a platform from which to shape an engaging tale of human greed, fallibility and darkness with prose that invokes Jim Thompson's relentlessness, Elmore Leonard's offbeat humor, and Ramsey Campbell's atmosphere. And yet, Williams' greatest strength is the creation of verisimilitude; after the final page, readers may well be longing to see this fictitious film."
— Daniel R. Robichaud, *Horror Reader*

"Fans of urban legends, splatter cinema, and sharp tools will want to get it on with *Crimson Orgy*. Austin Williams' debut novel pays respect to the cinematic trail blazed by H.G. Lewis—with sex, storms, and suspense."
—Rod Lott, *Bookgasm*

more...

D0951836

"Every once in a while, not very often, a book comes along that not only is a great horror novel, but also one that revels in the history of the field. Austin Williams is a new name in fiction, but he is right on target with *Crimson Orgy*. This is classic material for savvy horror fans and I give it my highest recommendation."
—Mark Sieber, *Horror Drive-In*

"A rambunctious homage to the not-so-halcyon days of no-budget exploitation filmmaking of the 1960s, told with a dry wit and a moralist's eye. Gene and Shel are great characters, and their swan song to the gore film genre is a cautionary fable for archeologists of the most obscure grindhouse fare who persist in believing that less always means more."
—John McCarty, author of *Bullets Over Hollywood*, *Splatter Movies* and *The Fearmakers*

"A ripping, tearing, cutting tale about the filming of a cult classic, and very much deserving of that status in its own right!"
—Curt Purcell, *Beyond the Groovy Age of Horror*

"*Crimson Orgy* is an entertaining read that accurately represents the exploitation film business in all its blood-soaked glory. Williams conjures up such cinematic exploits and unexpectedness well, and the story is well-paced. The characters each have distinct voices."
—Alyse Wax, *BlogCritics* and *SporkFashion*

"I give *Crimson Orgy* a 5 out of 5. Anyone with an interest in the way classic grindhouse style movies were filmed will enjoy this book."
—Mark "Red Hawk" Carpenter, *Happy Horror*

CRIMSON ORGY

AUSTIN WILLIAMS

Borderlands Press

All rights reserved. Published in the United States
by Borderlands Press.
www.borderlandspress.com

www.crimsonorgy.com

Library of Congress Cataloging-in-Publication Data

Williams, Austin [date]
Crimson Orgy by Austin Williams - 1st ed.

p. cm.

ISBN 978-1-880325-81-0

1. Exploitation cinema—fiction. 2. Florida,
United States—fiction. 3. Pop culture—fiction.
4. Horror—fiction. 5. Crime—fiction. I. Title

10 9 8 7 6 5 4 3 2 1

Manufactured in the United States of America
First Edition

CRIMSON
ORGY

"The chief enemy of creativity is 'good taste'."
- Pablo Picasso

"The dark side of human nature is a gold mine."
- Gene Hoffman

PROLOGUE

Excerpted from *The Ultimate Guide to Horror Movies*
Ed. Patrick Hooper
Silver Bullet Press, 1986, (2nd ed.), New York

Horror fans across the world have long coveted a print of Sheldon Meyer's infamous "lost" cult classic, *Crimson Orgy* (Stupendous Pictures, 1965). Shot entirely over the course of a single week, this ultra-low budget bloodbath is considered by many to be the holy grail of gore. Meyer directed only one horror movie in his entire career but its notoriety earned him a prime berth in the annals of the genre. Though his colleague in the Miami-based exploitation boom of the early '60s, Herschell Gordon Lewis, deservedly claims credit as the de facto inventor of the splatter film, (see chapter 2), many cultists find Meyer's work to be richer in tone and subtext than the frequently primitive offerings of the more prolific Lewis.

The intense fascination with *Crimson Orgy* began before the production even wrapped, when a member of the crew died of mysterious circumstances on the final night of shooting. The incident was attributed to a freak accident by local police in the tiny town of Hillsboro Beach, Florida, where much of the film was shot. But many in the Miami film community suspected a more sinister truth, that a gruesome death had been intentionally staged for the camera.

Encouraged by his producing partner, Gene Hoffman, to see the project through, Meyer reportedly suffered a massive nervous breakdown shortly after completing the final edit. He went into seclusion, taking the original 16mm negative with him. Despite a lengthy search that involved the hiring of at least one private investigator, Hoffman was never able to locate his director or his film.

For almost two decades, the only known evidence of *Crimson Orgy* was a series of outtakes and test footage totaling roughly ten minutes. These grainy, unedited sequences display a level of bloodthirsty ferocity that actually surpass the excesses of later splatter milestones such as *The Wizard of Gore* (H.G. Lewis, 1970,) *The Last House on the Left* (Wes Craven, 1972,) and *Cannibal Holocaust* (Ruggero Deodato, 1979).

Crimson Orgy was never released theatrically, but its legend was firmly rooted among horror enthusiasts coast to coast. With the advent of the VCR in the late 1970s, bootleg copies of a 76-minute cut, all of invariably poor quality, began appearing at fan conventions and memorabilia auctions. The first of these popped up at Splatterfest IV in Houston in 1982 and was widely duplicated for distribution by a private collector in Seattle. None of the original prints were ever located, and the level of completion of the 76-minute cut has been broadly debated.

Viewers who have seen *Crimson Orgy* come away with differing opinions as to the quality of the film, and the merit of its attendant legend. Some see just another largely inept piece of mid-'60s exploitation cinema, albeit one more stomach-churning than most of its kind. Others see a masterpiece of visceral horror that presages the "violent chic" adopted by mainstream Hollywood fare in subsequent decades. Even without the mystery behind its making, one could credibly argue that Meyer's film may well have attained the cult status it enjoys to this day.

Was *Crimson Orgy* the first snuff film in the course of American cinema, intentional or otherwise? Historians will probably never have a definitive answer. It's believed only two people were present on the set at the time of the "accident" and their lips are sealed.

Gene Hoffman died of a heart attack in the summer of 1973.

On August 8th, 1980, fifteen years to the day after wrapping the movie that made him famous, Sheldon Meyer took his own life with a shotgun.

MONDAY

Red lights flashed on the sand. Followed by blue. Red, blue, red, blue. The colors looked great but the pattern wasn't right. The beams of light should have been intersecting each other, one moving in a clockwise rotation and the other coming up to meet it from the opposite side. Instead, both red and blue were making circles in the same direction. First one, and then the other. It looked totally fake. A laughably bogus facsimile of a police car's emergency lights, reflected onto the nighttime beach.

Meyer was still bitter about not having an actual patrol car in the scene. Deputy Platt promised two weeks ago he'd be able to produce one. At least for an hour or so, long enough to pull off a master shot. The car was to be supplied gratis, like just about everything else on this miniscule production. There was only one condition, one so predictable Meyer said yes before the deputy finished asking the question. Sure, he could be in the movie. They needed a cop for the beach scene, anyway. Just having him stand there would save them the hassle of rustling up a police uniform. And the additional hassle of finding another slack-jawed resident of this backwater burg willing to stick around all night as an unpaid extra.

Mutual compromise: that's the only way to shoot a feature film for less than twenty grand.

It seemed like a fair deal all around. Everyone was happy. Until this morning, when Deputy Platt dropped by *Crimson Orgy*'s production office (room 217 of the Sand Palace Motel) and added a new clause to his verbal contract. He was no longer satisfied to just be *in* the shot. He wanted lines.

As in plural.

No lines, no patrol car.

Though he'd vaguely sensed it coming, Meyer flinched at this last-minute demand. It was barely past 8:00 when the deputy came calling, using his nightstick to pound on the door like it was a raid. Meyer had already been up for three hours, mapping out the day's shoot with producer Gene Hoffman over a pot of rancid coffee and a pack of Chesterfields.

Hoffman answered the door with a brisk, "Top of the morning, Sheriff. Coffee?"

Sitting at a card table they'd brought as a desk, Meyer couldn't help smiling. Hoffman had a rule for dealing with cops: always bump them up a rank. He knew damn well Sonny Platt wasn't the sheriff. There *was* no sheriff in the town of Hillsboro Beach, as they had discovered during their scouting trip two weeks ago.

Sheriff Fred Cates, based ninety miles away in that simmering bastion of civilization called Miami, was the big daddy in charge of Dade County proper. Meyer wondered if Sheriff Cates had ever set foot here in the far,

13

far reaches of his jurisdiction. What could have been the incentive? Within the 3.2-mile radius of Hillsboro Beach (pop. 347, mushrooming to 800 during the winter peak) the law started and stopped at the deputy's desk. And here he was, banging on the door with a ludicrous but predictable demand.

Deputy Platt didn't bother to correct Hoffman's mis-identification of his rank. He just laid it on the line in plain language. If they wanted a cruiser, he wanted a speaking part. He had better things to do than waste a whole night standing like a mute on the beach.

Meyer couldn't possibly imagine what those things might be. Calling Hillsboro Beach a sleepy little town would be an insult to sleep. It was more like a kudzu-covered morgue, snugly sandwiched between the Atlantic on the east and Intercoastal Waterway on the west. No man's land. Not too many beasts around either, if you didn't count the hordes of ravenous insects that asserted aerial dominance the minute the sun went down.

Sweating in the doorway, Hoffman caved instantly to the deputy's ultimatum. Meyer shook his head in anguish. Sure, it was the smart move if you were look-ing at the big picture. Which, to be fair, was Hoffman's job. Given Deputy Platt's status in these parts, it clearly wouldn't pay to give him a case of the red ass. They had seven full shooting days left. Still, Meyer would like to have seen his producer put up a show of resistance. For appearances, if nothing else.

Bidding the "sheriff" good day and reminding him to be ready to roll by sundown, Hoffman closed the door. He returned to his seat on the couch, which was deeply indented with the circumference of his gargantuan back-side. Dark ovals of perspiration stained his shirt under each arm, gaining width. Hoffman habitually lamented that his blood was too thick for Florida.

As disappointment took root, Meyer clutched his head tightly. A migraine was sending out its first feelers, promising a future invasion. This was going to be a very long week.

"So it goes," Hoffman said breezily. He resumed leafing through a stack of glossy 8 x 10 head shots. "Can't blame the local gentry for seeking a bit of the limelight."

"Disaster," Meyer moaned. "Sheer disaster."

"Bah. We'll figure out a way to make it work."

"I was envisioning a real economy of narrative for the scene. Almost like a silent, like *Nosferatu*. We talked about it on the drive down."

Hoffman made a soft grunting noise to communicate his empathy. He'd already accepted the situation and had mentally moved on.

Meyer was still clinging to his original hopes. He held his hands before his face to frame an imaginary shot. A battered copy of *Crimson Orgy*'s script sat on the sofa, but Meyer didn't need to reference it in order to map out the scene.

"We open on the two kids necking on the beach. Ace Spade approaches from the shadows. Shatters the boy's skull with a hammer. The girl screams. We cut to Frank and Hannah strolling down the beach. They hear the scream. Frank runs to check it out. Cut back to Ace burying a meat cleaver in the girl's belly. He opens her up and out come the intestines. He plays with them a little. Pins his calling card on the girl's dress and scurries off. Frank finds the girl's body. Gags. Notices the card. Pockets the card and goes to find a cop. Fade out."

Hoffman grunted again. "I like it. Simple. Classic." He was still pretty absorbed with rifling through the 8 x 10s in his huge meaty hands. Aspiring starlets, all of them. Bright eyes, eager smiles, creamy complexions. Each prettier than the last.

"It's perfect is what it is," Meyer continued. "Self-contained and beautiful. Plus we don't have to worry about sound, for a change. The wind can raise a hell of a racket out there after dark."

"I'm in total agreement, Shelly. It was a good, solid approach to the scene."

"Blown to hell because some bucktoothed law man thinks he's star material." Meyer dug a fresh Chesterfield from the pack on the card table and lit it furiously.

"You'll find a way to make it work," Hoffman repeated. "Remember when you rewrote the sponge bath scene for *Dirty Nurses* on the spot? Hell, it played better than the original."

"It would be nice to stick to the script. Just once, for the novelty."

"More interesting this way," Hoffman said. "Keeps the process fresh." He flipped to the next head shot and whistled appreciatively. "Well, what have we here?"

He held up the glossy for Meyer to see. A dark-eyed brunette wearing heavy mascara and a pout.

"Not bad," Meyer conceded.

Hoffman nodded. "I think she'd be perfect for the disembowelment scene, don't you?"

Later that afternoon, while Hoffman drove him to the set, Meyer sat in the passenger seat with a legal pad on his lap, conjuring some new dialogue. He was still anguished. Here they were on the first day of shooting and already they were being fucked with. The Deputy's strong-armed approach really left a foul taste in his mouth. It made him curse yet again the forces beyond his control that made it necessary to shoot *Crimson Orgy* in this pathetic anthill of a town. Instead of in Miami, where the veneer of professionalism might at times be maintained.

Well, he thought, *no point dwelling on that now.*

Hillsboro Beach had been Hoffman's call all the way.

16

Its proximity to Miami made timely film drops at the lab feasible, while still being remote enough to ensure privacy. And the town boasted only one bar, the Angler's Rest, which limited the possibilities of a drunk and unwieldy crew. This was especially important when it came to the movie's male lead, Vance Cogburn, who could sniff out a saloon within a hundred-yard radius and be counted on to knock back a fifth of bourbon and at least one cocktail waitress nightly, given half a chance.

Meyer's ballpoint pen skittered across the pad, futilely trying to stay within the lines. Hoffman seemed to deliberately seek out every pothole and gully in the winding two-lane road. The Ford Fairlane, a rental from the Hertz desk at the Miami airport, was pushing 70. Speed tended to make Meyer nervous, most acutely when he was not behind the wheel. Residual memories of an auto wreck he'd barely survived as a child sometimes yanked him out of sleep with a choked scream. Less often, they came over him when he was wide awake. The sickening lurch of his father's Packard sliding across a stretch of black ice on a frigid Illinois night. His mother's keening wail. Her head stuck in the spiderglass windshield.

And her blood.

Covering him.

Stop. Don't want to think about that, either.

The rented Ford chugged onward. A moss-covered telephone pole flew past Meyer's window in a blur. Bobby Darin was belting out a sappy doo-wop song on the radio. Insects of all shapes and size were meeting grim fates against the oncoming rush of the Fairlane's grille. Slowly, achingly, a fresh idea took hold in his mind.

Maybe he could turn the deputy's character into a savage satire of all the thick-necked, beer-bloated authority figures he'd met while preparing *Crimson Orgy*. First the patrolman they'd had the bad luck to encounter when grabbing a roadside shot on State Highway A1A.

Then the manager of the Sand Palace, who seriously jacked their room rates when he figured out what they were up to in room 217. On and on, culminating with the detested Deputy Platt.

All those good ole boys had nodded just a little too slowly when agreeing to whatever request Meyer presented. It was the basest kind of power trip, one he suspected held a whiff of anti-Semitism. "Sure, you can shoot your moving picture on our property, city boy," they'd all said. Promptly followed by the requisite shakedown. In 1965, the idea of gaining a permit to film a B-movie in some rural stretch of South Florida was unheard of. All you did was shell out a handful of cabbage to the local boss man and go get your shot.

They'd almost uniformly called him "city boy" but Meyer heard "Jew boy" in each lazy drawl. It stung, even though he knew it was at least partly the creation of his own imagination. When he casually floated this theory to Hoffman, his partner dismissed it as insupportable paranoia. Meyer knew he was right, but was also aware of Hoffman's enviable talent for blotting out anything that didn't support his view of the world.

Gene Hoffman made it a point of pride that he internalized absolutely nothing. He walked the earth with a kind of buoyant confidence that bordered on sociopathic. His 6'3", 350-pound frame may have had something to do with it, but it ran deeper than that. Self-loathing, or even basic doubt, would have taken far too much introspection for Gene. He never understood Meyer's crippling bouts with insecurity, but he made a game effort to put up with them.

Shel Meyer, for his part, couldn't stop spinning stories in his head. Asleep or awake, the wheels never slowed down. That was his greatest asset as a filmmaker, and his greatest weakness as a human being. Always assigning myriad meanings and interpretations to the simplest events. Reading between the lines when there weren't any lines to begin with. As long as he could channel that mental combustion into outward creation, Shel was OK. He needed a project at all times, and this morning Deputy Platt gave him a good one. Here was his chance at artistic retribution against each and every one of these bigoted provincial pigs.

The inclusion of an ignorant hick cop would serve the movie in more ways than one. First, the satirical angle. The drive-in teenyboppers wouldn't pick up on it, but if there was any way of convincing a legitimate film critic to take a peek at *Crimson Orgy...* Meyer dismissed the thought before allowing himself to complete it. Laughable. Screw the intelligentsia. They didn't pay to see movies, at least not the kind Stupendous Pictures made.

Back to the hick cop. A secondary function of this character would be to make their leading man a little sharper, by comparison. Vance Cogburn was a bartender at Augie's in Coral Gables who Hoffman insisted upon casting as the heroic protagonist, "FRANK BUTLER." Meyer suspected it was a payoff for some sort of unsavory transaction involving one of Augie's cocktail waitresses, but he didn't put up much of a fight. The kid definitely had the right look. Nice tan, two rows of even white teeth, a pompadour that floated over his forehead like it was filled with helium. Nonetheless, Meyer harbored deep concerns about Vance's ability to perform credibly for the camera. Tonight would tell the tale.

Fueled by his ripe enthusiasm, Meyer's pen lurched across the page as Hoffman plunged the front end into another pothole.

"Try to hit every one while you're at it."

Gene chucked a cigarette butt out the window and floored it. He did what he could not to smile, but it was a passable effort at best.

"Just keep writing, Shakespeare. We'll be there in a few minutes."

Flipping to a fresh page, Meyer continued to flesh out the scene. He deliberately used monosyllabic words as much as possible for the new dialogue. He hoped the lantern-jawed Deputy wasn't too thick to see this as a jab at his intelligence.

```
EXT. BEACH — NIGHT

TAMMY's body lies on the sand. Her stomach torn open,
blood and guts everywhere. FRANK kneels beside her,
examining the PLAYING CARD that's safety-pinned to
her dress.

A COP walks into the frame.

                    COP
          Hey! Who are you, pal?


                    FRANK
          I'm the guy who called
          for the police. Took
          you long enough to get
          here.


                    COP
          What do you know about
          this?


                    FRANK
          Nothing. I was taking
          a stroll with my girl.
          We heard a scream and
          followed the sound. She
          was lying here like this
          when we got here.


                    COP
          Where's your girl now?
```

                    FRANK
          I told her to wait by
          the car. She's got a
          weak stomach.

The cop looks down at Tammy's body.

                    COP
          This is the work of a
          sick maniac.

                    FRANK
          Brilliant deduction. Is
          that what they teach you
          at the academy?

                    COP
          Say, buster. I don't like
          your tone!

                    FRANK
          Sorry, officer. I guess I'm
          just a little rattled.

The cop shines his flashlight onto Tammy's blood-
splattered dress. CLOSE-UP of the playing card.

                    COP
          What's that?

                    FRANK
          I was wondering the same
          thing. Looks like the
          Ace of Spades.

                    COP
          Think it might be a
          clue?

                    FRANK
               (sarcastic)
          Well, you're the policeman.

Without hitting the brakes, Hoffman banged a hard left onto a dirt road almost entirely obscured by tall wavy grass. Meyer slammed up against the door, jabbing himself in the hand with the tip of his pen.

"For Christ's sake, Gene!"

Hoffman just chuckled. Unlike his partner, he loved being out here in the sticks. Everything about it. The briny tang lacing the air, the faraway cry of the gulls, and especially the utter freedom when it came to driving. As a boy, Hoffman had dreamed of a career as a stock car racer. A growth spurt shortly after his eighth birthday canceled out that ambition. He was wearing his father's old shoes by the time he was ten and had hair on his chest the next year. So much for stock cars.

These days, the closest Gene could come to that lost boyhood dream was to bomb around these South Florida sticks with a rented Ford Fairlane and a terrified director in the passenger seat. When they were back in Miami, Meyer refused to let Hoffman drive him anywhere. Here in the wilds of Hillsboro Beach, in the midst of a grueling round-the-clock production schedule, he had no choice but to put his personal safety in jeopardy. The show must go on.

The Ford bounced due east along what was really no more than a dune buggy path. In the rearview mirror, the sun was a blinding orange blur. Hoffman adjusted it so he could concentrate on the wheel. Thick sawgrass marshes began to loom taller than a man on each side of the path. After another fifty yards they were totally engulfed. Reeds and cattails tapped and scraped against the windows like living things trying to prevent the car's escape. Meyer took note of the effect. It might work, not in *Crimson Orgy* but maybe in a future project.

Then the Ford shot out of the writhing passage and all that lay before the bug-dotted windshield was a vast empty beach. Beyond, the blue patience of the Atlantic.

Hoffman parked at the top of the dunes, afraid to risk going any further onto the sand. As he killed the engine the two men sat there for a moment, listening to the breakers. Meyer was pleased to see the rest of the crew had already arrived. All three of them. A pair of pickup trucks sat by the water's edge. A white van was parked nearby, and two guys in tank-tops were hauling some lighting equipment out onto the sand.

"Looks like the boys are catching the fever. They're as excited as we are."

Hoffman snorted softly. "I wouldn't bank on it."

"Why not? They're on set ahead of schedule. It's not like they're getting a piece of the gross."

"They've been here all day, Shelly. I sprang for a few sixers of beer and told 'em they might as well enjoy the surf."

Meyer shot him a disapproving look.

Hoffman shrugged. "They had nothing to do until we start shooting. Why make them sit on their hands all day? A happy crew's a productive crew."

"What about a sloshed crew?"

"Relax. It's cheaper than feeding 'em."

True enough. Serving a crew meal more substantial than a bag of potato chips would have sunk their budget. The three-man team had busted its collective hump over the past few days, getting everything ready for the shoot. They'd earned some R & R. Meyer didn't begrudge them the day off. He was just reluctant to let go of the notion that they'd arrived early at the beach out of sheer desire to bring *Crimson Orgy* to life. The kind of desire he felt, even if he didn't entirely understand.

Shel got out of the car. He took off his brown tassel loafers and held them under his arm as he trudged across the sand toward the crew. It took Hoffman a good deal longer to make the trek. His tree-trunk legs sank into the sand ankle-deep with each plodding step. By the time he got there, Meyer was ensconced in his role as director. Setting up the Mitchell rack-over camera on its rickety tripod, supervising the placement of lights, barking out orders in his good natured way. Their trusty portable generator (fondly nicknamed "The Jenny") was pumping out enough power to light a sizable portion of beach.

After another twenty minutes, shooting was ready to commence. All they needed were some people to put in front of the camera.

The sun was gone by now, but still painting the sky a dreamy pink and purple melange. A breeze, one that simply pushed the hot air around instead of cooling it off, had risen. It sent little flares of sand into everyone's face. Meyer screamed at Cliff the Grip to keep the bonnet tightly secured over the Mitchell. Ricky was hard at work stirring a ten-gallon drum of fake blood with a large wooden spoon. They had learned painfully that the blood (a combination of cornstarch, red dye #12, and Kaopectate) would set into a hard paste if left to sit still for more than a few minutes. The actress who got doused in last week's color test shredded herself with steel wool trying to get the sticky gore off her skin.

Just as Hoffman was impatiently glancing at his watch for the umpteenth time, he made out a collection of figures emerge through the curtain of tall grass above the dunes. What a relief. Tonight's performers had decided to show up. When you can't afford to pay the cast with anything except praise, you never know for sure until it's showtime.

Vance Cogburn led the way, followed by two local teenagers who'd been brought onboard earlier in the week. Then came Jerry Cooke, who carried perhaps the film's most challenging role: the psycho killer, "ACE SPADE." It was truly inspired casting. Jerry was small and wiry, a bundle of skittish energy perpetually wrapped in a shabby black business suit, no matter what the weather or the occasion might be. It was his costume for the movie.

Jerry was understandably thrilled when Meyer offered him such a plum role. With his wild mop of dark curls and funereal pallor no amount of Florida sunshine could enliven, he made certain members of the crew a little uneasy with how well he fit the part.

Bringing up the rear was Deputy Sonny Platt.

On foot.

Meyer shot Hoffman an alarmed glance. The producer waved a placating hand and said, "I'll handle it. Prep the talent." Then he started jogging across the beach to meet the deputy, his heavy frame swaying from side to side.

Meyer greeted his four actors by the camera and went through a perfunctory explanation of what was to come. He kept glancing at the discussion between Hoffman and the deputy that grew more heated in the distance. When Hoffman threw up both hands in a "Why me, Lord?" gesture, Meyer knew they were screwed. His producer only reacted thus when a problem was deemed insurmountable. Wearing a toothy scowl, Hoffman led the deputy across the sand to join the rest of the crew.

Gene pulled Meyer aside and gave it to him straight: there would be no patrol car. An outdoor polka festival was taking place in nearby Pompano Beach. Platt was compelled to send two of his black and whites over to serve as backup in case the revelry got out of hand. That left the Hillsboro Beach Police Department with a single cruiser, which obviously couldn't be wasted here.

Meyer and Hoffman both smelled bullshit, but there was little they could do except take the deputy at his word. They were royally hosed. Night had fallen, no chance of recasting the policeman's role. Hoffman suggested he could stand in, make it a plainclothes cop. Meyer rejected the idea. Gene had already been tapped for another scene. His face wouldn't be visible, but Meyer was worried some keen audience members might recognize the producer's fleshy, pear-shaped body.

They would have to just bend over and let Deputy Platt have his way with them. The show must go on.

* * * * * * *

Crimson Orgy marked the sixteenth piece of filmed entertainment to come out of Stupendous Pictures. It was the most ambitious to date in terms of budget, narrative scope, and the audience it hoped to reach. If pressed, both of Stupendous's cofounders would admit what this movie really was: a shameless attempt to cash in on the gore film phenomenon that took over the drive-in circuit when Herschell Gordon Lewis's *Blood Feast* took everyone by surprise two years ago.

For about a decade starting in the early 1950s, Miami enjoyed a minor heyday as the "other Hollywood." Low-budget filmmakers flocked to the city for two reasons. The first was the same that drew their predecessors to Southern California forty years earlier: the climate. Advertising execs based in New York and Chicago liked to use South Florida as their winter retreat. A few of the more enterprising individuals figured they could make some easy money while on vacation, and have a few grins at the same time. Why not scour the beach for aspiring models who weren't especially shy in front of a camera and put together a low-budget flick? The first crew to act on that whim stumbled onto a highly profitable cottage industry.

The secondary attraction to Miami was its sheer distance from Hollywood, measured in more than miles. For the most part, the Florida movie crowd had absolutely no ambition of making it in the mainstream of the industry. Being on the fringe had its advantages.

Namely freedom, in terms of what they could shoot, how they could market it, and how to cut profit-sharing agreements with exhibitors. None of the rules by which legitimate studios abided had any currency in this tiny corner of the showbiz world.

These were exploitation pictures, some of the cheapest ever made. The critics didn't review them. The Academy took no notice. None of the major talent agencies came calling. And that's exactly how the tight little circle of Miami moguls liked it. They saw themselves as outlaws, the rustic cousins of the global filmmaking family. Too coarse and frankly too weird to sit at the big table, and they were not the least bit interested in gaining respectability.

Let Hollywood have its tinsel. Miami had a corner on sleaze. The grindhouses and drive-in theaters dotting every town in America thrived on the 16mm dreck oozing out of Miami like lava from a perennially active volcano. And for the first two decades of its existence, cinematic exploitation translated as sex.

Like everyone else on the Miami scene, Gene Hoffman and Sheldon Meyer got their start with a string of so-called "nudie cuties." A trend born in the late '40s, these racy featurettes managed to avoid the censor's knife with the use of some dexterous advertising. Billed as either hygienic educational shorts or nature films, they were nothing but pure exploitation to the core. A half-dozen production teams in Miami churned out scads of nudies per year, shipping them onto the B-theater circuit to substantial profit.

Stupendous Pictures joined the game in 1957. Gene Hoffman and Shel Meyer each ponied up half of the initial $8,000 needed to produce *Tawdry Tina's Big Night*, their first six-reel nudie. Hoffman produced, Meyer directed, and the two shared writing duties. *Tawdry Tina's* script was completed in a single evening with the help of some pep pills and a fifth of good Scotch. Meyer did most of the writing, Hoffman did most of the practical questioning.

"Tina" and her costars were cast during late-night missions to the Cottontail Club in South Beach. Shooting required all of two days, most of which took place in Gene Hoffman's swank art deco apartment building on Collins Avenue. Four prints were sent on the drive-in circuit: starting in the South, then rotating out to the Midwest. By the end of its run, *Tawdry Tina* had quadrupled its makers' investment. They were putting the finishing touches on their next picture when the tattered reels returned home.

One year and a handful of flicks later, Stupendous Pictures was an unqualified (if virtually unknown) success. Its output varied in quality only by degrees. Some were almost inspired, the majority barely endurable except by the most hormonally-addled members of the audience. But they all made money. At the outset of 1959, Stupendous's offices moved out of Hoffman's apartment and into a high-rise on Ocean Drive. It almost began to look like a professional outfit.

And that's when the first cracks in the partnership began to appear.

Shel Meyer made it clear during a Friday afternoon development meeting that they should spend a little more time and money on future projects. A failed novelist, he still clung to some vague notions of storytelling as a noble art form.

Gene Hoffman was constrained by no such concerns. Reeling the saps into the seats was his only objective. An avowed student of P.T. Barnum and William Castle, Hoffman understood the nature of ballyhoo. It was based on a trio of marketing entities that acted in consort: the title, the poster, and the trailer. If you put together a package that contained all three, you had a moneymaker.

In a series of increasingly rancorous debates, Meyer did all he could to insert some authorial touches within the rigid confines of the genre. The way he saw it, making a movie took a hell of a lot of time and effort, so why not use the storytelling device to make a point that went beyond mere entertainment?

"Sure, I can give you eighteen tits in seventy minutes," he would say when pitching a plot to Gene. "But why can't I put all that tit in a story that actually *says* something?"

"Say whatever you want, Shelly. Just make sure you can do it on 9,000 feet of raw stock, because that's all you got."

Meyer always delivered on that mandate, which is why Hoffman kept working with him. The partnership was so successful that neither man wanted to see it dissolve, no matter how severe their differences. A principled exploitation filmmaker is a contradiction in terms, as Hoffman liked to say. But as long as things remained on schedule and under budget, he could afford to let his director have some ideals.

Thus *Dirty Nurses* was more than a wall-to-wall series of sponge bath scenes. It was the cautionary tale of an arrogant brain surgeon whose chronic womanizing leads to his downfall and humiliation. *Bambi's Birthday Suit* was about a girl so traumatized by her repressive Catholic school background that on her eighteenth birthday she sheds her schoolgirl uniform to go forward into womanhood just as God made her. *The Libidinous Ones* centered around a group of neglected (though amazingly busty) suburban housewives who shrug off their inhibitions and launch a full-frontal public nudity campaign to reclaim their absentee husbands from the bowling alley and golf course.

(Toward the end of the 1970s, when a group of Parisian film students devoted an entire semester to studying the subtext of Sheldon Meyer's *oeuvre*, they hit upon a central theme: liberation through catharsis. Shel himself would have never dreamt of verbalizing his intent with such inflated language, though he would have been deeply flattered by the analysis. As for Hoffman, he probably would've felt grossly insulted by such a highbrow appraisal of the pictures bearing his stamp. "I make crap," as he liked to say, "but my crap always gives the ticket buyer his money's worth.")

As 1961 drew to a close, Stupendous Pictures saw the first clouds forming on the horizon. At least five other Miami-based production teams were keeping pace with their output. The market got dangerously crowded. Box office revenues slumped as the audience grew jaded. Blurry, handheld close-ups of rosy erect nipples and big bushy vaginas no longer packed them in like they did before. A new taboo needed to be breached if the exploitation racket was going to survive.

It happened in the summer of 1962, with *Blood Feast*.

Herschell Gordon Lewis and his producing partner, David F. Friedman, were no strangers to Miami exploitation. A former carney, Friedman had been one of the founding fathers of the underground film movement. Lewis was a straight-laced Chicago ad man who reluctantly got into the nudie game several years earlier. In hindsight, the moviemaking duo was labeled as nearly clairvoyant. They felt the winds of change blowing before anyone else, and they reacted with a radical shift away from the nudie format.

Blood Feast had its debut at Peoria's Imperial drive-in on July 9th. A sweltering, sticky night. Hot rods and convertibles filling every space of the dirt parking lot. Rowdy hooting and catcalls, kids running from one car to another. Friday night in middle America, straight out of Norman Rockwell. The audience doubtless was expecting a typical monster-on-the-loose potboiler, complete with wholesome teenagers, clueless authority figures, a man in a rubber suit.

What they got was something quite different.

"Nothing so appalling in the annals of horror!" the poster shrieked and, for once, there was some truth behind the ballyhoo. This was new territory, almost an entirely new medium. Storyline bordered on nonexistent. Just a series of disjointed shots, with no attempt made at generating suspense through conventional means. Endless stretches of tedium peppered with the worst acting and production value imaginable.

Then, the money shot. The screen ran red, and the drive-in fell utterly silent. But not for long.

By the end of the second reel, the balmy night air was alive with cries of outrage, shock, and horrified delight. A dozen cars peeled off the premises, sending up clouds of dry clay in disgust. A handful of furious patrons bull-rushed the box office, demanding a refund. But the vast majority sat riveted in their T-Birds and Mustangs. Necking slowed to a crawl. The concession stand stood deserted, packed with popcorn and weenies rendered indigestible by the happenings onscreen. People simply could not believe what they were seeing.

This wasn't entertainment. This was sick. And they couldn't get enough of it. The following night, a mile-long traffic jam stretched outward from the Imperial's entrance.

By the time a year passed, *Blood Feast* had played in forty-two cities with no signs of slowing down. In a brilliant promotional coup, Friedman printed the movie's logo on a million barf bags and shipped them to every venue running the film for ushers to hand out. The *Los Angeles Times* denounced Herschell Gordon Lewis's demented little home movie as "a blot on the American film industry." The revenue it generated, upwards of two million and counting, proved to anyone paying attention that in the world of exploitation, the nudie was yesterday's news.

There was a new bully on the block, named GORE. Tits and ass no longer ruled the inner city grindhouses, college theaters, and tattered outdoor screens of small town America. The real money was to be made in the gratuitous exhibition of *internal* body parts. Brains seeping through bits of shattered skull, intestines skewered, tongues ripped out of gaping mouths, livers limply hanging, eyeballs punctured and shishkabobbed. The taboo thrill of the gore flicks seemed oddly akin to that provided by the nudies: the human form presented in a way you knew you almost certainly shouldn't be looking at. A widescreen dose of anatomical peek-a-boo, in ultra-vibrant color.

Shel Meyer and Gene Hoffman went to see *Blood Feast* at the Rialto Theater in downtown Tampa. Pandemonium reigned. Many in the audience started shouting at the screen just prior to the gore scenes. They had clearly seen the movie before and were coming back for a second or third time.

Elbowing their way out of the theater in a slightly dazed state, Meyer and Hoffman wondered if they should reconsider their upcoming production slate. They decided to wait and see if this was just a fluke or something more.

The answer came quickly. Aside from repeat ticket sales, Hoffman noticed another key way in which the format created by *Blood Feast* differed from the nudies: the makeup of the audience. Gore seemed to be a true crossover medium. The droves of customers shelling out their money to see filmed eviscerations were comprised as much of women as men. Especially in the more rural regions of the country, *Blood Feast* turned out to be the ultimate date movie.

The math wasn't too tricky to calculate: twice the audience than even the most feverishly promoted nudie could ever hope to garner. Meyer and Hoffman reached an undeniable conclusion about the state of their industry.

Skin was out.

Blood was in.

They needed to get a piece of that action.

First, they needed a story. Nothing complicated. Just a basic narrative device allowing them to showcase four or five repulsively gruesome murders. That was all Gene Hoffman wanted. Shel Meyer agreed, but he was quick to note that simplicity didn't necessarily mean one-dimensionality. A lot could happen under the surface.

An idea had been brewing in his head for some time. He'd never spoken of it to Gene, didn't fully understand it himself. It actually made him a little uneasy to think about. But when the micro-moguls of Stupendous finally decided to make a gore movie of their own, Meyer knew he could use this vehicle to really get something out of his system.

He saw an opportunity to deliver a piece of filmmaking beyond what a populace already exposed to *Blood Feast* might expect. Oh, he would give the audience an eyeful. But the impact would be deeper than just visceral. This cheap little movie of his was going to be a statement. More than that. An indictment, written in the blood and entrails of a half-dozen pinup models.

TUESDAY (A.M.)

Barbara stretched out on a lounge chair, sunning herself. When she first lay down a little while ago, she could vaguely sense Cliff the Grip's gaze poring over every inch of her. Neither flattered nor discomfited by the attention, her awareness of it died quickly. As the sun, already scorching at this early hour, manufactured small beads of sweat along her brow and upper lip, she became lost to everything else around her. The sound of Cliff's soft grunting several feet away, the occasional rattle of a passing automobile, the hum of a vacuum cleaner canvassing a carpet somewhere on the Sand Palace's first floor... all of this dissolved in the intense splash of radiance across her skin.

She'd felt a bit guilty when deciding to spend the morning poolside. Her original intention was to devote at least an hour to running lines with Shel Meyer. It wasn't her idea, but when Shel suggested it she was happy to oblige. Even a bit relieved. Barbara knew it was in everyone's interest, especially her own, to log as much rehearsal time as possible before the cameras rolled.

Today was her first shooting day. Ever. It caused a mild panic attack when Meyer told her they were only able to shoot two takes for each setup, given their extremely tight budget for film stock. He would attempt to get everything done in a single take as often as possible. Her call time wasn't until noon, so maybe she'd be willing to spend a few hours getting the lines nailed cold? She was.

That plan got kiboshed when Shel woke her at 7:30 with a frantic phone call from room 217, all of three doors away. He couldn't make the rehearsal due to an emergency creative meeting with Gene Hoffman. "These things happen in the heat of battle, kid, you'll get used to it." Barbara thought he could've just as easily conveyed this information at 9:00, the time when they had scheduled to meet. But since the director was awake and hard at work, why should anyone else be allowed to sleep in?

Shel urged her to practice the lines alone. Not the same as interacting with another person, but time well spent nonetheless. (Keelhauling her costar Vance into a rehearsal was out of the question; the hard-drinking beefcake bartender rarely rose before 10:00 and wasn't worth much until noon.) Hanging up before saying the words Meyer wanted to hear, Barbara rolled over and was back asleep in less than a minute.

Waking an hour later, she resolved to follow her director's mandate. She had a job to perform, no matter how strange it felt. The whole situation still felt slightly alien. She'd hoped once they arrived at Hillsboro Beach and started shooting, this enterprise and her participation in it would take on a semblance of normalcy.

No such luck.

Twenty-two-year-old Barbara Cheston had landed *Crimson Orgy*'s leading female role in an act of faith that didn't make much sense to her. She was the beneficiary of something Sheldon Meyer felt deeply, but had a hard time verbalizing. Even after a meandering conversation over martinis at the Coconut Grove in South Beach, Barbara still had no clear grasp of his reasoning. All she knew was that Meyer felt convinced he'd found the ideal girl to play "KELLY DUNHILL," cub reporter for the *Sarasota Sentinel* who launches an investigation into some unsolved murders tearing apart a remote beach town.

Barbara's acting experience was precisely nil. Everyone else in the cast seemed to at least harbor some ambition of a career in movies. What they lacked in experience they were more than willing to overcome with scenery-chewing zeal.

So why had Barbara been hired, despite a lack of interest almost as glaring as her lack of experience? She'd given up trying to wring a coherent explanation out of Shel Meyer.

Gene Hoffman, at least, was refreshingly candid: "The camera eats you up, doll. In this racket, that's half the battle."

Maybe so, but there was no shortage of beautiful girls in Miami who would have employed any number of dubious tactics to land a leading role. In light of her recalcitrance (Meyer practically got down on his knees and begged her, in the end) why was she chosen?

None of it made sense, yet here she was. On the verge of stardom, as Gene kept reminding her until she told him to can it. Comments like that unsettled her. And they were hard to take seriously, in light of where this production was being housed.

Built in the late '40s, the Sand Palace was indicative of many cheap and dirty rest stops that popped up along

A1A to support the massive flow of tourists the highway ushered into South Florida. U-shaped, two floors stretching around a courtyard dotted with sun chairs, umbrellas and a kidney-shaped pool, the motel was aptly named in one regard: it sat right on the beach.

Unlike other fleabags situated on more desirable stretches of the coast, the Sand Palace hadn't seen full occupancy since a March weekend in '55, when a mapless group of vacationing churchgoers from Boston mistakenly assumed Hillsboro Beach was within walking distance of downtown Miami. Since that glorious three day peak, the Sand Palace had fallen on grim times.

The day Hoffman first checked it out, not one of the sixteen rooms was occupied. Hardly surprising, given the conditions. Decades of exposure to wind and rain had fostered deep cracks in many walls. The thin metal bannister leading to the second floor looked sure to snap under moderate pressure. Constant baking under the sun had warped the walkway to funhouse levels of irregularity. Even during the high season, it was unlikely this dump ever came close to capacity. Now, smack in the middle of a typically brutal Floridian summer, its deserted status seemed a foregone conclusion.

In spite of the Sand Palace's many shortcomings, Hoffman found it an ideal location. Within footsteps were long stretches of secluded beach where nudity and bloodletting could be captured without intrusion from uninvited gawkers. Ernest, the potbellied manager, let the crew have full run of the place, providing they didn't make a mess or disturb any confused motorists who might check in, God willing. Hoffman assured Barbara she'd recall the Sand Palace fondly as the launching pad of her mondo career in flicks. She knew he was trying to be supportive, but it had the opposite effect, making her feel like she bore too much responsibility for *Crimson Orgy*'s success.

So with a grim sense of obligation, Barbara set about practicing today's lines. Lying on the lumpy bed, she tried hard to keep her eyed locked on the pages. Despite her best efforts, she couldn't help noticing the sunlight blocked by the gauze curtains of 214's window was growing more intense. The room brightened by miniscule but undeniable degrees.

By the time the bedside clock read 9:30, the curtains had lost the battle. And so had she. The room was brilliantly lit from outside and Barbara's will lay in tatters. She flung the script aside and dug into her drawer for a bikini. A few minutes later she was stretched out by the pool, infinitely happier with life.

Cliff the Grip had watched her descend from the second floor. Whenever she was within sight, Cliff found it tremendously taxing to look at anything *but* Barbara. He was out here trying to solve a technical dilemma from last night's shoot. Rather than slave away in his van parked in front of the motel, he'd brought the necessary items to the pool with the now-redeemed hope of catching a glimpse of Miss Cheston.

A wooden pole, some flood lights, and a pulley were on the ground in front of him. Cliff was not optimistic about his ability to create anything spectacular with these materials.

When Deputy Platt showed up last night without the pledged patrol car, Meyer was apoplectic. Then he began looking for a solution. Cliff quietly volunteered one. His van was equipped with an impressive array of gear for such a micro-budgeted shoot. Most of it was left over from the commercial jobs that were Cliff's bread and butter. He'd learned how to use the bare minimum required for each of the ad gigs and saved the rest. Cliff did commercials strictly for the dough; his true loyalty lay with Stupendous Pictures and he kept himself free whenever he was needed by his two favorite employers.

Last night, he'd once again proved his worth by coming up with a solution to the patrol car crisis. Cliff proposed rigging a pair of 500-watt lights to the end of a six-foot pole and driving the pole into the sand. He'd cover one light with a red gel and the other with a blue gel, and when the cameras rolled he'd spin the pole around. If placed just outside the frame, this rig might create a believable impression of a cruiser's rotating cherry tops. Along with Deputy Platt standing there in his uniform and some siren sound effects added later, the colored lights just might do the trick.

Gene Hoffman threw an arm around Cliff, loudly congratulating the trusty grip and promising a lobster dinner as reward for such ingenuity. Shel Meyer agreed, and Cliff was greatly relieved to be set free of Hoffman's clutch so he could go about the task of actualizing his brainstorm.

The rest of the night had been highly unpleasant, with a foul mood permeating the set. Deputy Platt proved worse on camera than anyone could have imagined. "Wooden" was far too lively a description of his body language, and he was incapable of delivering a single line without running into some kind of snag. Not that it mattered; the night wind howled so fiercely, any chance of capturing usable audio was rendered impossible. All the dialogue would have to be looped when they got back to Miami. Since Meyer never wanted the scene to have dialogue in the first place, this was particularly vexing.

There was also a regrettable situation with the tub of pig's intestines brought out for the shot of the girl with her belly torn open, but Cliff wouldn't allow himself to even think about that. Maybe not for a long time.

Typically, he blamed everything on himself. What an idiotic idea he'd had with the headlights rig! Cliff felt physically ill for having let Mr. Meyer down. No amount of cheerful talk from Mr. Hoffman could lift his gloom.

Neither of his employers knew the soft-spoken Key Grip suffered from intense bouts of manic depression, one of them severe enough to land him in a sanitarium for nine months as a teenager.

By the time they wrapped and got back to the motel, Cliff knew he wouldn't sleep a wink. He needed to figure out a way to improve the rig. The thought of screwing up again panicked him, sending ripples of tension all throughout his muscled frame. And that was what brought him down to the pool when he had every right to be crashed out in room 113, which he shared with his co-crewmen Ricky and Juan.

Barbara's sudden appearance provided a blessed distraction. Only to replace it with something much worse. Cliff was totally captive to her presence, his stomach clutched in a spasm of happy misery that is the hallmark emotion of the lovelorn. Was it possible she was as perfect as she looked?

As if in answer, Barbara rolled over onto her stomach in a single fluid move. She undid her bikini top. The straps fell from each side of the chair, dangling a few inches from the pebbly ground. Her honey-blonde hair fanned out across her back and she languidly brushed it across her neck so it wouldn't get between the sun and her skin. She lay with her head nestled in the intersection of her crossed arms.

Facing Cliff, her eyes were serenely closed. One small foot rested on the heel of the other, five pink-painted toes stretching into a splay and then snugly curling. Cliff suppressed a small whimper. He'd completely tuned out his reason for being here. All memory of last night's debacle drifted from his mind. His sole focus lay in imagining what it would be like to be reincarnated as the wicker chair supporting Barbara's golden body.

Lost in his hallucination, he didn't notice she'd opened her eyes and was directing their icy blueness at him.

40

"Does this pose work for you, Cliff, or should I try something else?"

He froze, aghast.

Barbara laughed at his stricken expression. But her laugh was gentle, without malice. "It's OK. If I'm not used to being looked at by now, I'm in trouble."

Speech gradually returned to Cliff's sphere of command. "I'm sorry, Miss Cheston. No excuse for being rude."

"Apology accepted. I'm gonna get pretty upset if you keep calling me that."

"Sorry. Barbara." It didn't feel right coming out of his mouth. They were virtual strangers. But she'd already warned him to drop the formality.

"Whatcha working on there?"

Cliff was startled by the coils of rope in his hands. It took him a few seconds to remember their purpose.

"Oh. Just trying to fix this rig. Mr. Meyer says it looked faker than heck last night."

"How late were you guys out?"

"'Til about 3:00. Sun was almost up when we got back."

Barbara whistled. "You should be taking a day off."

"No such thing, once we start rolling. It's nonstop 'til Sunday night."

"Man. You guys are troopers."

Cliff shrugged, embarrassed by even such an oblique compliment. He smoothed his Fuller Brush mustache and tried to change the subject. "Big day, huh?"

Barbara turned over again. It seemed to Cliff he'd said something to break her relaxation and his gut twitched with remorse. She leaned forward with a sly grin, as if to impart a secret.

"Tell you the truth, I'm a little nervous. I should be studying my lines but I just can't do it anymore. After a while it starts sounding like a bunch of nonsense."

Cliff looked down. "You'll do great. Just probably some butterflies is all."

"I guess. I'm starting to think Sheldon's not such a great writer. Some of the things he has me saying are so *stupid*."

Cliff froze again. He was taken aback by this flagrant criticism of his employer. If anyone else had made such a remark he would have rudely rebuked them. But this was Barbara, his faraway Barbara, interacting with him so candidly.

"Mr. Meyer knows what he's doing."

"I'll take your word on that. I've never actually seen any of his work."

"Oh, you wouldn't be interested in the pictures he's made so far. They're sort of..." Cliff tried to think of the term Mr. Hoffman used to describe the nudies to potentially offended exhibitors. It finally came to him. "They have what you might call a selective appeal."

Barbara smirked ever so slightly. "Right, selective. As in, horny guys who like looking at beaver. You OK, Cliff?"

He was fine, despite almost choking on his tongue. The color of his face would have shamed the lobsters served at Finney's Seafood Hut down the road at A1A and Seabreeze Lane.

"Anyway, this picture's gonna be different," Cliff continued manfully. "Mr. Meyer and Mr. Hoffman are calling it a blockbuster in the making."

"Have you read the script?"

"Nah. It's not really part of my job."

"That makes two of us. I'm only allowed to read one scene at a time. I have no idea what the story's about."

"Mr. Meyer probably doesn't want you to get overwhelmed your first time out."

He said it a little too quickly. It sounded like a line that had been coached, and it was.

"Yeah," Barbara replied after a measured pause. She turned over to lie on her stomach again, breaking the visual connection. "That's what he told me, too."

There seemed to be a sense of finality to her words. Cliff was relieved. It was the most involved exchange he'd had with her so far, and for the most part he felt it had gone pretty smoothly.

* * * * * * *

The Angler's Rest looked like an outhouse, but at least it didn't smell like one as long as the front door was propped open. That was Vance's observation as he drained his third bourbon and slid the glass across the bar for a refill. Here, not even 11:00 A.M. yet, sat *Crimson Orgy*'s leading man, grabbing a few eye-openers while everyone else was preparing for a long day of shooting.

Fortunately, Vance's assessment of the bar was not openly stated but silently bounced around his head in competition with a half-dozen other thoughts vying for supremacy. Never an overly curious fellow, Vance's frame of concentration narrowed even tighter when he was drinking. With each beverage the number of contending thoughts shrank until only two general categories remained: food and sex. This morning, his mind was turning inexorably toward a late breakfast.

To be fair, the Angler's Rest didn't look much like an outhouse. Except for the fact that it was a wood-framed, one-story shack, cheaply made and likely to blow away in the face of a Category 2 tropical storm. How it had stood its ground for so long (since 1932, according to a smudged bronze plaque behind the bar) was a mystifying question. Cementing the outhouse association in Vance's mind was the crescent-shaped window carved into the front door. He'd noticed it when entering the bar for the first time, about a half-hour ago.

He shouldn't be here right now. When Vance signed his contract with Stupendous Pictures, he'd been amused to see an addendum stapled to the back of the paperwork, guaranteeing he would remain sober during shooting hours. Gene Hoffman assured Vance it was a mere formality extended to all-non union actors, but this was later proven to be the bullshit it sounded like at the time. Apparently his reputation preceded him.

Vance really didn't care. This whole project was just a lark, a chance to get out of town for a week and have a few grins. Who knew what it might lead to? If more parts came of it, great. If not, it would make a funny story for the fellas and ample cannon fodder for the broads.

Vance had considered an acting career, vaguely and without any real passion, since high school. It was hard *not* to consider, in light of how frequently he was asked if he'd ever been in the movies.

It was his look, that's what did it. Vance was handsome in a kind of plastic, blow-dried way that was tailor made for mindless drive-in entertainment of the late '50s and early '60s. The chin. The tan. The pompadour. It was all just begging to be filmed and projected larger than life. He had a nice deep baritone too, and his eight years as a lifeguard gave him the kind of rangy, sculpted frame that would sell plenty of popcorn in Des Moines.

So the movie star gig was something Vance mulled over from time to time, in between drinking, volleyball, and recreational cocksmanship. Ever since taking the bartending job at Augie's, he'd been propositioned almost nonstop. The legitimacy of these offers ran from respectable stabs at bit roles to outright solicitation, but Vance didn't give any of them much thought until Gene Hoffman said he could have the lead in a feature if he wanted it.

Hoffman had been a fixture at Augie's long before Vance started working there and he was liked by the entire staff. There was a certain no-bullshit heft about him that Vance respected. The guy was clearly no pole-smoker. Vance knew Gene's offer was above the board. He accepted on the spot, before even clearing the required week-long hiatus with his boss.

That's how Vance operated. On the spot, in the moment, damn the consequences.

Which is exactly how he found himself in the Angler's Rest, catching a pretty good buzz only an hour before he was due in front of the cameras. This was an overt breach of his contract. Part of him almost felt bad about it, but that feeling evaporated with the first swallow of Kentucky bourbon. The sweet taste of home. A Louisville boy who'd migrated to Miami in search of a more varied field of conquest, Vance remained stubbornly old-fashioned in certain essential customs. In a decade or so, maybe less, these were going to catch up with him in the form of crow's feet, exploded capillaries, a perpetual beer tan. But at this stage in life Vance wasn't worried about it. He wasn't worried about much.

With a yawn he wearily massaged his prominent temples. What the hell, last night had been brutal. Standing out there on the beach until damn near sunup. Spitting out the same stilted lines over and over. Dealing with Shel Meyer's shrill fussing over the most miniscule of details.

Vance didn't have much use for his director. In fact, if he'd had a chance to meet Meyer beforehand, he might easily have walked away. The man was impossible. A bundle of needy agitation, like some of the chicks Vance had known. Come to think of it, Meyer sort of carried himself like a girl. He ran like one, with his hands held perpendicular to his scrawny torso. It didn't seem likely he swished, not by the way he would perpetually drool and fawn over Barbara, but he was definitely halfway there.

45

With a few solid hours of acting under his belt, Vance concluded it had been a stone drag thus far. Of last night's many little dramas, none was more troubling than his run-in with that joke of a cop. He and Deputy Platt rubbed each other wrong from the word go. What began as a bit of good-natured ribbing turned nasty quick. Vance resorted to openly mocking the deputy after he'd screwed up three takes in a row.

Hoffman intervened just before the first punch was thrown. He yanked Vance aside, hard, to remind him Platt was the law around here no matter how ridiculous that might seem. Vance agreed to put a cork in the wisecracks, but he and Platt still plainly despised each other.

He knew it wasn't over. If the dumb cracker ever felt like putting the badge away, they could settle it as men. Vance hoped it would happen. At least he told himself he did.

With that thought chewing at his peace of mind, Vance took a hit off the fresh drink that appeared before him. Today's fourth, a dangerous number when you're on doubles. His eyes did a lazy lap around the bar in search of something interesting, but little had changed since he first walked in. The same pair of gnarled old fishermen still occupied the corner, speaking to one another in low mumbles. Probably telling lies they'd both heard a thousand times. The same rusted oyster tongs were hung from the ceiling, above an incredibly fake-looking marlin mounted on the far wall. A darkened juke occupied the corner, so covered with dust it appeared not to have been used for years. The floor was a bed of sawdust and peanut shells.

Painfully bored, Vance returned his focus to Sherry, the barmaid. A faded matron in a loud floral dress, looking like she'd washed ashore with the morning tide. Her graying blonde hair fell in uneven hanks, thickly matted in places as if plastered with wet sand. Lashes long and sharp enough to harpoon a dolphin jutted from above and below her tired eyes. A clown's red grimace was painted onto her lips. She seemed to be mocking her natural beauty, which was still evident if on the wane, by dolling herself up with such garish recklessness.

Vance had tried to strike up a conversation with Sherry when he sat down. No harm in getting on friendly terms with the proprietress of the only saloon within a manageable drive. But she was having none of his smarmy small talk. Her reticence, bordering on hostility, intrigued Vance. Few were the women who could stave off his high-wattage charm, especially if he chose to apply it with any vigor. Whenever he came across a resistant specimen, he unconsciously found himself paying far closer attention to her than to the phalanxes of all-too-easily-smitten lovelies who seemed to float his way even when he had no use for them.

Vance's eyes pored over every inch of the dilapidated barmaid, alert for any small hint as to the source of her distance. She wasn't a dyke, he was pretty sure of that. Something about her inept attempts at glamour (the lashes, the war paint, the dress worn tight over her bountiful breasts) indicated a certain interest in looking good for whatever salty crew comprised the Anger's Rest regulars. But if that was the case, why wasn't she offering herself up on the bar with tearful thanks to the gods of love for sending such a strapping young swain as Vance Cogburn through her front door? So far, she'd exhibited nothing close to gratitude for his presence.

This was troubling to Vance. Despite three attempts at playful innuendo, Sherry remained as inscrutable as the Atlantic that crashed against the continent just across the highway.

"How warm's the water around here?" he asked when he thought he caught her stealing a sidelong glance.

47

Sherry shrugged though the smoke of her cigarette. "Don't swim."

"Really. What do you do to keep that sweet bod in gear?"

"I usually beat the shit out of some silly drunk."

The way she said it, it didn't sound like a joke. Not a threat, either, of course. That would have been ridiculous. But there was no humor in her voice.

"Can't argue with the results, mama," Vance said before crushing his double in a pair of massive gulps.

He decided not to order another. Who needed this hag and her frustrations? He had a movie to make. Stardom to attain. Checking his gold-plated wristwatch, he saw he was due on set in roughly a half-hour. Time to bolt. They were probably already looking for him, and if he didn't skedaddle soon someone would think to check the Angler's Rest. It would *not do* to be found here.

Pushing himself away from the bar, he issued a terse wave to Sherry (who did not return it) and made his way to the crescent-windowed door.

Stepping outside, the bright morning heat hit him like an uppercut. Taking a moment to let his eyes adjust, he cursed himself for leaving his sunglasses in the motel room.

Vance half expected an ass-chewing by Shel Meyer when he returned to the set. Not that it mattered. The prospect of being bawled out by Gene Hoffman was more unsettling, but Vance figured he could handle even that. He had surprised everyone, including himself, with how good he was in front of the camera.

Vance overheard Hoffman using this fact to needle Shel Meyer when they fell into a constrained argument last night. That was a revealing bit of eavesdropping. It told him clearly he'd not been Meyer's first choice for the role of "FRANK BUTLER." Vance wasn't resentful but nor was he too concerned about pissing off the uptight director. On the other hand, it would be suicide to alienate Hoffman, his one true ally on the production.

Climbing behind the wheel of his battered '58 Impala, Vance decided he needed a new ride. That's what he would do with the check he got for his next role, which would be exponentially bigger than what he was making to appear in *Crimson Orgy*. When you start so close to zero, the only way to go is up. Or so Hoffman kept telling him.

Vance threw it in reverse and fishtailed out of the bar's dusty parking lot. He bid the Angler's Rest good riddance, though he knew he'd be back soon enough. Probably after tonight's wrap. Turning right onto the highway, he floored it.

The Impala's needle climbed to 80 and didn't let up. There was no need to rush, really. It was just kind of fun hauling ass out here in the middle of nowhere. Free as a bird. Vance's watch read 11:42. Plenty of time to make it back to the Sand Palace, gargle some mouthwash, and join the rest of the crew by the pool at noon. He was feeling great.

He was feeling so great it started to worry him.

Tightening his grip on the wheel, Vance regretted downing that last drink with such abandon. It was like injecting four ounces of Wild Turkey straight into his cerebral cortex. He could put back the sauce with the best of them, but he was just a man. And there was no denying he was lit up right now.

Taking a quick inventory, he assured himself it would not be noticeable. No bloodshot eyes staring back at him from the rearview mirror. His equilibrium felt respectable. Slurring seemed unlikely. Just to make sure, he started loudly voicing his lines from last night's scene. After two passes, he felt pretty confident in the clarity of his diction. But he was having so much fun, he kept on bellowing the cheesy dialogue with his right foot heavily planted on the accelerator. What the hell, an actor's supposed to rehearse, isn't he?

"Nothing!" Vance boomed over the engine's roar. "I was taking a stroll with my girl! We heard a scream and followed the sound! She was lying here like this when we got here!"

Vance was so absorbed with the oration he didn't even hear the siren until the patrol car was riding right up on his rear fender. Then he heard it just as loud as you please.

No, he thought, *it can't be.*

But there it was. The cherry tops that had been so desperately absent on the beach last night were in his rearview. He could clearly distinguish the pockmarked face of Deputy Platt behind the wheel. The man appeared to be grinning, though it was hard to tell with the sun blazing into the windshield.

Unbelievable. Of all the shit luck!

Cursing weakly, Vance started to edge his car toward the shoulder. Slowing down, he couldn't accept what was happening. Something inside wouldn't let him. Just as he was almost off the highway, he roughly veered back into the lane and hit the gas.

An automatic gut reaction, not a rational decision, it only enraged the deputy. Vance's head jolted back violently as the patrol car rammed his fender.

Jesus, you'd think I knocked over a bank, Vance thought before realizing he'd done something far worse. He'd humiliated the wrong hick. And Gene Hoffman wasn't around to pull his bacon from the fire this time.

The Sand Palace stood less than two miles away. The crew was there waiting for Vance, waiting to make him a star. He'd been feeling so good just seconds ago. The air itself was intensely ripe with promise. It didn't seem possible the day could take such a radical turn for the worse so fast.

After another quarter mile, Lance grimly hit the brakes and brought the Impala to a rest on the shoulder. No need to go through this in front of everyone.

He sat there, sweating, letting the engine idle. It suddenly seemed like the entire car reeked of bourbon. Reaching into his pants pocket, Vance realized with a jolt he didn't have his wallet with him. It was sitting on the night stand in his room, next to his sunglasses. Grabbing a handful of bills and leaving everything else in the motel felt like a brilliant decision an hour ago. Now it only compounded a nightmare.

Hearing a car door slam behind him, Vance couldn't help glancing in the rearview. He saw Deputy Platt loping forward with menacingly casual strides. The grin was undeniable. It had stretched into a leer of vaguely porcine delight.

Then the deputy was at his window, rapping a set of pink, hairy knuckles against it. Vance noticed his other hand was coiled tightly around a nightstick the size of a rolled-up newspaper. Its wooden surface, painted a dull black, was covered with small nicks and dents probably won off the skulls of countless fools who'd made the mistake of raising the deputy's ire.

A louder tap shook the window, rendered by the nightstick. Vance turned slowly to face him.

This was the same slit-eyed country jake who had seemed like such an inferior creature within *Crimson Orgy*'s power structure just hours before. The man Vance had openly mocked. The man who called him a "city slicker" with a mouthful of backwoods hate.

The man who was now in a position to seriously fuck Vance up.

51

TUESDAY (P.M.)

EXT. BEACH — NIGHT

Sun goes down over the horizon. ACE parks his dune buggy in front of his shack. Lifts a heavy BURLAP SACK from the passenger seat.

The sack is stained with GORE that SEEPS through the cloth.

A bloody DRILL BIT pokes out from a hole. ACE throws the sack over his shoulder and steps out of frame.

INT. SHACK — CONTINUOUS

ACE sets the sack down on a large construction table. Unties it.

CLOSE-UP of BETTY's corpse.

BLOOD AND BRAINS oozing from the side of her head, covering her shoulders. The DRILL buried in her ear.

Ace picks up two heavy WOODEN BEAMS and starts nailing them together.

DISSOLVE TO:

An 8-foot CROSS leans next to the table. Ace is using a paint brush to add some LETTERING to a piece of plywood. He nails it to the top of the cross.

ACE puts the cross flat on the floor and lays BETTY on top of it. He grabs a handful of rusty NAILS from an empty paint can.

FADE OUT: to the sound of HAMMERING.

FADE IN: EXT. SOUTH FLORIDA COUNTRY CLUB — DAY

A dozen people stand by the front entrance. Rich, gentrified WASPs: seersuckers on the men, floral hats on the ladies.

They are REACTING with HORROR to something outside the frame. A woman FAINTS and another man GAGS.

REVERSE ANGLE:

BETTY is crucified next to the Country Club's front door. GORE pours from her head wound, also from her wrists and ankles.

TILT UP to the SIGN at the top of the cross, reading: "Ever thus to bigots."

A POLICE CAR pulls into frame from the B.G. COP gets out and breaks up the crowd.

                    COP
          OK, what seems to be the trouble?
               (he turns, sees Betty)
          Oh, dear God!!!

COP runs to be sick in a trash can. He regains his composure and

A knock on the door startled Meyer just as he felt the scene was starting to cook. He ignored the interruption. But he couldn't continue typing until he was sure. His fingers hovered above the keys, hoping whoever stood outside 217's door might think the room was empty.

Craning his neck, Shel looked over toward the window. Judging from the pale light behind the curtains, it was approaching sundown. He wanted to get in a nap before shooting resumed tonight. They'd broken an hour ago and Shel returned to his room tired but satisfied. He only intended to spend a few minutes at the typewriter, but a half-hour had passed and he was just getting worked up.

The moment his fingers gingerly lowered onto the keys, another knock rattled the door.

"Who is it?" Meyer barked.

"Gene. Open up."

Meyer pushed himself away from the night stand he had converted to a writing desk. With the bedside lamp and alarm clock removed, there was just enough room for his trusty Underwood Model #7.

He unlocked the door for Hoffman. They exchanged mechanical greetings. Gene walked to the night stand and began reading the fresh page clutched in the Underwood's embrace. An infuriating habit of his, reviewing Meyer's work while it was still in the earliest stages of completion.

"Just a little fine tuning," Meyer said defensively. "I've decided we should see Ace starting the crucifixion, rather than open on the shot of her nailed to the cross. It'll raise every hair in the theater if we fade out on the sound of hammering."

Hoffman didn't offer any reaction, not even a grunt.

54

Meyer pressed onward. "Then we dissolve to some horrified onlookers at the country club. Hold on that for a little longer than necessary, the suspense will be murder. Then, ka-pow! We hit 'em with the beauty shot."

Hoffman sat heavily on the sofa and lit a cigarette. He still hadn't said a word, which alarmed Meyer. Usually Gene's feedback, whether praise or excoriation, came fast and without prompting. Silence was the most disturbing reaction of all.

"Won't take more than an hour to shoot the scene of him making the cross," Meyer soldiered on. "One master setup and maybe three inserts. I think it's worth it. It'll have one hell of a disturbing effect."

"What's with the country club?" Hoffman asked.

"It's an improvement, don't you think?"

"Shel... come on. The girl's supposed to be crucified in front of her parents' house. We got clearance for the location, we got the two extras we need. What the hell are you doing moving the scene to a country club?"

"Think it through, Gene. Think about the *context*. Why is Ace Spade killing these girls? What's he protesting against?"

Hoffman let out a long exhalation through his nostrils, producing a reedy whistle.

"He's protesting against an exclusionary society that won't accept his kind," he eventually answered, mouthing the words robotically. It was a direct quote from Meyer's pitch that Gene felt he'd parroted far too many times already.

"Damn right," Shel agreed vigorously. "Now tell me. What's a more vivid representation of that society than a racist country club? No Jews allowed, right? Darkies in white gloves hanging in the shadows, waiting to be bossed around. And the idle rich with their golf and their Mint Juleps and their cotillions. Tell me it's not perfect."

"It's not possible!" Hoffman shouted. "We don't have the location. We don't have the extras you've written in. We don't have the fucking *time*, Shelly."

"We'll pick up the exteriors on the drive back. I saw a golf course as we were passing through Pompano. Take us a few hours, tops."

"Are you listening to a goddamn word I'm saying? We can't afford this."

Meyer worked himself up to a standing position. He'd anticipated this response.

"Look, Gene. I know you've got a contingency fund, a little stash in case of the unexpected. Let's not hedge our bets on this one. Now's the time to swing for the fences, you've said so yourself."

Hoffman took a final monster drag and got up to stub out his cigarette.

"The contingency fund is gone," he said, returning to the couch. "We're operating with zero margin of error. That's what I came to tell you."

"What do you mean, gone?" Meyer asked. "Where did it go?"

"Into the deputy's back pocket."

"I'm not following you."

Another long exhalation from Hoffman. Sometimes Shel Meyer's naiveté was just ridiculous.

"Pull your head out of your ass, will you? How do you think I sprung Vance from the mess he was in?"

Meyer thought back to the events at the beginning of the day. His mind was reluctant to go there, to acknowledge what Hoffman wanted him to see.

The whole incident had been a little fuzzy, since his attention was stolen with prepping the morning's shoot. All he knew for sure was Vance had been late for his call time. The rest of the crew assembled in the motel's parking lot at noon as planned. Just as Meyer was ready to send a search party to that filthy gin mill down the highway, Vance's Impala came creeping in the driveway. Immediately followed by Deputy Platt's patrol car.

That seemed strange, but Meyer was so relieved he didn't pay much attention to the law man. Then he got so busy reaming out Vance for his tardiness, he failed to clock what was going on between Hoffman and the deputy. They were locked in an intense conversation, sitting inside the patrol car as it coughed black smoke from its tailpipe. Meyer assumed Gene was giving him a perfectly reasonable bag of shit about the other night, maybe trying to wring some future cooperation out of him in return.

Now, seven hours later, it seemed inescapably clear something else had been going on.

"Didn't you notice anything funny about Vance?" Hoffman asked, bringing Meyer back to the present.

Meyer shrugged. "He flubbed the first take or two. Seemed a little distracted maybe."

"Scared shitless is more like it. He'd just been fucking arrested."

"For *what*?"

"Oh, nothing serious. Speeding. Operating a vehicle without a license. Drunk driving. Resisting arrest. I think that was all."

Shel's head sunk slowly into his hands. "Jesus..."

"The little prick should be in a cell in Dade right now. Fortunately for us, our deputy friend's just as greedy as he looks."

"How much?"

"Exactly what we could afford in case of an emergency. Not a penny less. So let's be clear, OK? No rewrites. No new locations, no more extras, no new effects. We're gonna make precisely the movie we set out to make when we left Miami. If we're lucky."

A moment of anguished silence filled the musty room. Then an explosion: Meyer slammed his fist down onto the card table. Hard, like he was driving his knuckles straight into Vance Cogburn's mouth.

He hit the table's edge with enough force to flip the whole thing over in a summersault. All the items on top flew into the air like a flock of startled pigeons: the ashtray containing a dozen butts, a deck of nudie playing cards, two loose-leaf stacks of notes, a small collection of empty beer bottles. Everything came crashing and splashing down in scattershot disarray. A few dead cigarettes landed in Hoffman's lap, along with a nice spray of ash dusting his Bermuda shorts.

Hoffman was slack-jawed. This was by far the most violent thing he'd ever seen his partner do. Gene had occasionally sensed a slow burn underneath Shel's milquetoast façade, but it had never taken outward form. He honestly didn't think the guy had it in him.

Gene started laughing first, his whole chunky frame rattling with hoarse chuckles. The more he thought about it, the funnier it became. Killer Shel Meyer, slayer of cheap furniture. Too much.

Eventually Meyer broke up in tandem. He hadn't surprised himself with the outburst. His fists had shattered more than a few lamps, mirrors, and other inanimate opponents in their time.

After they'd regained their composure, Shel asked in a somber tone, "What the hell do we do now?"

"Follow the script," Hoffman answered matter-of-factly. "Isn't that what you wanted?"

"Are we absolutely sure Cogburn's in the clear?"

"Far as today goes, yeah. Gotta keep plenty of daylight between him and the deputy, though."

"I could strangle the punk, I really could. You should've let him rot in Dade, Gene."

"Oh, sure. With 1,000 feet in the can? Not even *you* could write him out of the script now. Besides, you gotta admit the kid's done a good job."

Meyer wasn't willing to concede this point, at least not out loud.

"Tell you the truth," Hoffman continued, "I'm more worried about Barbara."

Meyer was surprised to hear this. His mind again backtracked to the events of the day. Once Platt had driven off (*with his goddamned blackmail money!*) shooting began more or less as scheduled. They had three dialogue-heavy scenes to knock off. All involving Barbara.

First up was a lengthy scene in which Kelly Dunhill tries to get some information out of Frank Butler, without revealing her identity as a reporter. She has come to the seaside town of Palmdale on an undercover assignment, researching two recent murders. After learning Frank discovered the first victim while strolling along the beach with his girlfriend, Kelly approaches him at the public pool where he works as a lifeguard. During the scene, an attraction between the two becomes clear.

Meyer set up the Mitchell by the edge of the pool, where Barbara had been tanning herself a few hours earlier. After helping him prep, Ricky and Juan stripped to their trunks and started splashing around in the chlorine-choked water. They would be visible in the background of the shot, making this location more believable as a crowded public pool.

Shel wanted to get the whole scene in one master. They ran a few rehearsals, then started rolling.

It went fairly smoothly. Barbara's performance wasn't awful. After a rocky start, she improved noticeably. She may never make much of an actress, lacking any semblance of naturalism, but she remembered her lines respectably. A few of the later takes even showed a knack for improvisation, but Shel put the kibosh on that. He was not the kind of filmmaker who encouraged deviation from the pages.

59

After four nonstop hours, they'd nailed the scene plus two smaller ones involving Barbara and the father of the first victim, played by none other than Gene Hoffman. The crew broke at 5:30 to grab some rest before another long night.

A pretty good day, all in all. Sitting here in room 217 as evening crept in, Meyer was unsettled to hear his producer voice concern about their actress.

"The girl has absolutely no idea what kind of picture we're making."

"Well..." Meyer began cautiously, "she knows her character's tracking down a murderer."

"C'mon, Shel. She doesn't know it's a gore picture. Who knows, maybe she won't care. Maybe she'll groove on it. But we need to level with her soon. This idea of feeding her one scene at a time won't float."

"I don't know what you're worried about. She's already agreed to go nude for us."

"That's a whole different ball of wax. I'm telling you, gore scares people. They're not used to the idea of seeing mutilated bodies for kicks. We could have a real problem when Barbara finds out what this flick's really about."

"I've planned for that. She won't come near a drop of blood until Sunday night. By that point, it'll be too late for her to do much about it."

"I don't like this shit about keeping people in the dark," Hoffman rumbled uneasily. "The whole team should know the game plan, that's how we've always done it."

"We're doing a lot of things different this time, aren't we?"

Meyer smiled and patted Hoffman on the knee. Intended to be a comforting gesture, it was jolting. These two men did not share physical expressions of friendship. Gene Hoffman, for his part, was an incorrigible back-slapper, ass-pincher, and glad-hander. But he made a point of keeping his paws off Meyer because he

60

knew how uncomfortable such casual intimacies made the skittish director.

So there sat Hoffman, stunned for the second time this evening by a wildly uncharacteristic display from his partner. First a clenched fist smashing a table, now a clammy palm patting his kneecap. Was Meyer going through some kind of breakdown? Christ, that's all they needed to cement this production as an unmitigated disaster. A lush of a leading man in trouble with the law, a leading lady totally unprepared for what her role required, and a jabbering wreck of a director.

"Just relax," Meyer said after removing his hand and taking a measured step back. "You know I've dealt with problematic talent before."

This was true, but it didn't do much to put Hoffman's mind at ease.

"Lemme ask you something I've never really understood. Why are you so stuck on hiding the nature of this picture from her? If she's offended by the material, we just find someone else."

Meyer didn't reply. He didn't really have an answer, at least not one he could verbalize. There were, in fact, some very specific reasons he'd insisted on casting Barbara. He would have refused to make the film with anyone else. So intense was his desire, he decided back in Miami to play it safe and keep her in the dark about the objectionable elements of *Crimson Orgy*. Which were, of course, the whole point of the picture.

Realizing he wasn't going to get an answer, Hoffman rose wearily from the couch. He'd accomplished what he set out to do. Meyer was officially on notice they had no extra money to spend. Everything needed to go exactly according to plan if this project was going to come off. Now Gene wanted to go back to room 221 and pass out for as long as possible until everyone gathered for the evening's shoot.

"I had a funny feeling about this girl from the start," he said, turning at the door. The dying glow of the sunken sun backlit his huge body as it filled the frame. Meyer found himself automatically thinking it would make a good shot.

"You were gung-ho on her and I didn't fight you," Hoffman continued. "I knew how you felt about Vance. So far, I'd say both our instincts have proven sound."

"Sure," Meyer agreed. "Except for pissing away all our backup cash, your boy's been a dream."

"Just deal with Barbara. Let her know the score. Do it soon, or I will."

With that, he shut the door behind him, leaving Shel Meyer alone with his unspoken motivations.

* * * * * * *

Her eyes were open wide. They hadn't blinked in almost a minute. A look not of horror or pain but simple surprise was written across her pretty features. Her lips were parted, as if frozen in speech. Most of her face was hidden by the glistening red paint coursing down from her left ear, splashed across her cheeks, dripping from her nose and staining her perfect white teeth.

"Hold it just like that, Julie," the man's voice said from somewhere outside her field of vision. "That's perfect."

She heard her named being called, but couldn't connect the voice to any person. A disorienting sensation.

The stage blood tasted awful, but Julie didn't complain. It was caked uncomfortably close to her nostrils, emitting chemical vapors, but she remained still. She could feel it starting to congeal on her skin. Her most fervent hope was that the camera would stop rolling very soon and she'd be allowed to scrub it off.

At first, it was almost fun having the red paint dabbed across her head and shoulders. Shel Meyer handled this duty personally and Julie found herself laughing giddily as he splashed the phony gore on her with increasing abandon. Kind of like finger-painting with her little sister as kids. By the time he was done, it really looked like a hole had been drilled in the side of her head.

Then it was time to add the calf's brains. That was when Julie first felt a shiver of discomfort. The brains had been properly refrigerated, a lesson learned from the fiasco with the intestines last night. Stench wasn't an issue. It was how the brains felt against her skin. The tactile sensation of that chilled gray matter nestling against her neck and getting in her hair positively gave Julie the willies. She found herself wanting this to be over. Badly.

Then the heat of the 1K lights started to become oppressive. The glare was so intense it blinded her to the small collection of people standing behind the camera, watching her so intently. She knew they were there, could hear them mumbling amongst themselves, discussing her performance. She could discern the ticking hum of the camera but couldn't see that either. All she could see was a little part of herself, her bare legs from the knees down, white in the steaming glow of the lights.

She'd never felt so totally exposed in her life.

The experience of being in a movie had definitely stopped being fun. She wanted to be far away from here. She wanted to go home and take a long bath.

Despite her discomfort, Julie stayed focused and delivered what was expected of her: total stillness. The old fashioned hand-cranked "eggbeater" drill jutting from her left ear didn't wobble, even slightly. This was due to the fact that her chest lay dormant, evidencing no sign of respiration. She could have been a mannequin.

This girl is good, Meyer thought as he crouched behind the camera, peering through the viewfinder. Who cares if she can't memorize more than a sentence at a time? They didn't need her to. Julie possessed a far more important quality as an actress, one that was surprisingly hard to come by.

She died beautifully.

Meyer continued to pull on the Mitchell's zoom crank, gaining a wider perspective of the cramped room. After executing a smooth pullout, he zoomed back in to grab another for protection.

The part that was to be played by Julie—"BETTY" (a.k.a. "VICTIM #2") — was not a complexly nuanced one. It involved just four words of dialogue. All she had to do was say, "Good night, Mr. Johnson," walk to her car, get beaten over the head with a truncheon, and have a 1/2" drill bit bored into her ear. And then she had to be crucified. Most importantly, she had to be able to hold her breath for two minutes at a time.

Shel had always planned to shoot this one tight, opening on a close-up of the girl's eyes and pulling back about halfway to reveal her blood-splattered glory. He didn't have the option to include any wide shots, given the limitations of the "set" they were using.

Gene Hoffman's motel room was doubling as the interior of Ace Spade's secluded beach shack. The original plan to use a maintenance shed at the back of the motel proved unworkable due to space limitations. No way of rigging adequate light inside the tiny, dust-covered shed. They could grab it for exterior reference shots, but that was all. Another compromise that made Meyer's teeth grind. Hoffman shrugged it off. The show must go on.

Room 221 was actually a somewhat reasonable replacement, one that would have to suffice. Hanging some ratty bed sheets on the walls, covering the floor with a tarp and then sprinkling the tarp with wood shavings created a pretty good effect. A heavy work table and some rusty tools were brought in and scattered about, along with a few stacks of plywood. Cliff, Ricky, and

Juan dragged the bed and night stand onto the walkway outside the room.

It was a blatant fire code violation and they were anxiously keeping an eye out for any signs of Ernest the manager. Hoffman had assured him the Sand Palace would remain essentially untouched during the course of the shoot. This was a breach of that agreement, but they didn't have any choice. It was a calculated risk. Ernest spent most evenings snoozing in front of the black and white TV in his office downstairs.

As an insurance policy, Hoffman decided they needed a lookout. Given his variable grasp of English, Juan was the natural choice. He was stationed down in the courtyard, on the far side of the pool but still within view of room 221. Upon the first sign of life from the manager's office, Juan was to hoot three times.

Sure, it was an idiotic plan. No way they'd be able to haul the furniture back inside the room with any stealth. But just having Juan down there made everyone feel better, if for no other reason than it kept the noxious fumes of his hand-rolled cigarillos at a safe distance.

Back inside 221, the camera kept rolling. In the final cut, this shot would run well over a minute in length, accompanied by the mournful wail of a saxophone. It was the second murder in the film, after the one on the beach, but this was the first shown in a brightly lit environment. There would be no way to hide from the carnage. No shadows or wide shots. It was a full-blown assault upon the audience's senses, and Meyer wanted to make sure it knocked the stuffing out of every single paying customer.

To make the shot work, Meyer needed an actress who could play dead for an extended period of time. Julie was not discovered at the Cottontail Club like most of her costars. Meyer had to seek her out at a very unique location. He knew right away where to look.

Julie Baylor earned her living as a Weeki Wachee Mermaid, spending most of her days in a bottomless natural spring just north of Tampa. She, along with eighteen other young ladies, performed three underwater shows a day in one of Florida's most oddball tourist attractions. Audiences packed into the plush 400-seat Underwater Theater and watched through a panoramic glass wall as the comely gals frolicked and gamboled dreamily in their polyurethane fishtails, taking occasional pulls of oxygen from rubber hoses.

Since opening in 1947, the Weeki Wachee Spring had been a hugely profitable pit stop curiosity. Road-weary dads in desperate need of an adrenaline-boosting thrill appreciated the mildly racy show as much as rambunctious tykes.

Gaining full mermaid status required a grueling training regimen, designed to weed out the diehards from the wannabes. Candidates learned, among other skills such as swimming with both legs bound together and throwing a Frisbee underwater, how to hold their breath for two and a half minutes. It was no joke, and every mermaid depended upon her finned sisters to stay alive in their submerged showcase.

Two weeks ago, Shel drove to Tampa. After sitting through three consecutive shows trying to pick a stand-out among all the equally fetching creatures, he decided upon Julie. Getting near her was a daunting matter. He resorted to palming off a pair of ten-spots on the doorman protecting the dressing room.

Meyer did not excel at approaching talent. His natural body language didn't lend itself to such a delicate task. Too many tics and scratches, too much unconscious foot-waggling. Gene Hoffman was much smoother, especially in dealing with young women. His relaxed bonhomie tended to put them at ease. Even if they turned down the offer, they generally walked away from the encounter not feeling as if they'd been grossly propositioned. But Hoffman had been tied up on the phone with exhibitors the day Shel went to Tampa. They were running out of time and needed to wrap up casting immediately.

Julie was initially taken aback by Shel's ham-fisted offer to appear in his movie. Fortunately, he was able to convince the girl his intentions were not nearly as trashy as they first appeared. Julie reluctantly agreed to come to Stupendous's offices in Miami for a formal audition. Car fare would be provided. Shel disclosed little regarding her role, except to assure her no nudity was required.

The audition puzzled Julie. She didn't have to say anything, just lie on the floor for a few minutes holding her breath. Compared to working in the Weeki Wachee spring it was a piece of cake. They hired her on the spot: $50 cash, plus gas money to get down to Hillsboro Beach and back.

She'd arrived less than an hour ago, a bit late after missing the Sand Palace by a dozen miles and having to double back. Meyer barely let her kill the engine before rushing her to a spot behind the hotel where they filmed her saying her line and then being attacked by Jerry Cooke.

The manic force Jerry brought to the scene unnerved Julie. It wasn't that he hurt her when he ran up from behind and pushed her onto a grubby mattress positioned below the camera's range to cushion the fall. The guy was too small to hurt her. His hands felt almost gentle as they went through the motions of clubbing her and dragging her down. The prop truncheon was made out of soft foam.

Making Julie queasy was that he did it with so much relish. Acting is one thing, but what this little guy with the crazy eyes was doing seemed like something quite different.

Jerry sounded like a genuine madman as he stood laughing over her prone form. Rippling, jittery guffaws escaped his lips in deep gasps, like they'd been torn from some dark place inside. A very disturbing sound, especially since he seemed unable to stop it. Several minutes after Meyer yelled "Cut!" Jerry was still doubled over in a spasm of wild mirth, punching himself in the leg in an effort to regain control.

The attack scene only required one take, thank God. It all happened so fast, Julie barely had time to learn anyone's name. Then she'd been rushed into room 221 to set up the effects shot. And now here she was, in the middle of her big close-up. Frozen in a grim tableau, each second ticking by like mercury. The whole process had been disarmingly casual, yet at the same time frenetic and wild. Surely this wasn't how they did things in Hollywood?

"Annnnndddd... cut." Meyer clicked the button and the Mitchell's whir died. Julie remained in position. Still afraid to ruin the shot by breathing. Kind of sweet, the kid really was trying hard.

"You can relax, honey," Shel said, stepping around from behind the camera. "That's a wrap for Julie, everyone. Let's hear it for her."

The four people tightly assembled in room 221 applauded heartily. No one louder than Hoffman. Somewhat frantically, Julie started to scramble from the blood-soaked tarp, betraying just how uneasy she was.

Meyer stopped her. "Hold it! Let me get the rig off you, we need it for another shot."

Julie miserably lowered herself onto the sticky mess, waiting as Meyer tried to scoop up the calf's brains and place them in a plastic bucket. It didn't work too well. They oozed through his fingers like wet runaway worms, landing on the floor with a sickening plop. Julie thought she might scream.

Giving up on the brains, Meyer instructed her to hold still as he attempted to pull the killing device from her skull. The drill bit had been severed halfway with the help of some bolt-cutters and Cliff the Grip's muscle. The truncated bit had then been fastened behind Julie's ear with the help of some quick-drying adhesive known as spirit gum. It stuck out of her head at a nice 90-degree angle.

As Meyer tried to remove the drill, it dawned on him that perhaps he'd been a little overzealous with the adhesive. The damn thing felt welded on. Mustering as much delicacy as possible, trying not to yank out any hair, he found himself losing patience with the situation.

"Cliff," he called out. "Get over here."

Cliff was helping to break down the tripod so the camera could be moved outside. He immediately dropped that project and jumped at his director's command. Stepping delicately around the gross puddles on the tarp, he loomed over the kneeling Meyer and glanced down sympathetically at Julie. She had a look of mild panic in her eyes and her slender freckled legs seemed to be twitching of their own volition.

Cliff felt immensely sad looking at her, though he wasn't sure why. He tried to ward off a nagging feeling that there was something inherently wrong in filming this kind of material. Something about it was just *wrong*.

"It won't come loose," Meyer rasped over his shoulder as he made another tug at the drill. Julie couldn't help wincing.

"Did you use the spirit gum remover?" Cliff asked. "Never come off without it."

Meyer stopped pulling. He could feel himself starting to blush but was damned if he'd let his Key Grip see it. Standing up, he nodded brusquely. "Why don't I leave this in your hands? I could use a little air."

Telling Julie what a great job she'd done, Meyer disappeared out the door as fast as his feet would carry him. Cliff cast another apologetic look down at her.

"Hold tight. I'll have that off you in a jiffy."

He stepped away to find the spirit gum remover, leaving her there. No one had bothered to turn off the lights that still burned down on her. Waiting for Cliff to return, forcefully willing herself not to cry, Julie decided she didn't want to have anything to do with the movies. She had a great job at Weeki Wachee and that was more than enough limelight for her. She wouldn't even see *Crimson Orgy* if and when it ever came to her neighborhood drive-in. She didn't want to be reminded of this night.

Emerging onto the walkway outside room 221, Meyer was distressed to see both Ricky and Juan lounging on the bed that completely blocked passage in either direction. Juan had inexplicably abandoned his post. Meyer wanted to yell at the errant grip but he couldn't make out much within the mushroom cloud of foul blue smoke shrouding the immediate area. Besides, he didn't know how to curse in Spanish.

"OK, fellas," Meyer said, trying to sound friendly but in command. "Let's strike the set and get this stuff back inside. I'll hold the fort out here."

The two grips traded a disdainful look. They made a show of getting up as slowly as possible, then trudged into the room to start cleaning up the blood, brains, and wood chips.

Meyer sagged against the railing and reached into his pocket for a cigarette. Perspiration dried along his receding hairline. The illuminated pool below sent flickering blue shadows across the courtyard. He was feeling pretty jazzed about the drill gag. It was good to get one solid effects shot under their belts. Dailies from the beach shoot would be arriving from the lab on Thursday. He was afraid to think about how the slashed belly effect would look on film, but he was confident in tonight's scene.

It suddenly occurred to him that Hoffman had disappeared. Strange, but hardly cause for concern. He'd be back soon.

Meyer had sucked the Chesterfield down to its filter when a tap on his shoulder startled him. It was Julie. She still looked like an accident victim. Some of the blood had been wiped off, but the frizzy hair on one side of her head was thickly clotted. Meyer suppressed a shudder as he imagined the ordeal she would face in trying to get it clean. Maybe she should just leave it in for the night.

"Well," Julie said, extending her hand, "it was nice to meet you, Mr. Meyer."

Shel smiled. "Don't say goodbye so soon, kid. We'll see you tomorrow."

Any trace of warmth in Julie's eyes evaporated. "What do you mean? You said I was done."

"You are, for tonight. We need to pick up another shot in the morning."

"I want to go home, Mr. Meyer. I want to go home tonight."

"Impossible. Besides, way too late to drive to Tampa."

"I'll be OK."

"You don't understand. We've got a nice room set up for you here."

She felt herself yielding slightly. "My own room?"

"No, you'll be sharing it with Angela. She plays Victim #3. Have you met her yet? She's a peach, you two will get on like a house afire."

Julie's resistance shot back up a few degrees. They wanted to keep her in this ghost town and they couldn't even come up with a private room? It was an insult. She wasn't going to make this easy on Meyer. She'd already been paid and her car was waiting in the lot.

"Do I have to wear that... stuff again?"

71

"Of course," Shel said, using his hands to frame an imaginary shot in front of Julie's face, as if she could see the image he had in mind. "We've seen Ace kill you and take you back to his room. Now we're gonna see where he leaves your body. Trust me, it'll be one of the most memorable shots of the whole picture."

"I don't know. This is a little more than I bargained for."

"Sweetheart, everyone's tired. We've all had a long day. Go get some rest. We'll have coffee and donuts ready at 9:00."

"I'll stay, but I don't want to get all messed up again. I don't like it."

Meyer's patience was wearing thin. "Look, you agreed to play the part."

"You didn't say anything about putting brains on me!"

Her voice startled Meyer. It was almost a shriek.

"OK, calm down, Jenny."

"It's Julie!"

Shel looked over his shoulder nervously. Half expecting to see an enraged Ernest charging at him. Why was it taking so long to get the goddamned bed back in the room? And where the hell was Hoffman? The producer's suave diplomacy was badly needed to put out this particular fire, but it seemed Meyer would have to go it alone.

"I'm sorry, Julie," he said in his softest voice, placing a hand on her shoulder, which was sticky. "Please cooperate with me here. There's a hot shower and a comfy bed waiting for you down in 119. Just knock on the door, Angela will let you in."

"No one said I had to stay the night," Julie said, twisting her body to free herself from Meyer's grasp. His hand detached from her shoulder with a wet smacking sound. "I don't have anything to wear!"

"We told you to pack an overnight bag," he countered. "I remember it clearly."

"Well, I guess I forgot."

Shel grabbed her arm again, a little less gently, and started guiding her toward the stairwell. Enough was enough. He made a mental note to chew out Hoffman at the earliest opportunity.

"This whole thing will be over by lunch tomorrow and you'll be on your way home," he rasped in Julie's ear as he propelled her forward. "Get some sleep, relax, and we'll see you in the morning."

A gentle push on the back encouraged her progress toward the stairway. She seemed to have capitulated but was still muttering a blue streak of obscenities as she trudged down the stairs. Such coarse language from such a sweet-looking girl!

Meyer shook his head ruefully. Nothing came easy. Hire an eighteen-year-old kid from Tampa and she starts coming on like Elizabeth Taylor with a hangover. Unbelievable.

Retracing his footsteps, he was relieved to see the bed had finally been cleared from the walkway. That was encouraging. Maybe they'd be able to wrap for the night without facing some sort of catastrophe.

Stepping back into 221, Meyer froze in his tracks. The room was a certified disaster area. It was actually horrifying.

The bed and night stand were haphazardly crammed up against one another. Cliff, Ricky, and Juan seemed to be heatedly arguing about where the furniture had originally been placed. The tarp, still covered with several quarts of blood, was leaking all over the carpet. Someone had kicked over the bucket of brains. The floor was a virtual lake of gore, totally nauseating to anyone who might happen to stumble into the room unaware of what had been taking place for the last hour.

One such intruder was in fact present. Meyer almost swooned when he saw Barbara standing there in the middle of the muck. He was given a brief moment to notice her woven sandals were stained bright red, with wet flecks of crimson splashed onto her slender ankles. It was an arresting image.

She stood with her back to him, listening to the frantic conference among the grips. She must have heard him enter, or some facial expression from Cliff tipped her off, because she turned as soon as Shel closed the door behind him. He was now sweating direly. Suddenly the room seemed much smaller, more claustrophobic than it had while they were shooting.

No place to hide from it all.

The blood. The brains. The gore-encrusted drill.

And her, staring at him.

Barbara's face, usually a study in sun-kissed health, seemed almost anemic. Just as Meyer opened his mouth with a casual remark to defuse the situation, she beat him to it.

"What the hell's going on in here, Sheldon?"

WEDNESDAY

It was dark out there, and quiet. Deputy Platt sat in the cruiser, waiting on her. She was usually worth the wait. Platt felt certain this night had the potential to be a good one, if it ever got started. His lower back ached a bit. He'd been planted in the driver's seat for the better part of the day and was anxious to reposition his weather-beaten body in a horizontal and naked arrangement.

The Angler's Rest's neon sign reflected off the cruiser's windshield. Platt read the flickering letters through the dusty glass. He was bored and tired. And randy. What was taking so long? Almost an hour past closing time and the parking lot was empty except for Sherry's Grand Am and his own patrol car.

Platt took another look at the bouquet laying across the passenger seat. A sorry sight, so different from what he had purchased from that snooty florist in Miami this morning. The rose petals curled sadly into themselves, defeated. The whole thing was depressingly wilted and the ribbon tying it together had frayed into loose strands.

Platt damned himself for neglecting to keep the flowers in water. Why hadn't he been able to do at least *that*? It wasn't complicated, like police work, but the nuts and bolts of wooing escaped him. Such things must come easy to some fellas. The deputy was not among them. He was nobody's Romeo, as he had admitted to Sherry on numerous occasions. Once or twice she'd been kind enough to contradict him.

The deputy checked his watch impatiently. Almost a quarter to midnight. Should he just barge in? No. He wanted to surprise her as she walked to her car.

The skeeters were out with almost demonic force. The air itself thrummed, clouding one's vision and nettling the ears with an incessant buzz. Platt hardly noticed it. He grew up around here. By late childhood his skin was so accustomed to vampiric assault it turned a permanent mottled red. The only time mosquitos bothered him was when they got tangled in the thatches of hair protruding from his nostrils. That was one hell of an irritant.

Platt consulted his watch yet again. He started to worry. Maybe she'd just want to drive home by herself. Sherry wasn't much for sentiment, and the fact that he'd faithfully waited in this seething darkness with a surprise bouquet wasn't worth a bucket of spit to her. Platt felt his well-laid plans for getting laid start to slip away.

The neon sign went out. Finally, she was off duty.

Sherry emerged from the front door, turning to lock it behind her. Platt watched every move, trying to decipher mood from body language. She was tired, that much was clear.

Well, so was he, but he was determined to make this a special occasion. Those blue-ribbon tits pressed out dramatically against her gauzy dress as she stood silhouetted by a utility light. It was almost shocking to see such a ripe body on a woman her age. How did she do it? Above the neck she hadn't rebuked the clock with the same defiance, but Platt still found a lot to admire in her full lips and high cheekbones. He didn't think he could wait another second to get his hands on her.

Turning, Sherry saw the patrol car. A weary but warm smile sought purchase on her face. Platt got out, clumsily holding the bouquet behind his back. When she was close enough to touch, he presented the flowers with a grandeur that was endearing but kind of pathetic, given their ratty state.

"You're under arrest, for stealing my heart."

"You'll never take me alive, Deputy."

A smile lightened her smoky voice. She liked to address him by his rank. Knew he liked it, too. It was sort of tongue in cheek, but there was a certain degree of heat to her salutation. The allure of a man in uniform, all that.

"Feel up for a moonlight drive?" he asked. "Still a few minutes left."

"Depends on where you're planning to drive me."

"Wild, of course. 'Less you had a better idea."

She slapped his face in reply. Gently, but hard enough to slay the fattened mosquito that had landed on his cheek. It was a messy kill.

"Ouch," he said.

"Sorry. He was getting ready to suck you dry." Sherry paused for effect as she took the flowers from him. "And that's my job."

"Just go on and leave your car here. I'll run you back in the morning."

"Whatever you say, Sonny."

77

Climbing behind the wheel, Platt started to feel pretty good about the night's prospects. He had a real firecracker on his hands. Almost nine months and this thing was still roaring with the heat of a freshly conceived passion. No matter how many times they burned the sheets it damn near brought the house down. Platt was elated, and puzzled. He kept waiting for at least one of them to get bored with it, as had happened after barely a year of connubial relations with his ex-wife.

Sherry poured herself into the passenger seat and slammed the door. "Stab it, sugar."

He peeled out of the lot with as much noise as he could muster. Banged a hard right and they were headed south. The sultry night air came rolling in through the open windows. Sherry untied her ponytail and let her graying but still blonde locks sail free.

"Faster," she said, even as his foot continued to weigh down on the gas.

It was never fast enough for Sherry. She liked the speed with which Platt could legally tear up these roads whenever he had a mind to. She encouraged moonlit bombing runs like this one along the lonely stretches of A1A, telling him she considered it foreplay. She got wet when the speedometer ticked over 80.

"Reach under the seat," Platt hollered over the wind.

"What?"

"Under the seat! Little surprise for ya!"

Sherry ran her fingers along the grubby floor. They wrapped around a small felt box. Ripping it open, she shrieked. Inside was the coral bracelet she'd gone ape over during their trip to Miami last month. She never thought he could afford it.

Forget those wilted roses, he'd hit a homer with this one. Sherry started covering his cheek with kisses and moaning throaty thank yous into his ear. This was definitely more like it.

Pleased as he was, it occurred to Platt she should really thank Gene Hoffman. The thick wad of bills he'd forked over the other day had paid for the damn bracelet. Then again, maybe the pretty boy actor deserved the credit. Platt didn't like the thought that Sherry owed her new charm to that rotten punk. As he traced the chain of events back in his mind the deputy realized, if anything, Sherry should actually thank herself.

Strange.

Two weeks ago, when first approached by Gene Hoffman about the possibility of donating a patrol car, the deputy felt an electric charge run up his spine. He couldn't believe it. A bona fide movie producer, here in Hillsboro Beach. What were the odds?

Even a Hillsboro loyalist like Sonny Platt couldn't deny his place of origin was little more than a glorified sand bar with a scattering of poorly-designed buildings and a few hundred lost souls calling it home. There was no tourism to speak of, as the beaches were far narrower than in Pompano and other nearby communities. Fishing was abundant, evidenced by the profusion of rods strapped to pickup trucks in almost every driveway, but that wasn't enough to draw outsiders. Indeed, Hillsboro seemed to offer absolutely nothing that might tempt a motorist en route to Miami or Ft. Lauderdale to hit the brake and pay a visit.

That sense of seclusion was exactly what had attracted Hoffman, along with the fact that Hillsboro Beach was under the command of a tiny rustic Deputy's office, well beyond the gaze of the Dade County Sheriff's Department. Gene was convinced he could manipulate whatever badge-wielding rube was responsible for keeping the peace around here. As usual, his instincts proved sound.

Deputy Sonny Platt was an incurable moviegoer. Besides football and fishing, going to the Delray Drive-In in Ft. Lauderdale had been his favorite pastime since he was in short pants. Now, pushing forty, he was still smitten with the silver screen. Even after making deputy six years ago, Platt never missed a new attraction at the Delray. Every Friday night, he would make the twenty-mile drive and park his cruiser right up front. Sometimes he took a date, but usually he flew solo. He didn't like any distractions from the cinematic experience. A guy could stroke his woman anywhere, but the Delray was the only place in these parts where you could find entertainment like the kind Stupendous Pictures churned out. Platt had seen just about every nudie shot in Miami, without ever knowing how close he was to the source. He just assumed anything projected onto the Delray's screen came from Hollywood, CA.

So he'd been duly impressed when Hoffman came calling, but first wanted to make sure the man was legit. Grilling him for some credentials, Platt was amazed to hear him rattle off familiar titles like *Naked 'Til Sunrise*, *Cuffs 'n' Collars* and *Wiggle, Wiggle, Wiggle!* Platt needed no further proof and made every assurance he could grant the producer's request.

"You want a cruiser," he'd said. "Sure, no problem. Take all the time you need with it, my pleasure."

Not until Hoffman drove off with a sly smile did the deputy begin to feel he'd capitulated too readily. If they were in such dire need of his help, surely he was entitled to add certain conditions. He dialed the Miami number on Hoffman's business card and said he wanted to appear in the movie as compensation for loaning the car. The director, Shel Meyer, answered his call and agreed without too many questions.

Platt's initial delight turned to frustration when he thought about how easily he'd gotten his way. Started to think maybe he hadn't asked for enough. Did they take him for a total hayseed? Why not, he'd acted the part perfectly. Those thoughts tormented Platt until Monday the 2nd, the day of the shoot.

That morning, he'd driven over to the Sand Palace convinced he had every right to insist on a *speaking* role. These Miami hustlers weren't going to steamroll into Hillsboro Beach and have their way with the good folk who called it home. Not on his watch. If they wanted to shoot their movie in the deputy's jurisdiction, they'd damn well have to play ball.

Platt was again surprised and slightly dismayed that his ultimatum met with no resistance. Hoffman didn't seem to mind giving him some dialogue in the least. Platt walked away from room 217 scratching his head. It wasn't until he'd returned to the station that he started to worry about what he'd gotten himself into. Who the hell was he kidding? He was no actor. He'd never memorized anything since the pledge of allegiance as a kid, and that was no cakewalk.

Platt spent the rest of the day in a state of gut-jerking agitation. By the time he showed up at the beach, his nerves were completely shot. Still feeling he'd been manipulated in some way he didn't quite understand, he decided at the last minute to renege on his promise about the patrol car. It was a chickenshit move, sure, but somehow it made him feel better.

The night turned out much worse than even his most paranoid fantasies would have allowed. Platt was as woefully ill-equipped to perform in front of a camera as any human imaginable. Give him a shoplifter to tackle or a ticket to write and he'd do it without raising his heart rate. But this acting thing was another beast altogether. This was *scary*.

He simply couldn't get the lines out. A few times he came agonizingly close, only to crap out on the last word. It was bad enough having to deal with the antsy director but when the pretty boy with the pompadour starting busting his chops, Platt almost lost it. That kid didn't know how lucky he was to walk away without a serious pistol-whipping. If not for the calming influence of Gene Hoffman, some real blood would most definitely have stained the sand that night.

Deputy Platt drove home early Tuesday morning just as the sun was starting to rise, absolutely beside himself with feelings of impotent rage. He didn't sleep a wink, consumed with thoughts of Vance Cogburn's smirking face and snide wisecracks. At 10:00 A.M., still fuming, he drove to the station because he couldn't think of anything else to do.

Funny thing about revenge. Rarely presented itself as a realistic option, but when it did there was nothing better. Especially when it fell in your lap like a gift from Providence. Sitting at his desk, sipping cold coffee and thinking how much he'd love to knock Vance's dick in the dirt, Platt answered a call from Sherry at about 11:35. She had a hot tip for him.

Some young troublemaker, an outsider, had walked into the Angler's Rest, knocked back four double bourbons in rapid succession, then peeled out of the parking lot like a maniac. He was headed southbound in a banged-up Chevy, straight into the deputy's reach. And oh, yeah, the son of a bitch blatantly hit on her and then insulted her when she showed no interest.

Sonny was off the phone and scrambling for his keys before he could get a more detailed description of the guy. In his gut, he knew it had to be Vance. Five minutes later, as he floored it to tailgate behind that shitty Impala, his instinct was confirmed.

Damn, that was sweet! A total reversal of fortune in less than twelve hours.

Platt was ready to drive Vance down to Dade right away and bid him adios. But then the potential upside of the situation occurred to him. Satisfying as it would be to lock Vance up, the actor was far more valuable as a bargaining chip. Why not put the squeeze on that producer Hoffman? He'd have no choice but to peel off a few bills or see his leading man disappear.

Besides, if the pretty boy was sitting in a jail cell, Platt would not have an opportunity to settle his hash in a more private manner. So he drove Vance to the Sand Palace, turned him loose, and collected a handsome fee for his hide. Let the little shit think it was over. Platt knew the crew would be in town for a week or so. His time would come.

In the meantime he had his sweet, dirty Sherry. Sonny Platt was more than willing to pay the outrageous price of $250 for that gaudy coral bracelet, as long as it made her happy. She was worth every penny and more. Not only was she a banshee on the springs, she'd provided him with the means to let himself feel better about his awful night in front of the camera. Her quick-thinking phone call made it all possible, which is why she had essentially bought herself the bracelet.

Now, ripping down the highway on this final minute of August 4th, 1965, Platt grew aroused as he mentally replayed the whole tableau. Sherry's wandering left hand provided encouragement. They were less than four miles from his ranch-style house on Tidewater Lane and they couldn't arrive soon enough.

At the exact moment Sherry reached between his legs and found her uniformed man at half-mast and rising, the neon sign of the Sand Palace came into view. Platt pushed the needle over 90. Feeling Sherry's skilled fingers go to work on his fly, he gripped the wheel tight enough to make the veins on his forearms bulge. The car was rattling like a broken fan as it cracked 100.

Just for the hell of it, and to further incite his woman, Deputy Platt hit the siren and let the cherry tops blaze as they tore past the motel.

83

* * * * * * *

Vance was standing on the walkway in front of his room when he heard the siren pierce the still night air. It made him jump. He couldn't help it. His nerves were badly jangled. After spending the past hour pacing the cramped carpeted perimeter of room 226, Vance desperately needed fresh air. He'd stepped outside and was just beginning to relax a bit, enjoying the night despite the bugs.

Then he heard the siren's whine, and the tension knotting his spine returned with renewed force.

Vance really wanted a drink. His last taste of alcohol came with that ill-advised fourth bourbon in the Angler's Rest. He'd spent the remainder of Tuesday feeling so relieved about being set free, and at the same time so agitated by the arrest, he hardly thought about belting back a few until he was alone in his room at the end of the evening. By then he was so tired it almost didn't matter.

He still felt pure noxious hatred for that swine cop. But mostly he felt a crushing dose of apathy for this entire project and his role in it. Somehow his encounter with Platt had robbed him of the sense of fun he'd been enjoying, and he had a feeling it wasn't coming back.

A stiff cocktail would really offer some friendly companionship right now, but why torture himself thinking about it? The opportunity to wet his whistle was out of reach for the next four days. He was effectively jailed. On house arrest here in the wretched Sand Palace Motel.

He'd considered the idea of slipping out in the middle of the night. Just jump in the car, blaze back to Miami, and forget this whole thing. Considered it seriously, for a minute or two, before dismissing the notion as folly.

It wasn't a sense of obligation that kept him trapped. Vance's sole obligation was to the preservation of his own backside. Certainly he wasn't held by the hopes for impending stardom that seemed almost plausible less than forty-eight hours ago but now appeared to be the most delusional kind of pipe dream.

Fear was what kept Vance from walking away. Fear of Gene Hoffman. Vance wasn't in the habit of treading lightly around any man. He'd come away from enough brawls with his prized face intact to thoroughly trust his feint and jab. But when Hoffman cornered him yesterday after paying for his freedom, Vance folded. The elephantine producer shoved him against a poolside vending machine with enough force to shatter the plexiglass window.

Before Vance could react, those huge mitts were on him. He locked up, mesmerized by the insane force of Hoffman's rage. Vance could almost see the blood vessels explode in a darkening sphere around Gene's nose as he screamed about the deadly blow dealt to *Crimson Orgy*'s emergency fund.

The sudden change in demeanor was shocking. Until that moment, no matter what challenge cropped up along the way, Hoffman had been the coolest cat imaginable. Ready to tackle any tough situation with a laugh and a shrug. Apparently he had other modes of crisis management at his disposal.

So Vance decided it was not in his interest to breach his contract with Stupendous Pictures. The upshot of Hoffman's scolding was clear: any unsupervised foray from the Sand Palace would be met with savage retaliation. If Vance managed to keep his nose clean and finish the job, Hoffman might consider letting him keep the tiny percentage of the gross he'd been guaranteed in his contract. The key word was *might*.

Bad news on top of more bad news.

In a way he couldn't define, Vance felt this production was operating under a rotten sign. It was more than just his arrest. Small rivulets of tension were appearing everywhere, just below the surface.

He wasn't quite sure what was going down between Barbara and Shel Meyer, but it was ugly. Last night, he'd been woken up by a shrill yelling match outside his room. It started around 10:30, right after the crew wrapped Julie's death scene. Vance wasn't needed for that one, and since he was still licking his wounds from the events of the morning he decided to lay low in 226. Bored to distraction, he dozed off.

Barbara's voice tore him from a bad dream. Cracking open the door to his room, Vance saw her running down the stairway toward the courtyard, hotly followed by the director. Catching up to her just as she was about to reach the Sand Palace's entrance, Meyer grabbed her roughly by the wrist. She wheeled around and stuck him hard across the face. The lapping of the nearby pool amplified the sound, sent it pingponging off the walls around the courtyard.

Meyer seemed momentarily stunned. As Barbara turned away she bumped squarely into Gene Hoffman, who had just come through the entrance carrying two brown paper bags under his arm. From his second story vantage point, Vance could tell the bags contained liquor bottles. Fifths, by the size of them. He found himself unconsciously licking his lips.

Hoffman took prompt control of the situation. He waved Meyer away and assumed the brunt of Barbara's rant. Vance couldn't grasp all the specifics, but the gist of it seemed to be that she'd been misled. Lied to, in fact.

Hoffman listened patiently, not interrupting. When she ran out of breath he began speaking in low mellow tones, passively blocking her progress toward the entrance. Vance heard little of what he said but after a few minutes Hoffman had managed to bring Barbara back to a composed state. With a gentleness unusual for such a large man, he guided her back to her room. And didn't follow her inside.

The show seemed to be over, so Vance closed the door and sank onto his unmade bed. He lay in stillness, staring at the cottage cheese ceiling and trying not to think about the bottles tucked underneath Hoffman's arm. Eventually, sleep came.

This morning, it seemed like everything was almost back to normal. Barbara didn't show up for coffee and donuts at 9:00. Meyer made a point of telling the crew she wouldn't be needed today. Said he'd deliberately scheduled a day off after all the hard work she'd put in.

Shit, Vance mumbled under his breath, *who does this guy think he's kidding? Does he think there's a single one of us who didn't hear what happened last night?*

If others on the crew shared Vance's skepticism, they kept it to themselves.

Shooting started an hour later at a private residence a few miles north of the Sand Palace, where they filmed Julie's crucifixion. It was a painfully dull ordeal, with Meyer continually barking at the girl on the cross to keep still. Poor thing, how could she help flinching a bit? Must have been damn uncomfortable mounted on those wooden planks for such a long stretch.

Aside from boredom Vance had some ugly vibes to deal with, coming from all quarters. Hoffman just ignored him, but the mood from the rest of the crew ranged from aloof to openly hostile. Meyer was even more acerbic than usual. Julie was withdrawn and quiet, obviously counting the minutes until she could go home.

Vance exchanged less than a half-dozen words with Jerry Cooke, but that was par for the course. Jerry was beginning to treat his role as "Ace Spade" with almost deranged reverence. This morning, he announced to the whole crew that from now on he would speak to no one

87

unless addressed by his character's name. So much for bonding with his costars.

The behavior of the grips was even more perplexing. Vance had enjoyed a relaxed rapport with Ricky and Juan previously; today they made comically overt pains to keep him at arm's length. Vance was irritated but he tried not to let it show. He knew he had fucked up badly and probably deserved a day's worth of the cold shoulder.

The heaviest vibe came for some unfathomable reason from the brainless lump they called Cliff the Grip. Every time he turned around, Vance would see that moony mug glaring at him from some distant corner. It was like Vance had deliberately injured Cliff by getting pulled over. Idiotic. How could the guy take it personally? Must have something to do with his dog-like loyalty to Hoffman and Meyer. Hardly worth worrying about, so Vance just tried to tune Cliff out.

Once they'd wrapped the crucifixion and waved goodbye to a visibly quaking Julie, the crew drove up to an abandoned warehouse halfway to Ft. Lauderdale. This location served as the meat packing plant where Ace Spade works. Three scenes took place there, two of which they shot today. These involved minimal dialogue and Jerry Cooke nailed all of Ace's lines with a perfection that bespoke his previous acting experience. Weird as he was, there was no denying Jerry's talent.

Driving farther into Lauderdale, they stopped at a quaint Methodist chapel on the northern lip of the town. Numerous reconnaissance trips by Cliff had established the church was empty on Wednesdays. Here they filmed the third murder of the movie, the one where Ace Spade cuts out the heart of a preacher's teenage daughter and leaves it as a surprise in the alms box.

When Vance first read this scene in the script, he'd almost backed out of the project. Rationalizing his qualms away, he predicted it would be filmed in a suggestive rather than literal way. Turned out he was dead wrong, but there wasn't much he could do about it now.

The heart must have come from a pig or maybe a goat and it was a foul thing to behold. Cliff the Grip, obviously disturbed by the process, inserted two thin wires through the left ventricle. The other ends of the wires were wrapped around the fulcrum on a pair of bolt cutters. When the bolt cutters were opened and closed, the heart appeared to pulse grotesquely, oozing thick gouts of stage blood from the open arteries. Cliff refused to operate the rig himself, saying it was just too much for him. Vance sympathized; he could barely even look at the thing.

Angela Billings, the girl playing "BETH" (a.k.a. "VICTIM #3") didn't seem at all bothered by the proceedings. A mousy little brunette with about a pound of dark mascara circling her eyes, her biggest challenge was to not ruin the shot by giggling as Jerry Cooke reached into her red-drenched shirt and pulled out the throbbing ticker that by all rights belonged in some unfortunate farm animal.

Angela's hysterics only served to fuel Jerry, who was always on the borderline of uncontrollability, especially when shooting what Meyer called the *wet* scenes. They were both crippled with mad laughter as Jerry placed two fingers on the bleeding heart like a doctor getting a pulse reading. Shel had to shout at the top of his lungs to get their attention and remind them this wasn't a game. They got it on the fourth take.

Angela actually gave a decent performance, except for one shortcoming. Meyer was disappointed with her scream. In fact, it was the third time this week he'd been unhappy with the screams he was getting. None of the actresses seemed capable of generating the kind of ear-splitting wail he was listening for.

89

For his part, Hoffman thought all the girls had been admirable screamers. He didn't understand Shel's disappointment. A scream's a scream, ultimately. Some are more piercing than others, some evoke pity rather than terror, but they all get the job done. The audience isn't going to sit there and say to themselves, "Gee, I didn't buy that scream. That girl was clearly faking it."

Such was Gene's assessment. Shel did not share that breezy view. This sonic absence in the film was becoming an obsession. He kept telling his actresses he wanted to hear a scream of pure, undiluted terror and agony. No one seemed to understand what he was getting at. When pressed for specifics, such as pitch or length, he could only say, "I'll know it when I hear it. It's got to be *real*."

His frustration worried Hoffman, who took advantage of a quiet moment to remind Shel they could always capture some decent screams at the office in Miami and loop it in later. Meyer wasn't too pleased with that idea. He was intent on capturing it in the camera.

"What difference does it make?" Hoffman asked. "As long as it sounds right, who cares if we pick it up in a studio?"

"That misses the whole point, Gene. We need to feel the terror of the moment. The real terror, as it happens."

"Oh, for Christ's sake."

"Don't worry," Meyer said, chucking him on the arm. "By the time we wrap, I *will* hear that perfect scream. We all will."

How can you be so sure? Hoffman wanted to ask, but Shel had already walked away to set up the next shot.

A quick insert of Jerry dropping the heart into an alms box was all they needed to wrap at the church. Vance was relieved to get out of there. A lapsed Methodist whose parents never missed a service for any catastrophe short of a death in the family, he felt acutely uneasy being a part of this operation.

90

On the drive back to Hillsboro, they pulled off eight moving road shots: four of Jerry driving Ricky's white pickup (with a sign taped on the door reading "Hoffmeyer Quality Meats") and four more of Vance driving the rented Ford Fairlane, supposedly in hot pursuit at twenty miles per hour to keep the lens relatively still. It was the first time he'd appeared in front of the camera all day.

By the time they dragged themselves back to their rooms at the Sand Palace, it was almost 11:00. Vance was exhausted but couldn't sleep. It had been one hell of a strange day. Just as the clock was getting ready to turn over to August 5th, he heard the wail of Deputy Platt's siren rip through the darkness.

It shook him. It reminded him he was a prisoner.

Listening to the siren recede in the lonely distance, feeling the fetid air like an invisible hand on his sweat-soaked brow, Vance calmly and rationally determined he needed a drink. Right away. Hoffman had to give him just one, as long as Vance promised to go promptly to bed. Those two fifths he spied under the producer's arm last night must still have some life in them.

Vance walked down and knocked on the door of 221. No answer. For the hell of it, he tried the knob. He couldn't believe it was actually unlocked.

Emptiness inside.

Maybe Hoffman had stepped away for a meeting in Meyer's room. Maybe he was giving Barbara some turkeyneck. What difference did it make? Either way, the situation was perfect. Vance could slip in, take a relaxing slug or two, then mosey back to his room without anyone the wiser. Whole operation wouldn't take more than thirty seconds.

What the hell. Fortune favors the bold.

Vance stepped inside, quickly pulling the door closed behind him. The bathroom light was on, adding some murky visibility through a crack in the door. Otherwise the room was dark.

He started rifling through the mounds of debris that cluttered almost every available square inch. The floor was all sticky with some kind of dark paint. No wonder Gene was so pissed about losing his contingency fund. He'd have to pay the motel for a total refurbishing of this room.

Papers, empty beer bottles, all kinds of crap sandwiched themselves between Vance and what he was looking for. Then he saw them: two fifths of Jameson's. One of them half-dead, the other with the seal still intact.

Vance lunged for the open bottle, spun off the cap and took a good long pull. The whiskey rolled down into his gullet with a beautiful burn. He breathed deeply before helping himself to another.

Recapping the bottle, Vance started to feel damn good about himself. Almost scary how fast that old bulletproof confidence came roaring back with a few swallows. It wasn't just the immediate glow that lifted his spirits. It was his self-discipline. No man with a true drinking problem could walk away after two measly hits. No, sir. Vance had it under control.

To celebrate this realization, he uncapped the bottle and took two more robust slugs.

Agghhh. Maybe not such a great move. The bottle was noticeably closer to empty than it was a minute ago. Oh, well. Nothing Vance could do about that now. He set the bottle back and rearranged the debris around it.

Turning to leave, he tripped over a small metal box by his feet. Flailing wildly, he narrowly missed splitting his head open on the corner of the dresser.

The box shone in the dusky light by his ankles, almost laughing at the pratfall it had created. Vance was oddly drawn to it. He bent down to run his hands over the smooth metallic surface. It was like a safe with no lock, or a ridiculously heavy case for a small musical instrument.

He opened the box and immediately gagged at the feculent odor that wafted forth. Inside was a bundle of gauze, stained dark red all around one end. It was about the size of an arm, but Vance didn't let himself indulge that idea. Hoffman may be a semi-shady character, based upon some of the stories he'd heard from the waitresses at Augie's, but Vance wasn't prepared to believe the man was carrying around a severed human limb in a metal box. It must be another animal organ. That was the sensible conclusion.

No amount of rationalization could kill his curiosity. He had to know.

A few tugs at the gauzy dressing told the tale. Vance swallowed, his throat suddenly dry again. It was a human arm, all right. Torn asunder just at the shoulder. Still half-fresh, exhibiting signs of some early decay. Bloody ligaments dangled around the curved end of the protruding humerus.

Vance couldn't determine the gender. Small rows of fine black hairs running along the forearm were not definitive. It could have been a sturdy woman or a less than average-sized man.

He unpeeled the gauze a bit more, moving from the elbow toward the hand. The dressing was wrapped tightly with medical tape around the wrist, keeping the hand fully covered.

Get out of here, the rational part of his brain cried.

He couldn't. For some illogical reason, Vance needed to know if this revolting piece of human wreckage was male or female in origin.

As gingerly as possible, he found an opening along the loops of tape and started peeling it back. The gauze fell away from the flesh freely, offering a clear view of what lay underneath.

93

It was a woman's hand, balled halfway into a fist. Long, elegant fingers. Chipped polish on the nails. Vance leaned in closer, plugging his nostrils between his thumb and index finger. He was tempted to touch the skin, to see if it was as real as it looked. Was it possible the thing was a prop? He wanted to believe it but there was just no way. Not with that stench.

Get out of here!

Vance almost felt the arm, but stopped himself just before making contact. He moaned sickly as he noticed something that had escaped his attention.

The woman's fingers were wrapped around a pair of eyeballs.

At the exact moment he felt those four swallows of whiskey rocket from his gut to his mouth, bringing with them the cheeseburger he'd wolfed for dinner, Vance heard the door open. Gene Hoffman's huge shadow fell over him, blotting everything to black as Vance passed out in a geyser of his own vomit.

THURSDAY

Barbara was an excellent driver. Shel had to admit it. He didn't hold to any chauvinistic opinions regarding women behind the wheel, but he was less than thrilled when she'd reached for the keys to the Fairlane and said she wanted to drive. The way she said it sounded less like a request than an order. Acutely aware of the thin ice he was on, Shel handed over the keys without a word.

They drove down to Miami to pick up eight rolls of film Ricky dropped off Wednesday morning at Yale Lab on Grove Avenue. Meyer was anxious, to put it mildly, to see what they'd gotten in the can over the course of the first two shooting days. In just a few hours he would have no choice but to sit down and take a long, cold look at it all.

His mind stayed focused on the potential surprises waiting for him as Barbara jammed the car down the A1A quite a few miles over the speed limit.

Normally, Shel would have dispatched one of the grips to make this pickup. Hoffman suggested the three-hour round trip might provide a good opportunity for the director to mend fences with his leading lady.

Gene had miraculously been able to cool her down the other night, but she was still irate about the way she'd been treated. She held most of her contempt for Shel, because he was the one she'd worked with most closely in preparing for the shoot.

It was a tense drive. They hadn't spoken except in formalities since their embarrassing altercation in the courtyard two nights ago. He thought the day off he gave her would help to melt the ice, but that didn't seem to be the case. She certainly hadn't apologized for slapping him.

Minimal small talk was the most Meyer could get out of her until they entered the city limits. The skyline of pastel high-rises and gently swaying palms seemed to act as a tonic on both of them. It really felt good to be back on home turf.

Shel directed her to the lab and by the time she parked the car they were speaking freely. The chinless, acne-plagued clerk at the counter barely processed the pickup order, so intensely was his gaze fixated on Barbara. She did look especially stunning in a see-through top and white painted-on Capri pants. Meyer gave the clerk processing instructions for the six new rolls he was dropping off, then lead Barbara over to a leather sofa in the lobby.

He beseeched her forgiveness for concealing the whole truth about *Crimson Orgy*. Shel was a master at supplication and eventually his earnest pleas found a response. He made quite clear that she would not have

96

to sully herself with any animal parts or phony blood. She was the heroine of the picture, and so of course she would survive all the way until the closing credits.

As they sat on the sofa waiting for the film to arrive from the vault, Barbara told him exactly how she felt about the situation. She wasn't nearly as offended by the nature of the movie as she was by the insult paid to her intelligence.

"I really wish you'd been straight with me," she said.

"You're right," Meyer agreed hastily. "It was a bad way to handle it. I wanted you for the part and I wasn't sure how you'd react if you knew the whole story."

"Try asking. Jesus, how long did you think you could keep it from me?"

"I wanted to put it off as long as possible. I figured the more deeply you got involved in the role, the easier it would be to handle the material."

"So you're a coward, as well as a liar."

"That's what I've been trying to tell you. I acted like a total shitheel, but only because I knew you were *the* girl to play Kelly."

"What does that mean, exactly?"

"You're just the right one, that's all. I can't imagine anybody else for the part."

"That doesn't make much sense, Sheldon."

"I've learned not to worry too much about logic. Instinct is the master in this game. Rely on logic and you end up with mediocrity."

He really hated the way she rolled her eyes at that one.

"Well, now that I'm in the loop, tell me the whole story. Pretend you're pitching *Crimson Orgy*. What happens?"

"It's a thriller," Meyer said with a shrug.

"Right. And?"

"A maniac calling himself Ace Spade is butchering the daughters of the wealthiest families in a small Florida town. He leaves a calling card with each victim. Our heroine, a reporter for a local paper, starts an investigation when she senses the police isn't doing all it can to solve the murders. She teams up with a lifeguard who found the first body and together they track down the killer. They fall in love along the way. As a twist at the end, the girl winds up saving the guy from the killer instead of vice versa. Ace Spade meets a poetically brutal death. Our lovers embrace. Credits roll."

"OK, I get it. That's how the movie's going to play. What's the *story*?"

"I just told you the story."

"No. Why does it all happen? What's underneath?"

Meyer casually reached into his pocket for a cigarette. He had a little trouble lighting it. "You're losing me, Barbara."

"Don't dodge the question, you know what I mean. This thing's personal for you."

"That's ridiculous. It's a dumb drive-in flick."

Meyer wished he sounded more believable. Barbara obviously wasn't buying it.

"What's underneath?" she repeated. "Why does Ace Spade do it?"

An unexpected wave of gratitude rolled over Meyer. He could feel himself blush. Throughout this entire process, no one had ever asked him that. Not even Hoffman, during their endless bullshit sessions. It sort of amazed him someone cared enough to inquire.

"Benny's a nice kid living on the outskirts of a small elitist town," he began uncertainly. "Born to a Jewish couple of modest means. His mother's a seamstress, his dad drives a produce truck. They're definitely on the fringe of the community, but they're not alone. A small Jewish enclave exists at the indulgence of the WASP plutocracy. It's a ghetto, basically."

"Keep going," Barbara said.

"On his eighteenth birthday, Benny's house burns to the ground. Both his parents die. The fire truck shows up about an hour too late. Benny manages to escape just as the house collapses. In tears, he begs the firemen why it took them so long to arrive. There's been a string of recent fires in the Jewish neighborhood. Arson is suspected in all of them, yet the fire trucks never seem to arrive on time. Benny pounds his fists against the captain's chest, crying, 'What took you so long?'"

Meyer paused to kill the cigarette.

"The fire captain says they were tied up with important business at the station. Benny asks what could be more important than putting out a house fire. The captain reaches into his pocket and pulls out a deck of playing cards. Looks the boy in the eye and says, 'Poker, you little kike.' Benny rips the deck from his hand. The cards fall to the ground and the captain walks away. Benny sinks to his knees, sobbing. He stays there all night, curled up in front of his charred house. When he opens his eyes in the morning, the first thing he sees is a card lying face-up."

Barbara nodded. "The Ace of Spades."

"Exactly."

She waited a moment to see if Meyer had anything more to offer, but apparently he was done.

"That's so much more interesting than the plot of the movie," she finally said.

"I know, but it won't sell tickets. It's just a basic revenge story."

"Yeah, but the motivation adds a whole other layer. It makes the movie more than just a bloodbath. Why not put it in the script?"

"It's in there, tucked away. Suggestively, not literally. Maybe one or two people will pick up on it. The drive-in crowd won't give a damn *why* Ace Spade does what he does. They're paying to see the action."

She raised an eyebrow. "What was that you said about mediocrity?"

"Look, I hear you," Meyer replied, trying not to sound defensive. "I wish I had more freedom to tell the story the way it should be told, believe me. I'm working with a formula here."

"OK. Fair enough."

He placed a hand on her arm. "Sorry. I know I get a little heated. This is a major sore spot between me and Gene."

"Forget it, but tell me this," she said, retracting her arm. "I know it's not part of the movie, I'm just curious. Who's burning down the Jewish homes?"

Meyer dismissed the question with a wave.

"Doesn't matter. The point is, nothing is done to stop it. No one cares. That's why Benny decides to take retribution against the entire town."

She let that sink in as Shel got up to collect the film cans from the counter. He paid the clerk and Barbara held the door for him as he carried them out. She got back behind the wheel and started the engine. Meyer strapped on his seat belt and waited.

Before she put the car in gear Barbara turned, her eyes locking onto his. "I've got one more question."

"Sure," he said, not liking her tone. "Anything you want to know."

"Why does he only kill sexy young chicks?"

*　*　*　*　*　*　*

Shoot the messenger. That's what Gene Hoffman wanted to do. It wasn't a realistic option, but he liked to indulge in the fantasy. It gave a definable channel to his rage, which seemed important at the moment.

The messenger was on Hoffman's transistor radio. His name was Ken Dillard. He was the meteorologist for

100

WKLN, the Miami station that was the only communication available on the FM band in Hillsboro Beach. Hoffman had just spent the past three minutes listening to Dillard's monotone voice spitting out disastrous tidings, and if he never heard that nasal drone again it would be too soon.

Hurricane Estelle was brewing in the Atlantic, creating all sorts of potential mayhem 900 nautical miles across the waves from where Hoffman now stood. After several days of stationary churning, Estelle finally heard the starting gun and was on her horse. She was moving north by northwest at approximately nineteen miles per hour. If unbroken, her trajectory would drive directly into Miami before rolling north up the coastline. Landfall was estimated at forty-eight hours. Residents of both Dade and Broward Counties were already being warned of a likely forced evacuation.

Shutting off the radio and tucking it in his pocket, Hoffman stepped out of his room. He wandered down to the parking lot in front of the motel. A breeze that under other circumstances would have felt like a blessed relief caressed his face and ruffled his baggy shorts. For the hell of it, he licked a bratwurst-sized finger and held it in the air. Undeniably cooler than the past few days, probably below the 80-degree mark. Strong gusts blew up from the oceanside of the highway.

Well, this was perfect. Just what they needed. Hoffman had expended so much mental energy over the past four days trying to anticipate and contain any number of man-made crises that he hadn't even allowed himself to consider something more elemental. Surely God was too occupied with larger matters to pay any attention to what was going on in Hillsboro Beach, FLA.?

Apparently not.

It didn't seem possible. Hurricane season didn't officially start until the end of the month. Meyer and

Hoffman had taken great care consulting the Maritime Almanac when they plotted *Crimson Orgy*'s production timeline. While a mean summer storm was not out of the question, historically speaking, early August was considered a relatively safe zone. What the hell was Estelle doing? How dare she crash the party just as things were getting interesting?

Hoffman walked back through the Sand Palace's arched entrance. His mind was whirling with questions, calculations, and strategies.

What was the shrewd plan? Clearly, to grab as many shots as they could today, then pack up and head back to Miami to sit out the storm in the relative safety of the South Beach offices. It might actually do the production some good. Give everyone a chance to recharge their batteries.

Hoffman dismissed the idea upon quick reflection. It presented an unacceptable risk, that no one would be willing to return to Hillsboro after enjoying the comforts of the city.

There was always the hope Estelle would be downgraded by the time she made landfall. Definitely within the realm of possibility. But if the crew decided to stick it out and she retained or even increased her power, they would be dangerously exposed. Nowhere to hide around here. Hillsboro Beach was a very naked little community. The Maritime Almanac noted that these coordinates hadn't been visited by a serious 'cane since 1928. It was catastrophic. The entire town, as it existed at the time, was decimated. The rebuilding of Hillsboro Beach did not commence until '31, the year of its incorporation.

Hoffman was reasonably sure he was the only one on the crew who'd heard the forecast. No one else at the motel had access to a radio. Meyer and Barbara were still on the road and the Fairlane's radio hadn't been working since Shel smashed his foot into it after the first night's shoot at the beach. He might have picked up the news in Miami, but Hoffman considered that possibility dim. All of the director's limited attention was no doubt focused on picking up the film and pacifying Barbara.

They were due back any minute, in fact. Hoffman pondered his next move. The proper thing was to notify his partner as soon as possible. Shel had a right to know, and his input should be recognized. But something made Gene loathe to share the information. Maybe it was because he could sense how tense the director already was. If Shel got another piece of bad news, he might just crack. Hoffman had always maintained a full disclosure policy on previous productions, but he'd never seen Meyer so tightly wrapped before.

It surely had something to do with where they were shooting, so far removed from the soothing urban familiarity of Miami. But Gene intuited something deeper than that. It related to Shel's almost religious devotion to this project. Meyer had no interest in simply matching the accomplishment of *Blood Feast*. He wanted *Crimson Orgy* to surpass it, to slaughter it. In terms of money, sure, but also in terms of what the film would show. What it would *say*. This had to be a celluloid celebration of carnage unlike anything ever attempted before. That was their only chance to stand out in the exploding gore market.

So the argument went.

Hoffman agreed, but he didn't really get it. How could anyone invest so much of his soul, his sanity, into a junky little picture like *Crimson Orgy*? It didn't make sense. Much as he secretly admired Shel's artistic convictions, this time they were dangerously close to spiraling out of hand.

Mulling this over, Hoffman decided to walk to the manager's office. The salty dog in charge of the Sand Palace must've weathered a few heavy blowers in his time. He would have the proper perspective on the situation. If Ernest planned to keep the motel open for business, Hoffman intended to follow suit with his own endeavor. Obviously there was some risk involved. What else is new in the world of pictures?

As he was crossing the courtyard, Hoffman noticed Vance lying on a sun chair by the pool. Working on the tan, despite the gathering clouds.

Hoffman altered his route and walked over to sit down in the chair next to him.

"Don't get too brown, kid. We need your skin to match for continuity."

Vance ignored him.

"How you feeling?" Hoffman asked.

"Crackerjack. Thanks for asking."

Gene chuckled. "You've had a rough ride, all right. Can't say you've got my sympathy."

"Who asked for it?"

"Drop the attitude, you little prick. I'm tempted to mop my floor with your face."

"Sorry. I offered to clean it up."

"Forget it, that room's a lost cause. I'm moving into 227." Hoffman paused to light a smoke. "Right next to you, champ."

"I'll try not to snore too loud."

Hoffman smiled. He couldn't help liking the way, despite having fallen apart so utterly, Vance still kept the old guard up.

"How bad are the shakes today?"

Vance allowed a short but telling pause before replying, "Come again?"

"You heard me."

"I think you've got the wrong idea, man."

"Been around enough juiceheads to read the signs, believe me. I'm not out to persecute you, kid. I just want to know how deep you're in."

104

Vance either didn't feel the need to defend himself or couldn't think of anything to say. Hoffman let a quiet moment pass, watching a sea gull circling in the patchy sky above.

"I like you, Vance. Like to see you get your act together before you wind up with your chin on a gutter. Them pretty looks won't last long, the way you're going. And then what do you have to fall back on?"

Vance snorted. "If this is what making flicks is like, I say the hell with it."

Hoffman laughed deeply. "Come on, have a sense of humor. Your wounds are all self-inflicted."

"Maybe so, but I didn't count on working with people who keep cadavers in their luggage. What else you got stashed away, Gene?"

It was a taunt, a weak one. Hoffman didn't take the bait.

"I explained that to you last night. You were pretty busy puking so I'll tell you one more time."

Vance tried not to show how attentively he was listening. He didn't remember much about last night after discovering the arm. He awoke to Hoffman slapping him across the face and throwing a glass of cold water on him. They exchanged a few words, then Hoffman guided him to the door. Vance stumbled back to his room and collapsed on his bed without bothering to shower. When he awoke this morning, the whole incident was blurred beyond a clear comprehension.

Hoffman let him wait a moment before explaining. "I know a guy works at a morgue in Miami. Don't ask where, doesn't matter. We need an arm for the scene where Ace sends a surprise Easter basket to the judge. Planned on using a mannequin and maybe we will. Shel wants a real one, just in case."

"How long are you gonna let it rot? It's half green already."

"It arrived by courier yesterday. We shoot it tonight. Then we get rid of it."

"How about packing it in ice?"

"How about doing your fucking job and let me do mine?"

Vance grabbed his shirt from the back of the chair and put it on. The sun had disappeared behind a massive cloud formation. A chill wind cut through the air.

"Well, I guess it all makes sense. Except for one thing. The eyes."

Hoffman shrugged. "Little practical joke from my friend. I didn't even know about it 'til you opened the case."

"A joke," Vance said, remembering the shock of discovering those glazed yellowing orbs clutched in the disembodied hand. "Funny stuff, Gene."

"The guy's got a weird sense of humor. He works in a morgue, what do you expect?"

"OK, forget the body parts. That's not the only screwy thing going on around here."

"What else?" Hoffman asked, shifting his weight and emitting a screech of protest from the chair. "Don't hold your tongue, kid. Spill it."

"Jeez, where do I start?"

"Pick somewhere."

"OK. What about Barbara?"

"What about her?"

"What she's doing in this movie, man?"

Hoffman shook his head. "If you gotta ask me that, I guess the stories I've heard about you aren't true."

"OK, she's a fine piece," Vance said. "Anyone can see that. She can't act worth a damn."

"Is that right, Mr. Barrymore?"

"I may be an amateur, but at least I get the lines out. She's hopeless. And it's pretty obvious she thinks *Crimson Orgy*'s a joke."

106

"What are you so worried about her for?"

"I'm just trying to figure out why she's here."

"You already answered that. She's a tomato."

Vance paused before deciding to continue. Did he really want to get into this?

"I overheard Meyer say something the other day," he said cautiously. "I can't figure out what it means."

Hoffman snorted, displeased. "Eavesdropping on the director. You're really trying to make his shit list, huh?"

"I wasn't eavesdropping. We were wrapping at the beach, I was carrying some stuff to the van. Meyer was talking to that little freak Jerry." Vance raised a sardonic eyebrow. "I mean 'Ace'."

"So what'd he say?"

"Jerry asked him the same thing I asked you. What's she doing here? Why did he cast her?"

"And?"

"Meyer said Barbara's best quality is that she doesn't know anyone in Miami. He said there's no one to come looking for her."

Hoffman's mammoth face was impassive. "Is that all?" he asked.

"Kind of an odd thing to say, don't you think?"

Gene turned to face him. Vance tried to look away but couldn't quite do it.

"Are you sure you want to know what he meant by it?"

* * * * * * *

Meyer didn't have an answer to Barbara's question about the gender-specific nature of Ace Spade's victims. At least not one that satisfied her. They were speeding back to Hillsboro Beach and couldn't get there fast enough to end this conversation, as far as Shel was concerned.

It seemed like such an obvious question that he'd never bothered to consider it. He was following a formula with this project, one that had ancient roots but could most recently be traced to the phenomenal success of *Blood Feast*. All the victims in that flick were shapely young women. Therefore, the same would apply in *Crimson Orgy*. If it ain't broke...

That was the rational answer Shel told himself. Made perfect sense but it wasn't the kind of thing he felt comfortable verbalizing. After all, his film aspired to be more than just a rip-off of another man's work. And, to be very truthful, when he first sat down to write the script it had never occurred to him on any level to make Ace Spade's victims male.

Of course he kills sexy young broads, Shel wanted to say to Barbara. *That's what the audience is paying to see.*

He didn't say that. Instead, he sputtered out a few lame sentences about the long-standing tradition of damsels in distress throughout the history of art and storytelling, all the way back to the Greeks and before.

She was having none of that.

"We're not talking about a woman tied to the train tracks who gets rescued at the last minute," Barbara retorted, her foot jamming down on the accelerator. "The victims in your movie get *run over* by the train. And then you show us their mangled bodies. That's the basic idea, right?"

Meyer ceded her point, all the while deeply resenting the way she was personalizing the movie as if it was an expression of his innermost psyche.

Looking to deflate the tension, he tried a different tack, rambling about the magician's custom of using female subjects for grisly illusions.

"Ever see a man get sawed in half at a magic show?" he asked, feeling like he'd scored a solid point.

"No, but it's the same thing. At the end of the trick, the girl comes out of the box unharmed."

"I think you're mixing two different points. I'm not going to defend the socially redeeming aspects of *Crimson Orgy* because, clearly, there aren't any. All I'm saying is, it's always the woman who's in danger. That's how it works and there's no way I can change it with this shitty little picture."

"You disappoint me, Sheldon. I thought you had higher ideals."

"Personally, I'd be just as happy to make a flick about a bunch of men who get killed, if I thought it would make any money."

Barbara took her eyes off the road to look at him.

"Would you? I'm not so sure."

"What are you saying, I hate women? That's absurd."

"I never said that."

"You're thinking it, though."

"Well, do you?"

"I won't even answer that. It's an insult."

"How come you've never been married?"

"How come *you've* never been married?"

"I'm twenty-two. You're..."

"It doesn't matter. Just because I've never been married doesn't mean I hate women."

"OK, don't get sore. I'm just teasing."

"Besides," Meyer said, regretting the words even as they were leaving his mouth, "Gene's never been married, either."

Barbara laughed out loud, slapping the wheel. "What does that have to do with anything?"

"I'm just saying."

Meyer could feel himself blush for the second time today. What a talent this woman had for making him squirm! She seemed to do it without even trying, and it obviously brought her great amusement.

"That's so cute," she said, still laughing. "He's like your big brother, isn't he?"

"I was only using him as an example of someone my age who's not married."

"Well, we're not talking about Gene. And besides, he definitely doesn't hate women."

"What makes you so sure?"

"It's obvious."

Meyer's jaw was tightly set. "Ol' smoothie Hoffman," he muttered.

Barbara shot him a mischievous look. "Jealous?"

"Forget it. I thought you wanted to have a serious conversation."

"OK, sorry. Let's have a serious conversation."

"Why don't you start, because I don't even know what the hell we're talking about."

Barbara smiled. "What makes me so sure Hoffman loves women? Well, for one thing, he didn't write *Crimson Orgy*. You did, and you have to take responsibility for it."

"He's producing the goddamned thing. With his own money."

"Yeah, but it's just business to him. It has a whole other meaning for you."

"And what's that?"

"That's what I'm trying to figure out."

Meyer struggled to spark a Chesterfield against the wind.

"On second thought," he said, "let's forget the conversation. Silence is golden, so they say."

He was so consumed with lighting the cigarette he didn't see the look of disappointment on her face. He thought she just enjoyed taunting him. She was actually trying to understand him.

The rest of the drive was spent in silence, two people sitting inches apart but lost in their own thoughts. Still, they couldn't help trading weary smiles as the Fairlane pulled into the driveway of the Sand Palace.

"Is it me," Barbara asked, "or does it feel like we just left this place?"

"Keep your chin up. Only three more days to go, after tonight."

"I know that's supposed to be encouraging, but..."

"I know. It's not."

They laughed and she patted his arm in a friendly manner.

"When it's all said and done, I'm sure I'll look back and smile."

"That's the spirit," he said, giving her hand a squeeze. It wasn't much in the way of physical contact, but at least she didn't recoil. They seemed to be growing more comfortable around each other, despite the aborted conversation.

They got out of the car. Barbara started walking to her room while Shel unloaded film cans from the trunk.

He called her name as she entered the courtyard. She turned.

"Thanks," he said.

"For what?"

"For sticking around."

She gave him a little wave and disappeared into her room.

Meyer lugged the eight cans up to 227 and kicked the door open without bothering to knock. He knew it would be unlocked. Hoffman always kept the door unlocked, whether at home, work, or in the john. It was a foible that had driven Shel to distraction numerous times throughout their partnership.

Hoffman had prepared for the screening. A spotted bed sheet was suspended across the wall, held up by clothes hangers. The rickety old projector they'd used since the days of *Tawdry Tina* was set up on a chair.

Meyer loaded the first reel and Hoffman killed the bedside lamp. Neither man said anything. It was a ritual they had, never to speak until seeing how the first few shots turned out.

Things began on an optimistic note. The wide establishing shots of the beach looked good. Worthy of a legitimate B-list Hollywood cinematographer. The light was perfect, the focus nice and deep. Hell, you felt like you were standing right there on the soft cooling sand as night came creeping in.

After the wide stuff came a few motion shots of Vance running across the beach upon hearing the girl's scream. Those looked great, too. Beautiful right-to-left pans that didn't have a single serious wobble.

Shel was feeling pretty excited until they got to the second wide shot, the one that was supposed to include the patrol car. Cliff's stopgap solution had not worked out.

Meyer almost couldn't believe how phony the colored lights looked. At the time of shooting, he was so distracted by the hundred other decisions of the moment that he'd somehow blocked it out.

Now, sitting in the calm of room 227 with nothing to distract his attention from the flickering images on the sheet except his own crushed expectations, he began to realize just how costly Deputy Platt's last-minute power play had proven to be.

"Turn it off" he said, feeling a migraine set in. "I can't take any more."

"Don't you want to see how the intestines look?"

"Not now."

Hoffman rolled his eyes. He wasn't nearly as critical as Shel. Sometimes he thought Meyer deliberately looked for flaws rather than allow himself to enjoy all the things that turned out well. Some kind of psychological flaw at work.

112

Still, Hoffman obliged the request. He knew his director's temperament well enough by now. If Shelly needed to blow a gasket over some insignificant detail the audience would never notice in a million years, best to let him do it and then move on.

"Awful," Meyer moaned from the pit of his clenched hands. "Not worthy of a dinner theater in Boise. A five-year-old would laugh."

"You're overreacting."

"You're *under*reacting!"

"Fine," Hoffman said, now annoyed himself. "I'm gonna take a piss while you brood."

He lumbered into the bathroom, leaving the door wide open. Meyer drifted off into an incensed reverie that was interrupted by a frantic knock on the door.

Cliff the Grip stood outside, looking like he'd just received a bit of truly awful news.

"You should be catching a few winks," Meyer said. "Another long night in front of us."

Cliff groaned an unintelligible reply that was lost in the shrubbery under his nose. His face was chalk white, streaked with sweat.

"You need something, Cliff? We're sort of busy."

He noticed the swarthy Key Grip was holding a ragged copy of the *Miami Ledger* in one hand.

"Thought maybe you should see this," Cliff said in a low mumble. "I can come back later."

"Don't tell me it's more bad news," Shel said, taking the paper from him.

From the open bathroom door, Hoffman witnessed this exchange and bolted into action. Barely bothering to zip up, he moved as quickly as his heft would allow. He immediately assumed what Cliff had in his hands was a weather report about Hurricane Estelle. He wanted to divert or at least soften the blow of this information before Meyer received it.

Too late. Meyer was reading the paper with widening eyes.

"Don't panic, Shelly," Gene began in his most assuring tone. "I know all about that bitch and I think we can work around her."

Meyer looked at him dumbly. "Work around her?"

He handed over the paper. Hoffman's eyes scanned the page. He didn't see anything about the hurricane. Then he noticed a small headline in the lower right corner.

TRAGEDY AT WEEKI WACHEE SPRING

One of Tampa's most popular tourist attractions was the scene of a tragic accident last night. Julie Baylor, one of 20 young women who perform underwater as the "Weeki Wachee Mermadis" died in a bizarre accident when the air hose she used for periodical doses of oxygen was severed on a coral outcropping. Bob Goldnut, proprietor of the attraction, stated that in its 18-year existence no such event has ever occurred, and none of the 45 women who have worked as mermaids have ever suffered injury. The accident happened in full view of a capacity crowd, including many young children, who watched in horror as Baylor struggled for air but was unable to reach the surface of the bottomless natural spring. Several other mermaids attempted to help her but their efforts were insufficient to

Hoffman stopped reading as Meyer took the paper back.

"Jesus Christ."

Cliff the Grip shifted from one foot to another, like he had a bad case of the trots.

"She never wanted to be here," he said, almost moaning the words. "She didn't like what we made her do, I know it."

Hoffman was taken aback by these remarks. Further taken aback to see Cliff glaring at Meyer with what looked like murderous rage.

"Let's not make this mean anything, OK?" Hoffman said. "It's just a coincidence, a terrible coincidence."

"She didn't want to be here," Cliff repeated.

"She knew what she was getting into and she was paid well for it. Isn't that right, Shelly?"

Hoffman glanced at Meyer for backup but none was coming. Shel appeared almost as stricken as Cliff. Hoffman sensed a bad scene unfolding, and he moved quickly to end it.

"Let's get something nice and crystal clear," he said calmly. "This is a hell of a sad thing, she was a sweet kid. But it's got absolutely nothing to do with what we're doing here."

Neither of the other two men said anything.

"Are we clear on that?" Hoffman asked, looking at Cliff but speaking to Shel.

"Yeah," Meyer eventually said. "Sure."

"How about you, Cliff? Are you with the program?"

Cliff shuddered like he was experiencing some sort of internal combustion. Worlds were colliding. His deep, personal loyalty to Stupendous Pictures was bumping up against an even deeper impulse brewing in his gut for the past three days. Ever since that first night on the beach, when he heard that girl scream as Meyer showered handfuls of pigs' intestines onto her.

This is wrong, Cliff couldn't stop thinking. *What we're doing is wrong!*

"It's like we're cursed or something," he finally said.

"Oh, for Christ's sake," Hoffman spat. "That's the biggest load of crap I've ever heard. You surprise me, Cliff."

Meyer didn't seem as dismissive. "What do you mean?" he asked.

Cliff matted down his mustache with a heavy calloused palm. He couldn't look either of his employers in the eye.

"Well, first we lost the patrol car. Then Vance got arrested. Then we had to pay all our backup money to the cop. Now this."

Hoffman snorted. "It's a good thing you don't write the script. If that adds up to a curse in your book, you'd have 'em snoring in the aisles."

Cliff felt himself getting angry at Gene Hoffman for the first time since he'd known him. Really, really angry.

"OK, then. What about the hurricane?" he asked.

Hoffman felt the bottom of his stomach drop out. This was pretty much the *least* desirable circumstance for Shel to hear about Estelle.

Before Hoffman could rebuke the loose-lipped Grip, Meyer had wheeled on him. His eyes bulged with indignation and something not far from panic.

"Hurricane, Gene?"

FRIDAY (A.M.)

She didn't know why she was doing this. There was no reason, but it felt good. As a little girl she'd been able to trick her mind into thinking it was somehow detached from her physical being, without ever losing contact with her senses. In a very literal way she could watch herself from a vantage point outside her own body, while at the same time soaking in everything around her. During especially painful moments, it became an escape mechanism.

This isn't real, she could tell herself. And believe it.

Her gift was a secret she shared with no one. A talent she'd lost well before adolescence but didn't start to mourn until adulthood. *Why did it go away?* she would sometimes sadly wonder. Maybe only the malleable, undeveloped mind of the very young can perform such metaphysical gymnastics before being hardened by experience. Or maybe she just got out of the habit.

Whatever the case, on this unbearably humid Friday morning she seemed to have reclaimed her childhood gift. At this very moment her mind was floating somewhere near the ceiling of room 214, looking down at her body and thinking that what her body was doing felt very, very good. Even if it didn't make much sense.

Barbara was standing naked with her hands planted on the dresser, letting Vance take her from behind. The heavy wooden frame creaked into the wall with each thrust. Her toes sank into the shag rug, curling tight for extra traction.

Vance was like a metronome, counting out an unbroken beat. Barbara liked it this way, but her knees kept getting pushed against the hard surface of the dresser. They'd been going for a good while now, and it was starting to hurt. Worse, it was distracting her.

She turned around, letting Vance slip out.

"What's the matter?" he asked.

"We've gotta try something new. I'm getting creamed."

"Huh?"

"Look at my kneecaps."

Vance got down onto his knees so he could examine hers. They were pink and slightly chafed from banging into the dresser.

"Poor baby," he commiserated, before taking her left knee into his mouth and biting. Barbara shrieked with laughter.

"Get off!" she cried, pushing him away. He fell back onto the bed and lay there. She stood before him, hands on her bare hips and a playful grin on her face. Letting him drink her up while she did the same. This thing started so suddenly, with such an unanticipated explosion, they really hadn't taken the time to visually appreciate one another. Which was a shame, considering what an exceptionally good-looking pair they made.

This was just a matter of time, Barbara told herself. Then she let her mind float away again. No longer content to just look, she crawled on top, locking her thighs around his waist and guiding him into her.

Vance groaned.

"Jesus, I really needed this," he said.

"Oh, yeah? Then how come I had to initiate it?"

"Well... you didn't seem all that interested in getting to know me better."

He barely got the sentence out. Barbara was rising and falling, rising and falling.

"What makes you think I am now?" she asked.

Vance didn't answer. By that point, neither one of them could talk.

About twenty minutes later, Barbara was pulling her hair back into a ponytail while Vance snored on her bed. She smiled as she asked herself why this had come to pass.

Why him? Why now?

Maybe it was because she shot her nude scene last night. Not the first time she'd disrobed for a camera, but it was the only time she'd actually enjoyed it. The three or four still photo shoots she'd done over the past few years felt sleazy and awkward. They were strictly for the cash, whereas her nakedness in *Crimson Orgy* had a sense of fun to it.

The scene was less than a minute in length. It simply showed Kelly Dunhill coming back to her hotel room, undressing, and stepping into the shower. Single camera setup, no dialogue, no frills. Just Barbara's unreal body exposed in a bright fluorescent glare.

They shot it in her own bathroom in 214, which Meyer thought would make her more comfortable. He cleared the set. Even Hoffman stepped outside. The scene didn't

119

require any synch sound and Meyer himself worked the slate. It was just the director and his starlet working together in unusually intimate circumstances.

Barbara wasn't self-conscious in the slightest. She'd already dropped her blouse during the audition at the office in Miami. But last night she found herself held hostage to an odd nervous tic. She kept wanting to smile as she slid her dress down her legs, unhooked her bra, then removed her panties for a quick glimpse of flaxen fur before closing the shower door behind her.

Meyer started to get a bit impatient after she blew three takes with her ear-to-ear grin. "It's totally out of context for the scene," he explained. "Just try to make it natural."

Barbara had to bite on her tongue hard enough to draw blood on the fourth attempt, but they got it.

It was only after she'd put on a robe and Meyer thanked her that Barbara realized how aroused she was. She'd never gotten any kind of charge from the photo shoots, but, for some reason, taking off her clothes for the purring Mitchell really flipped her switch. She found herself impatiently waiting for Meyer to pack up the camera gear and leave the room so she could masturbate. As soon as he left, she bolted the door, let her robe fall to the floor, and pleasured herself while sitting on the edge of her bed.

It was good. It was something she'd been craving all week.

So maybe that's why she found herself back on that same bed this morning, having sex with a virtual stranger.

At least he's a cute stranger, she thought as she watched Vance doze.

She tapped his foot.

"Come on, movie star. Sleep it off in your own room."

Vance pretended not to hear. She leaned in close.

"Hey. You gotta scram."

"What's the rush?" he asked, opening one eye. "Afraid someone might find me here?"

"Maybe."

"I don't think you've got anything to worry about."

"Just the same, I'm asking you to go."

"A few more minutes."

"Vance, this was nice. Really nice. Don't ruin it, OK?"

The other eye opened. "OK, dear."

Vance rolled onto his feet and started pulling up his chinos. Barbara sat on the edge of the bed, watching him. She liked watching him. He surprised her. She'd heard what a slayer of women he was from Gene Hoffman, who essentially warned her that Vance would at some point make a concerted effort to get in her pants. Thus informed, she'd been on guard from the moment they were introduced.

It never happened. Aside from some gentle flirting, Vance had basically let her be. She realized she'd put up a bit of a preemptive cold front, but his reticence, bordering on shyness, perplexed her. Of course, she didn't know what Vance had been through over the past few days, didn't realize he was forcing himself to adopt a much lower profile than usual. She simply chalked up his quiet manner to a respectable upbringing. Even found herself mildly irritated not to be receiving more overt interest from him.

About 9:00 this morning, as she went down to the pool to catch a little sun before the crew gathered at 11:30, she was inwardly pleased to see Vance lying in her favorite tanning chair. He gallantly surrendered it and stretched out on a towel. They chatted about nothing for a while. It was the most relaxed interaction they'd shared so far. The sun seemed to melt any barriers. The lapping of the pool was almost hypnotic.

Vance asked Barbara about her background, her childhood. He actually seemed interested. Surprising herself almost as much as him, Barbara interrupted his questions by taking his hand and leading him to her room. Such a forward move was hardly typical for her. Until it happened she hadn't given much carnal consideration to Vance, except in a vague way of admitting he was a fine specimen.

Now, an hour and two orgasms later, she was relieved not to feel any regrets. Sure, it was a fairly irregular decision. Perhaps a little reckless, but so what? It felt good, it was harmless, and they both obviously had some steam to let off.

"Mind if I ask you something?" Vance asked as he pulled his T-shirt over his head. "It's been on my mind all week."

"Shoot."

"What the hell are you doing here?"

"It's my room, isn't it?"

"You know what I mean. You don't seem like the kind of person who'd come within a hundred feet of *Crimson Orgy*."

"I don't know," she said, retrieving some panties from the dresser. "Someone offers you a role in a movie, it's hard to walk away."

"Yeah, but you don't seem all that interested in it."

Barbara shot him a look.

"Don't get me wrong. You're doing a great job. It just seems beneath you."

"Thanks, Vance. That's actually pretty sweet."

He looked at the smile on her face, thinking about the conversation he had yesterday with Hoffman. Part of him felt obligated to share it with Barbara. A more dominant instinct told him to keep his mouth shut.

"This movie," he said. "It's kind of sick, don't you think?"

Barbara nodded. "When I walked into that room the other night and saw those brains..." She shuddered.

"That's nothing. Hoffman's been carrying around a goddamn arm in a box. A human arm."

"Yeah, OK." Her face conveyed doubt with a trace of amusement.

"Saw the damn thing with my own eyes," Vance said, the words evoking an unbidden image of the grim discovery. Vance forced it from his mind, deciding not to share that part of the story with Barbara.

"I'd think I'd rather not hear any jokes like that. Not right now."

He slid on some sandals and gave her what had to be his most serious look.

"It's no joke. And here's the weirdest part. Gene told me they need the arm for the Easter scene."

"Which scene?"

"You know, the one with the 'blood-soaked basket'."

She gave a small shrug.

Vance smiled. "Did you even read the script or what?"

"Not all of it. I'm not allowed to."

"What does that mean?" he asked, feeling a small shiver of alarm he couldn't quite place.

"I only get one scene at a time. Doesn't make much sense, but that's the way Sheldon wants it. Why are you looking at me like that?"

Vance offered a shrug of his own, hoping it appeared casual. "Nothing, I just didn't know that's how you were working."

"So what about the arm?"

"Well, supposedly they're keeping it in case the prop arm doesn't look right."

"Yeah. And?"

"There *is* no prop arm."

"I'm still not following".

"It doesn't exist, Barbara. No mannequin, or anything like it. At least I couldn't find one in the shed. I checked this morning, before you came out."

"Hold on. You've been snooping around?" she asked incredulously.

"A little."

"*Why?*"

"I don't know. Bored, I guess."

All of the sudden Vance felt mildly embarasssed. He stepped to the door and laid a hand on the knob.

"Anyway, I've been thinking," he said with a turn. "What kind of sick nut would put this stuff in a movie? Hearts cut out while they're still beating. Disembowelments. Crucifixions. It's insane. I mean, little kids go to the drive-in."

"Sheldon says blood is the oldest form of popular entertainment," Barbara replied.

"Is that right?"

She leaned forward to mimic Meyer's slightly nasal voice as she repeated one of the canned lines he'd fed her: "'A grand tradition, from cave paintings to the Roman Coliseum to *Crimson Orgy*.'"

She trailed off, giggling.

Vance smiled. "He really laid that on you with a straight face?"

"Uh huh. I think he meant it, too."

"The guy's got a screw loose. You ever catch that look he gets sometimes? Like he's just ridiculously *into* the whole thing?"

Barbara thought for a moment.

"No, but I've caught him mouthing Jerry's dialogue a few times."

"Jerry," Vance said, shaking his head. "Talk about another basket case. Where the hell do you think they found him?"

"He's been nothing but sweet to me."

124

"Sure, as long as you call him Ace."

"That is a little weird," she conceded. "He told me it's this new style of acting. Says Marlon Brando does it in his movies."

"Christ. We got a crackpot director who thinks he's feeding Christians to the lions, and a screwy two-bit actor thinking he's Brando." He tuned the doorknob, then released it. "How'd we get roped into this loony bin?"

She walked over and grabbed him teasingly by the ribs.

"Are you saying you're scared, Vance Cogburn?"

"No. I'm saying you're the only one I trust around here."

"You really know how to make a girl feel special."

"Don't be so flattered. Everyone else belongs in a straight jacket."

Barbara smiled and kissed him. She hadn't gotten around to throwing anything on above the waist and Vance's fingertips started making the rounds.

"OK, handsome," she said, pushing him away. "Get lost. Mind no one sees you on the way out."

"Catch you on the set."

Vance opened the door, performed an exaggerated show of making sure the coast was clear, and was gone.

* * * * * * *

The wheels came off a little before noon. It happened so fast, no one was quite sure who to blame. Vance had a big mouth and his judgment was definitely suspect, but there was no excuse for Cliff's reaction. By the time things settled down, an ugly pallor had settled over the entire crew.

Everyone gathered by the pool at 11:30 to be subjected to a pep talk by Gene Hoffman. The producer didn't know if anyone else shared Cliff the Grip's despairing view of this production, but he wanted to make damn sure spirits stayed reasonably high in the face of all the mounting bad news.

One thing Cliff definitely had shared with his crew-members was word of Estelle's imminent arrival. No more keeping that monster in the box. Last night, Hoffman eventually managed to assuage Shel Meyer's concerns, though it took him until almost midnight. Now he felt the need to play wet nurse to the rest of his crew. He couldn't afford anyone going AWOL at this point. They still had two dozen scenes to shoot, and less than three days to do it.

Hoffman began his spiel with some standard-issue flattery about what a fantastic job everyone had done so far. He acknowledged there had been a few curve balls along the way, but what else was new in the world of filmmaking? And yes, he conceded, there was a tropi-cal storm headed roughly their way but no one needed to panic about that. He'd just heard the latest weather report predicting Estelle would spin back out over the Atlantic long before she reached Hillsboro Beach. Even if she decided not to cooperate, they would have plenty of time to pack up and drive north to safe accommodations in Ft. Lauderdale. But Hoffman was quite confident such a drastic move would not be necessary.

It was hard to tell if his sunny estimation made an impact. A collection of blank stares greeted his words. He forged on, disingenuously implying that everyone could count on some form of equity in *Crimson Orgy*'s box office take. Specific percentages would be discussed later on an individual basis.

Just as he was winding down with his customary chant of, "Fame and Fortune for All!" the shit really hit the fan. Vance stood directly behind Barbara during the speech. Close enough to gently press his crotch against the small of her back. She didn't seem to mind, as long as no one else noticed. She pushed him off once or twice, but Vance could tell by her body language that she was enjoying it. What on Earth is more fun than sharing a secret sexual connection in front of a group of clueless people who think they know the score? She even pretended to reach around and scratch her back, allowing her fingers to brush against the hard-on straining his chinos.

He should have employed greater restraint. The whole point was to enjoy a *silent* flirtation. But he couldn't help himself. Vance leaned forward and whispered something absolutely filthy in Barbara's left ear.

Very unfortunate timing.

He delivered his randy message at the exact moment Hoffman stopped chanting to catch his breath. What was intended as a private communication became a publicly broadcasted obscenity. Everyone heard it, but no one heard it louder than Cliff the Grip, standing protectively to Barbara's right.

A split-second of awkward silence passed before Cliff's left arm snaked around Vance's throat in a chokehold. Vance was so jolted he could barely hear Cliff bellowing at him to apologize. He couldn't oblige even if he wanted to. Cliff was throttling him hard enough to turn his face an alarming shade of purple.

Hoffman rushed forward to break it up but Cliff's hold was too strong. Vance's vision was strobing in and out as his brain cried for oxygen.

A black-out loomed.

It wasn't until Cliff felt Barbara's hand on his shoulder and heard her calmly telling him to let go that his arm relaxed a bit.

Vance made immediate use of his freedom. He buried a sharp elbow in Cliff's gut. As the Grip doubled over, Vance spun free and kicked him squarely in the groin.

Every man within earshot winced at the dull thud and the strangled gasp that followed.

Cliff reeled backward, knocking into a table on which several hundred dollars' worth of lighting equipment sat. The table collapsed and it all came crashing onto the pebbly ground. Another sizable chunk of the budget, lost in an instant.

Chaos reigned before everyone took a collective time out and calmed down. Meyer helped Cliff into a chair and told him to take long, slow breaths. Then he went in search of a first aid kit. Vance barely escaped a beating from Ricky and Juan, thanks to timely intervention from Hoffman. The two crewmen may have liked the actor, but they understood the hierarchy of the production team. Their loyalty definitely lay with their Key Grip.

Jerry Cooke was so wound up from the action he spun around the courtyard like a motorized top, shadow boxing and wildly slashing the air with an imaginary knife. Barbara retreated to a quiet corner, feeling somewhat nauseous. And furious with Vance.

Hoffman considered giving everyone a brief cooling off period but Meyer overruled him. They had a big day ahead of them. Four daylight scenes, all of which were technically straightforward but entailed substantial dialogue. Then an hour break at dusk before reassembling for a night shoot that promised to be especially daunting.

Their plan entailed breaking into the Fairview Cemetery, just outside of Hillsboro, to shoot the movie's penultimate murder scene. Hoffman had sought permission from the proprietor but got stonewalled. Too bad. When you're making a feature on a shoestring, you ask nicely first, and when you don't get what you need you just grab it.

Juan already refused to take part in tonight's shoot, claiming it grossly contradicted a number of religious convictions. Hoffman agreed to let him have the night off. It made more sense to tackle a single scene with one man short, rather than risk losing Juan permanently. His pay would be docked, however.

Things eventually got back to normal by the pool when Hoffman forced Cliff and Vance to shake hands. They trudged out to the parking lot and cramped themselves and the unbroken equipment into the four available vehicles. Vance tried to climb into the van next to Barbara, but she slammed the door on him.

Seeing no other place to sit, he climbed into the passenger seat of Juan's pickup. The cab was filled with evil fumes from his cigarillo. Vance just rolled down the window and didn't say a word.

The caravan started rolling out of the Sand Palace's parking lot. Hoffman took the lead in the Fairlane with Barbara in the passenger seat and Meyer in back. Vance really wished he could hear the conversation they were having. Ricky's pickup truck pulled out next with Jerry Cooke riding shotgun, followed by Cliff's van.

Juan sucked down on the foul thing clenched between his teeth and tossed the butt out the window. As he ground the gearshift into first, he spoke to Vance without looking at him.

"You know he's gonna kill you, right?"

FRIDAY (P.M.)

Estelle was proving to be a wily, capricious bitch. She was confounding the meteorologists with her erratic behavior. Only an hour after stating she would undoubtedly strike the coast sometime Friday night, Ken Dillard came on the air at about 2:00 P.M. to report she had stalled once again and might not make landfall until midday Saturday.

The uncertainty was driving Hoffman nuts. Not that it made a whole lot of difference. Even the most apocalyptic forecast wouldn't change his plan now. When he told the crew earlier today that Estelle was expected to spin off over the ocean, he'd been lying. None of the many weather reports he'd listened to over the past twelve hours predicted that. They all agreed she was definitely going to hit the coast of Florida. Just a question of when, and where, and how hard.

Hoffman ponderously weighed his options before deciding to lie. He knew the safety of the crew was in his hands, and he didn't take that responsibility lightly. But those hands of his were tied. This movie needed to wrap on schedule, if it was going to wrap at all. By Sunday night (or, more accurately, early Monday morning) the final shot absolutely *had* to be in the can.

Like a blood-bloated vampire on an all night spree, this production would deteriorate to dust with the first rays of the sun. At that point they would be out of time, out of money, and out of personnel. Most members of the cast had regular jobs and lives to resume. Their week-long discounted stay at the Sand Palace would be expended. And there would be nary a dime left in the production coffers.

One way or another, we will finish on time, Hoffman thought grimly.

Do or die.

Or both.

In all his years as an exploiteer, Gene had never worked on such a tense set. He hardly agreed with Cliff's inane theory about a curse, but there was no denying they'd been dealt a run of foul fortune right from the start. Hoffman didn't see any way of lightening the mood, and he knew returning to Miami ahead of schedule would be tantamount to shelving the project. He wasn't prepared to do that.

Crimson Orgy was the costliest movie he'd produced so far and he wasn't about to kiss off the expense. Besides, he still believed it would be a big earner if they could just finish the damn thing.

With that resolve, he turned off the transistor radio and decided not to turn it on again. *Que sera, sera.* A gambler at heart, Hoffman felt there was just no way he was going to meet his end at the hands of some skirt named Estelle. He always figured he'd wind up getting shot in the back or dying in his sleep, depending on how long his luck held out.

Buoyed by their producer's eternal optimism, the crew trudged onward. Blissfully ignorant of the potential devastation heading their way.

After picking up two scenes on the beach a mile or so from the motel, everyone loaded back into the caravan and headed further south. This time Vance rode with Ricky. He didn't put much stock in Juan's warning, delivered as it was by a wetback. Just the same, he made a point of keeping Cliff within his field of vision at all times.

At around 3:15 they stopped at a road stand where Hoffman sprung for burgers and malts out of his own pocket. He felt it was a worthwhile investment to derail or at least forestall some sort of mutiny. A well-fed crew is always more apt to stick it out.

While everyone was eating, Hoffman tapped Cliff on the shoulder and invited him to a private conference. The Key Grip had seemingly not recovered from this morning's fracas. Physically he appeared fine; Hoffman had to wonder what kind of equipment the man was packing if he could just shrug off the kind of nut-shot Vance laid on him.

It was Cliff's mental state that the canny producer found disturbing. He'd clearly blown some sort of fuse. His eyes were glassy and unfocused. He followed instructions accurately but with a dull, labored gait unusual for him. And his attention never seemed to leave Barbara. Ever.

Since the beginning of the shoot, Hoffman had noticed the way Cliff looked at her. He didn't give it much consideration. Hell, everyone looked at her that way. But after this morning, Gene started to suspect there was more than the expected lustful admiration behind Cliff's gaze.

Standing outside the road stand's restroom, he tried to draw Cliff out on the subject, to no avail. The only thing his Key Grip was able to communicate with any clarity was that, as far as he was concerned, it wasn't over between him and Vance.

Hoffman sighed wearily. That was the last thing he wanted to hear.

"Go ahead, take the kid apart," he said. "Just keep your cool until we wrap. I need you to be all business until Sunday night. Do we have an agreement?"

Cliff nodded, barely seeming to process the words. *It's like trying to have a conversation with a fucking mental patient*, Hoffman thought. If Gene had known about Cliff's history with institutionalization, he may not have made that association so glibly.

The meal finished, the crew loaded back into the cars and drove to a public park just north of Pompano Beach. It was a shady, meandering stretch of thick grass and gentle trees. Thankfully empty, except for a few picnickers.

This was where they were to shoot the big love scene between Frank Butler and Kelly Dunhill. Naturally, it could not come at a worse time. Barbara and Vance had kept their distance from each other all afternoon. They hadn't had a chance to patch things up during the continuous shooting.

Barbara wasn't really mad at him anymore. Thinking through the situation, her anger had been redirected to Cliff. Why in God's name did he react like that? What illusions was he laboring under, *vis-a-vis* their relationship? She'd tried to be friendly, had chatted him up once or twice, but so what?

The truth was, most of the time she hardly even noticed Cliff was around.

That was all changed now. After he'd stepped in to violently defend her honor, she found it difficult *not* to notice him. During the first two scenes they shot this afternoon he was always lurking nearby. He had this expectant look on his face, as if waiting for her to clarify something urgent for him. His suffocating scrutiny reminded Barbara of the way her father used to look at her mother, right before the beatings started. She couldn't take it.

During a quick break while Meyer reloaded the camera she quietly thanked Cliff for sticking up for her, but tried to make it clear he'd acted inappropriately. She didn't need his help, or his protection.

"Do you understand what I'm saying, Cliff?"

"Uh, yeah," came the opaque reply. "I thought you'd be offended by what he said, that's all."

"Vance was just kidding. You know how he is."

"That's no way to talk to a lady. I don't care if he's kidding or not."

"Look," she said, losing patience. "If it doesn't bother me, why should you care?"

"You shouldn't be here, Miss Cheston. I mean Barbara, sorry."

She didn't have time to ask what he meant by that before Meyer called out that they were ready to resume work.

Barbara cast an admonishing glance at Cliff and walked over to the camera. Here they were, ready to stage what was supposed to be a sexy embrace under highly dubious circumstances. How could she relax with the glassy-eyed Key Grip mooning around? Hoffman sensed her discomfort and told all nonessential crew members to keep a healthy distance as they filmed the delicate scene.

The script called for Kelly and Frank to seek refuge in the park after snooping on Ace Spade and almost getting caught. Inflamed by the excitement of their close call, the two protagonists start making out in a passionate but tasteful style.

Barbara and Vance stood woodenly a few feet from one another as Meyer doped out the scene for them.

"OK, you'll enter from the left," he said, framing the shot with his hands. "Deliver that first batch of dialogue. Then take a seat on the grass. You'll run through the next few lines, then start kissing. Clear?"

"Just like that?" Barbara asked.

"Just like that. Make it real, like you really find him attractive."

As Meyer walked over to the camera, she glanced at Vance.

"Still mad at me?" he asked.

"Yes," she said, attempting not to smile and failing. "Furious."

"Try not to let it show. This scene's supposed to inspire all the kids in the audience to start necking. You don't want to be responsible for ruining a million dates, do you?"

"I don't want that on my conscience, no."

"Me neither. So let's make this good."

Meyer locked in the composition he wanted for the shot and called for quiet on the set. A little boy flying a kite near the picnickers refused to cooperate, so Gene Hoffman marched over to stifle him.

"OK, here we go," Meyer said to his two stars. "Remember, Frank and Kelly have been desperately attracted to one another since the moment they met. They just had a very close call. The adrenaline's running high. Before they even know what's happening, they're in each other's arms. So make it spontaneous and give it some heat."

Barbara and Vance traded a glance. He was looking at her with a raised eyebrow that seemed to say, *I told you this guy had a screw loose.* She bit her tongue.

"Are you two ready?" Meyer asked.

"I'm ready, Sheldon," she said, her eyes still on Vance.

"I'm definitely ready."

"All right." Meyer crouched behind the camera as Ricky held the slate in front of the lens. "We're rolling. Annnnndddd... action!"

Vance and Barbara stepped onto their marks and delivered their lines. Perfectly, like a couple of old pros. They sat on the grass. He took his hand in hers as they walked through the rest of the stilted, phony dialogue. She leaned into him. His arm was around her waist. They started kissing. It was the most natural performance they'd given so far.

Once their lips touched, it became real. Neither was enough of an actor to fake it. In their minds, they were back in Barbara's room at the motel, just like this morning. Clothes in a heap at the foot of the bed. Suppressing their moans in consideration of the thin walls. All over each other, every which way.

Hoffman had crept back after bribing silence from the young kite-flyer with a shiny nickel. Standing behind the camera, he watched the scene with a huge grin on his face. He was fond of both Barbara and Vance, despite it all. The kids looked good together. Hell, he hoped they *were* screwing, as long as it didn't create any further interference with the shoot.

Barbara's fingers were tracing a teasing path along the hairs on Vance's forearm. Grabbing his wrist gently, she guided his hand under her shirt and placed it on her left breast. She'd decided not to wear a bra, at Hoffman's suggestion. Vance's thumb and forefinger closed around her erect nipple.

"OK, take it easy," Meyer said from behind the camera. "No need for overkill."

Shel was comfortable giving direction in the middle of the shot because he planned to run music over the soundtrack during this part of the scene. But his actors paid him no mind. Vance was caressing her breast vigorously and Barbara was making a moist circle around the perimeter of his mouth with the tip of her tongue.

"Hey, come on," Meyer said nervously. "Tone it down, I'm serious."

Their ardor only increased. They were legitimately going at it. Vance's free hand dropped casually into Barbara's lap, way too close to her pussy for Meyer to feel comfortable with.

"Shit!" he cried from his crouch. "Cut!"

Meyer killed the camera and stormed over to where they sat.

"What do you think you're doing? This isn't a stag flick."

Barbara laughed. "What are you getting so uptight about? You said you wanted heat."

"Heat, not smut. What's with putting his hand on your tit? That could get us in deep shit with the censors."

"Don't yell at her, man," Vance said. Then he lied, "It was my idea."

"I don't give a fuck whose idea it was. When I give you a direction, you damn well better follow it. Both of you."

Barbara wasn't smiling anymore. "Let me get this straight. You're happy to show people being tortured, mutilated, and killed. But you're scared to show a little heavy petting?"

"Don't jerk me around, Barbara. We've been through too much today."

"You gotta admit, she has a point," Vance said.

Meyer took a deep breath. "Listen, kids. The game we're playing here's got some very specific rules. There's only so much I can get away with. Personally, I'd love to shoot you two frolicking all day. You know I'm no prude."

"So what's the problem?" Barbara asked.

"The problem is context. Bare boobs are fine. A man's hand on a boob, that's trouble."

"My shirt was on."

"Not the point. I can't show him feeling you up, clothed or otherwise. It's called obscenity and it could land me in jail."

Barbara started to launch another argument about the obscenity of the violence in *Crimson Orgy* but stopped herself. What was she trying to prove? She could have walked off this production if it bothered her so much. It did bother her. But she was in deep now and she might as well just see it through.

"Sorry, Sheldon," she said. "Let's try again."

They reset for another take. This one went well, with the kissing restrained to an acceptable degree.

Acceptable to everyone except Cliff. From his exiled position some fifty feet behind the camera, he could see every smooch and cuddle all too clearly. Jaw set tight, heavy breaths made his mustache shimmy with each exhalation. His huge hands toyed with a trusty pocket knife, opening the blade and closing it. Cliff barely noticed when he slashed his thumb, sending a trickle of blood down his tightly flexed forearm.

* * * * * * *

Estelle finally arrived. A little ahead of schedule, depending on which forecast you listened to. Her timing was actually quite considerate. They had just pulled off their last setup of the afternoon, around 6:30, when the sky grew dark and heavy. The graveyard shoot would have to be rescheduled for Saturday night, but that wasn't a total disaster. Hoffman and Meyer were still reasonably

138

hopeful they could get it all done by the end of the week. They really didn't have any choice. It was time to move indoors, brace themselves, and hope for the best.

By the time they got back to the motel and started unloading the equipment there was no denying the hurricane's proximity. Hefty gusts of cool wind peppered with raindrops appeared out of nowhere, strong enough to make the oak-solid Gene Hoffman swerve like a drunken man.

Estelle was obviously planning on a dramatic entrance. Shel grudgingly admired her sense of theater. He was sitting in his room as night fell, banging away on the Underwood. A new scene had been niggling at the corner of his mind all day and he wanted to get it on paper before the heat of fresh inspiration cooled.

The scene had nothing to do with *Crimson Orgy*. It was for another project, one he'd never mentioned to Hoffman.

If he ever managed to get it all down, this would be something of a departure for him. No blood, no death, no illicit skin. In short, no pandering to the dark side of human nature. Just a sunny, optimistic tale about a little man beating the odds. This was the kind of story he'd tried to create as a novel years ago, only to be crushed by his own inability to believe in happy endings.

Tonight it just seemed to come to him, as easily as anything he'd ever written. Maybe he had matured somehow? Or maybe he'd just grown more willing to delude himself. In either case, Shel was greatly excited to see the words that had escaped him for so long driven into the page by the Underwood's keys.

He'd pulled the blinds aside to watch the storm as it crashed across the motel. As frustrated as he was about the delay Estelle created, he still found himself drawn to her power. Storms had always fascinated him, even as a little kid. They were God's own electric show. Sky-rending cracks of lightning were terrifying, but they brought a cathartic thrill as well. Kind of like horror movies.

The dirty window pane was already speckled with raindrops that grew larger and louder as time passed and Estelle drew closer. Meyer liked listening to the rain against the window. It provided a nice syncopation to the hammering of his fingers on the keys.

After an hour of steady typing, he leaned back in the chair and stretched his arms behind his head. Glancing at the window, he was startled to see Barbara peering in at him through the shimmering glass. She looked like a ghost out there. Her face appeared to be stained with tears, but it was probably only the rain.

She waved, almost shyly. Meyer got up to open the door. Upon closer inspection it really did look like she'd been crying. Her eyes were pink and puffy.

"What's up?" he asked in a friendly voice.

"Nothing, really. I was just wondering what you were doing."

"Sitting out the storm, like everyone else."

She hesitated. Her hair hung in a wet tangle that didn't look like it was created solely by the weather.

"Mind if I sit it out with you?" she asked quietly.

Shel was a bit taken aback but he said, "Of course not. Can't stand out here or you'll catch your death."

With a small nod she stepped inside the room and he closed the door behind her. Meyer was tempted to ask why she wasn't seeking companionship in Vance's room, but he held his tongue. Their heated performance in the park made it pretty clear to anyone with a working pair of eyes that something was going on between the two stars.

Even Jerry Cooke picked up on it. Before the love scene started rolling, Jerry had been contenting himself by strangling a novelty rubber chicken he'd bought at the road stand. Eyes squinting, tongue protruding grossly with concentration, Jerry wrung the synthetic neck hard enough to burn the skin on his palms. The look on his face was scarier than anything Shel had been able to capture on camera so far, but it went unnoticed by the busy crew. When Barbara and Vance started their on-camera make-out session, Jerry forgot all about the chicken and watched them go at it with the same gape-jawed look.

Driving from the park back to the motel, Meyer and Hoffman had a private discussion about the situation. In general, they tried to discourage liaisons among their employees, at least during the production process.

(That policy was instituted after an ordeal during the shooting of *Wiggle, Wiggle, Wiggle!* when Meyer enjoyed a steamy affair with a young starlet lasting just under four hours. Turned out the girl was also sleeping with their leading man, who took a territorial view of his bedmates and came close to clobbering Meyer when he observed him emerge from her dressing room with lipstick all over his mouth. Hoffman tore the enraged actor off the director and promptly fired him, but not before twisting the cuckold's arm hard enough to dislocate his shoulder.)

They certainly didn't want a replay of that situation, but given Vance's disastrous attraction to the bottle Hoffman figured they were better off if his energies were focused on alternate sources of pleasure. Shel reluctantly agreed.

What Meyer didn't know was Barbara had just left Vance's room with a slammed door and tears of anger misting her eyes. She'd gone there hoping Vance would be able to distract her from the intense fear collecting in the pit of her stomach since she learned about the storm. Barbara was only four when Hurricane Dora tore through Mobile, decimating large swaths of the city. Though she didn't remember the storm itself, she never forgot her mother's wild-eyed fear every time threatening clouds would form on the horizon. She'd inherited that fear on a powerful if not quite rational level.

So she sought out Vance with very specific hopes. Just some warm conversation, a friendly voice, maybe a few laughs.

Vance disappointed her keenly. He only seemed able to offer one kind of distraction, and she was in no frame of mind for that.

His initial movements were rebuffed gently. She knew it was reasonable for him to have some expectations, but she hoped he would set them aside once she made it clear they weren't going to be met tonight.

No such luck. Vance was oblivious to the cool reception that greeted his overtures. He didn't seem to understand her mood was a million miles from sex. He advanced, she demurred. He persisted, she rebuffed him again, less gently. On it went, until they both snapped at each other. Vance made a few particularly crude, cruel remarks.

Looking at him cooly, Barbara determined she was dealing with an overgrown adolescent. Maybe that's all he ever was. Or maybe he was just as scared as her, and sex was the only escape that would take his mind off the frightening possibilities Estelle presented. Either way, he'd blown it. The fleeting pleasure of this morning, and its brief reverberation during the love scene at the park, faded into nothing. She was done with him, and that's exactly what she said as she made for the door. He presented a few choice words in reply but she barely heard them.

She found herself standing on the walkway outside Vance's room, looking for a direction. The thought of going back to her own empty room was unpalatable. She craved company at that moment as keenly as she sought solitude most of the time. Barbara had always been her own best companion, ever since childhood when she would blot out the unpleasantness of her home life by drifting into her blissfully detached reveries.

Feeling the rain sting her face, she knew that old evasive tactic wouldn't work. So she walked down to Shel Meyer's room and stood outside, watching him type through the wet window pane. She didn't quite have the nerve to knock, and was ready to walk away when he happened to turn his head and notice her.

"I'm not interrupting you, am I?"

Meyer took a quick glance at the typewriter and shook his head. "Nah. I was getting ready to take a break."

Barbara sat down at the foot of his bed, facing the window.

"Storms scare me," she said.

"Really? I kind of like them. They remind us how miniscule we are, with our everyday cares."

"I always thought it was strange the way hurricanes have names. Why not tornados? Earthquakes?"

"I think it's because of the long gestation time," Meyer said, taking a seat next to her. "Quakes strike instantly, without warning. Same with tornados. We get a chance to get to know hurricanes before they punish us. By naming them, maybe we hope to alter their course. Like we can deal with them on a personal basis, begging them for mercy."

"Hmm. Interesting theory."

"Probably just bullplop. It's the first thing that came into my head."

She turned to look him dead in the eye. "Should we beg Estelle for mercy?"

He had to look away. "I don't think so."

"Can't hurt, can it?"

"I'll pass, just the same," he said.

Then he added, without knowing why, "Estelle was my mother's name."

"She's dead?"

143

"Yeah. Long time ago."

"My grandmother basically raised me," Barbara said, also not knowing why.

"Is that right?"

"Yeah. My mom was very loving but she just wasn't equipped to be a parent. She had enough to deal with, keeping away from my dad."

Shel reached for a cigarette and lit it. "How do you mean?"

"He..." she began, stumbling a bit. "He wasn't good to her."

"They're no longer married?"

"No. He left, thank God. Must have wanted someone new to beat up. By that point, my mom wasn't really all there, you know?"

"I'm sorry."

"It wasn't so bad after a while. I love my grandmother. She was seventeen when she had my mom, and my mom was only sixteen when she had me, so it wasn't like she was some old lady. She was strong, still is. She ended up taking care of us both."

Barbara repositioned herself to avoid Meyer's smoke. Turning her head, she almost cried out. Then realized the naked torso she saw propped against the far wall belonged to a mannequin. Half-hidden by the dresser, it had escaped her notice until this moment.

Topped with a mane of dark curls, its chesty, thin-waisted frame was tilted at a slight angle, plastic legs splayed unnaturally on the floor. The head dropped forward, as if drugged or dead.

So much for Vance's crazy suspicions, Barbara thought as a wave of bemused relief seeped through her. He must have been kidding about the severed arm, just to give her the creeps. Of course he was, the jerk.

"Where's your mom now?" Meyer asked, reclaiming her attention.

"In Mobile. Same place she's lived all her life."

"Do you get to see her much?"

"Not as often as I should. It's hard for me to go back there."

Meyer put two pieces together in his mind. "You mean it's easier to be a stranger sometimes."

Barbara nodded, startled to hear her own words coming out of someone else's mouth. "I forgot I told you that, but yeah."

"At the Coconut Grove. We were talking about why you moved here."

"I remember now."

Watching the raindrops splatter against the window, Barbara thought back to that first meeting with Meyer. A strange experience. Just getting the call from him was unnerving. She'd only moved into her Miami apartment two weeks before and hadn't given out her number to anyone. As Meyer introduced himself over the phone, he explained he'd seen some photos of her in the December issue of *Cheesecake* and called the publisher in Los Angeles to get some contact information on her. Barbara had given the publisher her Miami address the week before so she could receive a new check to replace one that had bounced. Based on the address, Meyer was able to dig up her phone number.

She remembered sitting there in a dark booth at the strangely empty Coconut Grove, listening to Meyer ramble on about making movies. Out of sheer nervousness, she ordered three martinis in rapid succession. By the time Meyer wrapped up his spiel she was fairly drunk.

That's when she started telling him about herself... the transience of her life since leaving Mobile three years ago... living in a different city with each changing season... modeling and cocktail waitressing to get by... working as a go-go dancer at the Whisky in L.A., a bunny at the Playboy Club in Chicago... not making any

145

lasting connections, and not seeking any. Looking back on it now, Barbara realized what an intensely personal conversation she'd had with Meyer on their very first meeting. It embarrassed her.

A strong gust of wind rattled the pane and she flinched.

"When it gets a little stronger I'll close the blinds," Meyer said.

Trying to shake herself into the present, Barbara asked him, "What do you think the real Estelle would have to say about *Crimson Orgy*?"

"I have no idea."

"Do you think she'd be proud of you?"

"It's impossible to say."

"I wish I knew what you're trying to do with this movie, Sheldon. I really do."

She was looking at him with a calm intentness he found unsettling.

"When I was six," Meyer said, "I was in a car accident. My father was driving me and my mother home from the movies. We'd gone into Chicago to see Chaplain's *Gold Rush*. You ever seen it?"

Barbara shook her head.

"It's a classic. Chaplain understood the pain underneath all humor. The biggest jokes in the movie come from starvation, insanity, loneliness. Anyway, we were driving home in my father's Packard. Bitter cold, late November. We lived in Winnetka, north of the city. It was sleeting heavily and the roads were frozen. I was sleeping with my head in my mother's lap, my feet were stretched on my father's lap under the steering wheel. I don't know what happened, if another car started it or if he just lost control. We went skidding off the road, down an embankment and slammed into a tree. The passenger side caught the impact. I don't remember the collision. I just remember waking up to my father yelling.

146

I'd never heard him make noises like that. My head was still pinned in my mother's lap, I was trapped between her and the dashboard. The collision had sent her head straight through the windshield. My father tried to pull her back into the car. She was stuck on the broken glass and I was trapped underneath. I started screaming until my father made me shut up by punching my legs. He managed to pull her back in and the blood just started raining down on me. Her neck had been cut on the glass. She was unconscious, maybe already dead. My father got out and tried to flag down a passing car. I was so cold I lost all feeling in my extremities. Maybe it was shock. Finally someone pulled over and agreed to drive us to a hospital. We headed back into the city. I don't remember the drive except that it was warm in the car. A woman held me in her arms in the back seat and I remember her stoking my hair. When we got to the hospital I sat waiting on a hard bench as all the adults disappeared behind a pair of swinging doors. The blood had dried on my hands, my clothes, my face. I was surprised how dark it was. A nurse asked me if I wanted some cocoa. I must have drifted off because the next thing I remember is my father waking me up. He was crying, which I'd never seen before. They were tears of anger, not grief. He told me my mother was dead and then he took me home."

Meyer stubbed out his cigarette. The wind seemed to have eased a bit. *Maybe we're in the eye of the storm*, he thought.

"It wasn't until I was about twelve that my father told me why my mother had died, at least in his opinion. The people who picked us up had driven us to a Catholic hospital. It was the closest one, apparently. My father said the woman at the desk refused to admit my mother because she was Jewish. My father explained she was born Christian, had only converted when she got mar-

147

ried. Didn't make any difference. Then a nurse saw how badly she was injured and they wheeled her into the ER. So they did admit her, but my father was convinced they didn't give her the best treatment available. He was sure they let her lie there on the gurney, dying as they tended to the other patients. When you're twelve years old and your father tells you something like that, you tend to believe it. Like I said, she may have already been dead. I pray to God she died at the moment of impact. But as far as my father was concerned, the people at that hospital killed her and I can't completely shake that suspicion myself. He told me that many times. He also said if my feet hadn't been in his lap when he was driving, the accident never would have happened."

Meyer turned away from the window. A disembodied palm frond lashing against the glass had almost hypnotized him as he told the story. He was startled to look over and see tears in Barbara's eyes.

"Hey, I'm sorry. I didn't mean to lay that on you."

"It just seems crazy to me," she said. "This movie. Why in God's name would you want to relive that?"

"I'm not reliving it. I'm trying to take ownership of it."

She let that sink in for a moment. "So it's supposed to be... therapy?"

"No. More like creative bargaining."

Barbara didn't follow. She felt like he was trying to get through a barrier, to communicate something to her.

"That's the purpose of art," he continued. "It lets us renegotiate our contract with God. We don't have to go through life just reacting to whatever He throws at us. Instead of simply surviving it, we can interpret it. Reshape it. Spit it back into the world on terms *we* dictate. It doesn't own us anymore, *we own it.*"

Barbara nodded. "I wish I could say I understood."

Now it was Shel's turn to feel embarrassed. "I've been rambling long enough. If Hoffman heard me, he'd never let me live it down."

"I'm not Hoffman," she said, taking his hand in hers.

He smiled at the understatement.

"No, you're not. If I ever make that mistake, I really need to see an optometrist."

She tried to laugh.

"Thanks for listening," Meyer said.

"Thanks for telling me the whole story."

Barbara still held in his hand. She was stoking his palm lightly with the tips of her fingers. Meyer felt a chill roll over him.

"I doubt it makes this picture any less repulsive to you," he said.

"No. To be honest, it doesn't. But I'm going to help you finish it anyway."

"You've been very understanding so far."

She smiled at him, but it was not a smile of mirth, or happiness.

"Whatever you need me to do," she said. "Just tell me."

* * * * * * *

Three miles south of the Sand Palace Motel, Sonny Platt's house was ready to face whatever Estelle had up her sleeve. The deputy had reinforced all the walls, shuttered the most vulnerable windows, and even constructed a safe room with his bare hands when he bought the one-story "hacienda" last year. Right now, he was running a straight-up prevent defense. The hatches were battened down, the larder fat with provisions. He'd instructed his three junior officers to keep their radio frequencies open for any contingencies.

149

Yes, Sonny had everything he needed to ride it out. Most of all, he had Sherry. At the moment, she was riding him.

She'd gotten here less than ten minutes ago and they hadn't even made it to the bedroom yet. Sherry was wound into such a hyperactive state by the promise of a good mean storm, so inflamed by the potential for real devastation, she had Sonny's pants around his ankles virtually seconds after she came barging through the front door, dripping wet and howling like a loon. She made no bones about the fact that danger turned her on. Whether driving at reckless speeds, jumping nude from a fifty-foot bridge into the Alapahoochie River upstate, or flipping a defiant bird into the face of a hurricane... it was all just foreplay to her.

They were on Sonny's couch in the living room, having a wild time of it. Sherry worked him like a stick shift, going from reverse all the way up to fifth and back down again with the dexterity of a Daytona champ. She was timing herself with the weather, hoping to climax in harmony with a house-rocking clap of thunder.

"That's right, Mr. Deputy," she moaned. "You're hitting just the right spot there."

Sonny wasn't as into it as he wanted to be. A man who took home ownership to be much more than a mere privilege, his attention was distracted by nagging worries that he'd overlooked some important storm safety measure. In all honesty, he was hoping Sherry would get off soon so he could casually slip away for a last-minute inspection while she sank into her inevitable post-coital slumber.

Trying to make the most of it, Sonny gamely followed Sherry's momentum. There wasn't much for him to do, just lie on his back and let her spring up and down like a yo-yo in the hands of a mental patient.

"Oh, God! Yeah, right there, baby!!"

Sonny voiced a few uninspired oaths in return, just so she didn't have to carry the load all by herself. He really was a terrible actor, delivering these phony lines as miserably as he'd done Monday night on the beach. His eyes were focused on the windowpane to the left of Sherry's bobbing head. One corner of the glass didn't appear to be fully sealed to the casing.

Damnit! How long was this going to take?

Sherry was slower in getting there than usual. After many many pumps, Sonny felt her torso start to shudder with inevitability.

Thank God. A few more thrusts and he could get back to doing something important.

Sherry was right there, teetering on the edge. She thrust her head back in a posture of sexual triumph, one hand buried in her hair and the other painfully grabbing onto the deputy's face. A finger smelling like stale beer got wedged under his nose.

Just as she started to come, Sherry screamed, "Yes, yes!! Fuck me, Vance!!!"

It was out of her mouth before she could stop it.

A split-second of silence after such a racket can last forever. Sonny stopped whatever it was he'd been doing, feeling his entire body deflate.

Enraptured as Sherry was, she fully realized what an egregious gaffe she'd committed. Her only option was to attempt to cover it up with more incoherent moans, occasionally throwing in a syllable that rhymed with the verboten name that had escaped her lips.

Sonny Platt wasn't buying it. He couldn't quite believe what he'd heard, but bad news always arrives with the awful force of credibility. She could have said any name in the world: his father's name, any or all of the other cops at the station, that slick fisherman she'd been dating before Sonny started pursuing her... they all would have been sweet music compared to the name of that goddamn pretty boy who he'd almost managed to forget about until two seconds ago.

Sherry collapsed onto his chest and lay there, mainly so she wouldn't have to look him in the eye. The deputy didn't say anything, just waited for her to regain her breath. His anger did not arrive instantly, it came seeping in gradually. He could feel the muscles in his neck tighten like steel cables.

Sherry finally sat up so he could see her. Reaching forward, he placed one hand firmly on her damp throat. It was not a lover's touch, and her eyes revealed more fear than a hurricane could ever induce.

"What was that you said?"

SATURDAY (A.M.)

Things started to get hairy sometime after midnight. The final hours of Friday were just the warmup. At around 12:30 the power went out, all the way from Pompano to Ft. Lauderdale. The wind gathered strength at a frightening degree of acceleration. It sounded like the Sand Palace was stuck between two freight trains that roared by with terrible velocity. Rain pounded against the walls in near-horizontal sheets. A palm tree fell violently in the courtyard, its frond-covered head smashing through a window on the first floor.

It became pretty clear no one was going to sleep through Estelle's party. Except Gene Hoffman, who could sleep through a nuclear blast and probably just murmur for someone to turn down the TV. Everyone else on the *Crimson Orgy* team was wide awake and they would remain so until some measure of calm returned. Didn't matter that they were all exhausted to the point of semi-hysteria, and that the worst part of production still lay ahead of them. No one even considered trying to drift off. They simply did whatever was necessary to get through this thing.

Shel was back at the night stand, typing away with the aid of some flickering candles. His shadow danced on the wall behind him like a tipsy goblin. He was having trouble summoning the optimistic words that came so easily earlier in the night. The creative window that had miraculously opened for him seemed to have slammed shut once again.

Barbara was lying in his bed, curled up under the covers. They'd stopped talking hours earlier, but he told her she was welcome to stay as long as she liked. Had that kind offer not been extended, she would have gladly imposed herself. There was no way she was going to be alone tonight.

Initially, Shel thought her presence might inhibit his work, but after a while he forgot she was even there. Around 1:30, when he took a break to smoke a cigarette and look out the window, her voice startled him. She asked him to keep typing. The sound of the keys soothed her. Though he'd essentially run into a wall, Shel agreeably banged out some sheer gibberish for her benefit.

Ricky and Juan were camped out with their flashlights in room 113, playing cards and killing a bottle of tequila. Cliff wasn't around. He'd stepped out sometime around 11:00, not saying where he was headed. The two junior grips were frankly glad to see him go. He'd been acting in a bizarre manner all day, saying nothing except to bark orders and screwing up the most menial of tasks. When Ricky offered a bandage for his sliced thumb, Cliff gave a cold stare that seemed to neither see nor comprehend the offer.

Dealing out another hand of five-card draw as the storm raged, Ricky assumed Cliff was up in Hoffman's room, trying to lift his spirits with a dose of Gene's unshakable sanguinity. Juan figured he was out in the van, devising some sort of handmade weapon to use on Vance. Neither of the men voiced their opinions. They just shuffled the deck and passed the bottle. At around 12:45, when that felled palm tree blew out the window in the room next door, Juan gave up on the cards and fell to his knees in fervent prayer. Ricky just scooped up the deck and started playing Solitaire.

Two doors over, Jerry Cooke sat in the dark, pulling the heads off some Barbie dolls.

Up in 226, Vance was lying on his empty bed, cursing himself. He'd really acted like a jerk when Barbara came by earlier. Now he was feeling bad about it. His throat was dry and he couldn't keep his hands still, but he didn't want a drink as much as he wanted to wind back the clock. If all she was looking for was someone to talk to, he should have been more understanding. Shit, he liked talking to her, which was more than he could say about most of the girls he banged.

It would be nice to have Barbara in his room now. They could stay up all night, goofing on Meyer, getting to know each other better. If he'd only been a little less insistent, they probably would have ended up naked before sunrise.

Vance didn't lament a lost sexual opportunity as much as he felt genuinely stricken to let Barbara down. There was something in her eyes when she showed up at his door tonight, something he hadn't seen before. Only now did he understand it was fear. Well, sure, why not? She was terrified at the prospect of being stuck in the oncoming path of Estelle. Who wouldn't be? She'd come to him for reassurance and he drove her away by being a self-centered asshole.

155

Vance spent at least an hour knocking himself around with these and other thoughts of self-reproach. Eventually, he'd had more than he could take. He picked up the phone and tried calling her room, but didn't even get a dial tone. The lines must be down. Throwing the phone against the wall in disgust, Vance lay back down and forced his eyes closed.

A little after 2:00, determined sleep would not come, he rose from the bed. It still wasn't too late to make amends. He was going to brave the storm, walk down to her room, and check on her. A selfless act of concern for another's wellbeing, that's what was called for. If she agreed to open the door, he would apologize and offer to keep her company for the rest of the night on a strictly nonphysical basis. Or whatever.

Vance opened his door and was rocked back on his heels by a powerful blast of cold, wet wind. It was much stronger than he expected. They were still within the storm's outer perimeter. He reconsidered his plan. Sheer insanity to step outside at a time like this.

Then he thought about Barbara again. Her room was only twelve doors away. He'd make it.

Vance had to use all his strength to pull the door closed. The walkway swayed under his feet. His entire body was soaked after being exposed for a few seconds. Shielding his eyes from the blinding rain he trudged ahead, struggling not to be blown over the railing.

Clutching it for support, Vance looked down into the courtyard and saw at least four palm trees had been flattened. They lay on the wet ground like broken men. Tremendous waves were leaping out of the pool, turning the courtyard into a swamp.

Vance had to count the doors he passed to keep track of where he was. Visibility became impossible as the rain seemed to actually thicken. Barbara's room was 214. He inched onward, turning the corner after passing Meyer's room. By his count, he had three more doors to go. Each step was a mammoth trial as the gales pressed him flat against the wall. When he'd passed the tenth door, he knew he was almost there.

He stopped in his tracks when he saw a large lump planted on the walkway in front of 214. Shapeless, it looked like a pile of debris wrapped in a plastic tarpaulin flapping madly in the wind.

Maybe a bag of trash blew up from the dumpster, Vance thought.

Then he saw an arm sticking out of the plastic.

For a dizzying moment, Vance flashed back to his grotesque discovery in Hoffman's secret metal box.

The arm moved.

There was a person wrapped inside all that flapping plastic.

In another instant, Vance knew who it was. The only fool crazy enough to station himself outside Barbara's room in the middle of a goddamned hurricane.

"Cliff!" Vance called out over the wind.

The top of the heap turned in his direction. Vance could barely make out that brushy mustache, shiny with rain, within the dark recesses of the tarp.

"What the hell are you doing?" Vance yelled.

No answer. Leaning his back against the door, Cliff struggled to rise to his feet. Vance extended a helping hand that was slapped away. Once Cliff reached his full height, he took a heavy step forward. Vance saw it wasn't a tarp he was wearing, but a jumbo-sized parka. His head was wrapped in the hood, raindrops pouring down in front of his eyes.

"Go away!" Cliff roared.

Vance could barely hear him. "Are you out of your mind? You need to get inside."

"Leave, Vance!"

"I want to see her first," Vance said. "Step aside."

Cliff reached out and shoved him back, hard. The wind seemed to help, causing Vance to retreat three steps. He regained his footing and squared up with the Grip again.

"She doesn't need you!" Cliff shouted. "I'm watching out for her!"

"Step aside, Cliff!"

Vance didn't see those big hands moving until they were locked on his throat. Strong fingers closed around his windpipe. Cliff was screaming something that got lost in the wind. He pushed downward as he squeezed, driving Vance to his knees.

Vance sent a blind a fist into the hood of Cliff's parka. He must have hit something because his whole hand exploded in pain.

Cliff wasn't phased. He kept forcing Vance down. Flailing desperately, Vance dug his other hand into the darkened hood, scratching and tearing at whatever his fingers touched. He felt his thumb scrape across an eye. It was enough to make Cliff's hold relax for a moment, long enough for Vance to regain his balance.

He still couldn't free himself from the choke hold. Cliff used his superior weight to push him against the railing.

Vance flinched as the iron grille gouged his lower back. Cliff took one hand off his throat to grab him by the leg, just below the knee.

He started to lift up, pulling Vance over the railing.

Vance's eyes swam in his head. He caught a blurred image of the ground below. The drop was more than than twenty feet. Cold wet cement waiting to greet his fall.

Vance used both hands to free his throat and tried to push Cliff back. It was no match.

"Stop!" he cried. "Jesus Christ, stop!"

Cliff had his leg almost over the railing.

Vance felt the terrible pull of gravity.

He was helpless, thrashing in blind panic.

In a gut reaction, Vance jerked his head forward full-tilt, smashing into Cliff's face. His forehead landed like a hammer, breaking the nose.

Cliff staggered back, inadvertently pulling Vance with him. He clutched his face with both hands.

Vance lowered himself into a crouch and rammed into Cliff, driving him back against the door of 214.

The force of both bodies colliding was more than the worm-eaten frame could handle. The door gave with a splintering groan and the two men went crashing into the room.

Vance landed on top. Pinning those wide shoulders with his knees, he put his throbbing hand on Cliff's throat and drove the other hand into his face. Repeatedly, until his knuckles were dotted with blood.

Then he started in with his elbow.

It went on for some time.

Vance finally stopped, gasping for breath. Cliff was motionless beneath him, his face a dark mass of hamburger. Vance rolled off and staggered onto the bed.

Only then did he notice the room was empty.

Jesus.

He tried to curse, but couldn't find the breath. They nearly killed each other and she wasn't even here.

Vance lumbered to his feet, using the dresser for support. The same dresser that played a role in a far more enjoyable physical entanglement just yesterday morning. It seemed like a year ago.

He glanced down at Cliff. Still unconscious, lying in a wet heap and again looking like a pile of trash in an oversized bag. Vance prodded him with his foot. He thought he heard a weak moan, but there was no movement.

Stumbling over to the shattered door frame, Vance braced himself for the winds and stepped back outside,

159

leaving Cliff prone in the abandoned room as the rain came pouring in.

* * * * * * *

Against all odds, the Sand Palace was still standing when the sun came up. The courtyard was a wasteland of leaves, fallen trees, broken glass, and huge dirty puddles. Less than two feet of water remained in the pool. The sun chairs were scattered all about, flipped over, a few hanging from the second story railing. One of the umbrellas had been launched like a javelin into the window of the manager's office.

Other than that, the place looked fine.

Gene Hoffman was the first member of the crew to awake, probably because he'd been the only one to get a decent night's sleep. Estelle didn't leave Hillsboro alone until almost 4:00 A.M. Most of the Stupendous team was able to doze off on individual schedules sometime after things calmed down.

It took Barbara the longest amount of time to sleep. Shel Meyer climbed into bed next to her around 3:00. He made no advances, just leaned over and softly kissed the top of her head. Within minutes he was snoring like a table saw cutting through sheet metal. Rather than return to her own room, she spent the next several hours tossing and turning, launching the odd kick at Meyer in a futile attempt to turn him over to a less sonorous position, and finally drifted off sometime around dawn.

Surveying the courtyard in the morning sun, Hoffman looked at his watch. Not even 8:30, might as well let the troops sleep in a little longer. He walked the perimeter of the hotel, admiring the damage. Quite a little blower, by the looks of it. But certainly no hurricane. Hoffman estimated Estelle to have been a paltry Category 5 tropical storm by the time she laid a lick on the

Sand Palace. Just like he'd been banking on. Had she still retained full-blown 'cane status, they would all be scattered across South Carolina by now.

You still got the instincts, kid, Hoffman thought to himself as a satisfied grin played across his face. *You know just how far you can push it before it's time to run.*

Looking up at the sky, he didn't see so much as a cloud. It was going to be another smashingly hot day. And a productive one, by necessity. They had quite a bit of ground to make up after their early wrap. Gene decided to hop into the Fairlane and drive down to the little diner in Pompano that made the really good coffee. He was going to pull out all the stops for this morning's crew breakfast: muffins, bear claws, cream-filled eclairs, the works. Yesterday was filled with tension, not the kind of environment he liked to shepherd. He'd make sure this new day started on the right note.

The Fairlane was halfway out the driveway when he noticed that Cliff's van was gone. The other crew vehicles sat in the same spots where they'd been parked yesterday evening, but the rust-coated white van was nowhere to be seen.

Strange, but no cause for alarm. Cliff was an early riser by nature.

Maybe he ran out to get some... for the life of him, Hoffman couldn't finish that sentence in his mind.

Was it possible the van had blown away? Hoffman craned his head to get a 360-degree view of the immediate environs. No, that couldn't have happened.

He still didn't think anything was amiss. Not really. But just to set his mind at ease, he pulled back into the driveway and decided to check in on room 113.

The door opened after some pounding and a bleary-eyed Ricky stood before him. Over his shoulder, Hoffman could see Juan sleeping in an upright chair. The other bed was empty and appeared not to have been slept in.

161

Hoffman felt a fleeting stab of guilt for shacking up all three guys in a single room.

"Morning, Ricky," he said. "Quite a night, huh?"

Ricky nodded and yawned at the same time.

"Sorry to rouse you so early. I was wondering where Cliff went."

"Don't know, Mr. H. He stepped out last night, before the storm got real bad. Thought he might be up in your room."

"No, he never came by. His van's not out front."

Ricky raised a tired eyebrow.

"That's a little weird," he said, reaching into the back of his shredded boxers to scratch his ass.

"Does he ever go out in the morning, before we get started?"

"Not as far as I know. Usually he's at the pool by the time I'm up."

"I see," Hoffman said, hoping the concern didn't show on his face. "Well, I'm sure he'll be back soon. Grab some more z's. We won't assemble 'til 10 or 10:30."

Ricky nodded and closed the door.

Hoffman crossed back over the courtyard, taking care to avoid the mammoth pools of muddy water. Under normal circumstances, he wouldn't be too concerned with Cliff's absence. But after the events of yesterday, the odds of their loyal but slightly unbalanced Key Grip going AWOL seemed at least even. Hoffman's fists clenched as he made this calculation. They could probably survive with one man down, but all of the lighting equipment was in that van. Its absence, if prolonged, would be an utter catastrophe.

Hoffman heard a door open on the second floor and looked up to see Meyer stepping out of 217. *Shit!* Gene definitely didn't want Shel to learn about Cliff's disappearing act until he'd had an opportunity to look into it himself.

Going into preemptive mode, Hoffman climbed the stairs to meet Shel on the walkway.

"Well," Meyer said, a wide grin on his face. "She did her best but we're still here, eh?"

Hoffman returned the smile. "I told you that bitch didn't have anything on us."

They shook hands as Hoffman arrived in front of 217. Shel tried to pull the door shut, but was a second too late. Hoffman caught a glimpse of Barbara's sleeping body just as the door closed.

"Tell me I didn't see that."

"Nothing happened," Meyer said quickly. "She just wanted some company during the storm."

"I'll bet. Are you out of your mind?"

"Relax, OK? I didn't touch her."

"Just spent the night chatting, huh? Telling ghost stories and such?"

Meyer thought about it for a moment. "Yeah, kind of. We actually got to know each other. She's a brave kid."

Hoffman snorted. "Anyone who'd share a bed with you deserves the fucking Purple Heart."

"What are you so pissed about?"

"C'mon, Shelly. After all the shit we just went through?"

Meyer had a quick answer that was cut off.

"Get her out of there," Hoffman said dismissively. "Do it soon."

"OK," Meyer agreed, then made a move to step around Hoffman. His progress was halted with a firm hand.

"Let's talk about the title for a minute."

"What about it?" Shel asked, looking alarmed.

Gene almost retreated. He didn't really want to start this particular argument, which he'd already decided to put off until they finished cutting the picture. This was just a grasping attempt at buying some time to get a handle on the Cliff situation.

"It doesn't... it's not as clear as it might be," he forged ahead.

"*Crimson Orgy*," Meyer said petulantly. "Two words. How much clearer can it be?"

"What about *Blood Orgy*? It's a little more direct."

"Too close to *Blood Feast*. We talked about this."

"I know. I'm just worried the audience won't know what crimson means."

"That's ridiculous. It's a basic word."

"If we were playing to a reasonably literate group, I'd agree with you. That's not our core. I'm worried about confusing the drive-in crowd."

"The poster should clear up any confusion."

"Shelly, we're taking a shot at a whole new level with this one. Why throw up roadblocks?"

"I don't think the title's a roadblock. I think it lands like a right hook."

"OK," Hoffman said slowly. "Let's use history as our guide. Which nudie did the best box office?"

"*Naked 'Til Sunrise.*"

"And after that?"

"*Her Nudeness.*"

"Correct. And number three was *Bambi's Birthday Suit.*"

"So it was. Good picture."

"Which one made the least money?"

Shel saw where Hoffman was going. "I can't remember," he lied. "*Bathtub Beauties,* I think."

"You know damn well it was *The Libidinous Ones.* And you know why, too."

"Of course." Meyer said in a hammy theatrical tone. "We broke Gene Hoffman's third rule of motion picture promotion: no words over three syllables in the title."

"You're the one who broke the rule, my friend. I made the mistake of letting you." He sorted derisively. "'Libidinous.' What kind of faggola uses a word like that?"

164

Meyer turned away, pretending to stretch his neck so Hoffman wouldn't see the hurt look he could feel on his face.

"Crimson's only two syllables," he said lamely.

"Doesn't matter. We need something about blood or gore in the title. Something literal."

"I disagree. Orgy's literal, bordering on vulgar. We need to balance it with something a little more... associative. Half the exhibitors in the country would never touch a picture called *Blood Orgy*. And you might as well kiss the South goodbye."

"All the better," Hoffman said, taking a quick shine to the idea. "We'll put it on every lobby card and one-sheet: 'Banned in seven states!' That's gold."

"I thought you were worried about losing our core. The South *is* our core."

"That was for the sex pictures. We're selling death this time. Much broader reach."

"I still think *Crimson Orgy*'s a smarter bet."

"Fine," Gene said, fresh out of patience. "I knew it was a mistake to bring it up."

He jerked his head in the direction of Shel's room. "Get her out of there."

"Let her sleep another hour. We're sending Cliff to the lab, anyway."

Hoffman took a deep breath. "No one's going to the lab."

"What do you mean? We've got six rolls waiting for pickup and another four to process."

"We'll do that when we're back on Monday. No time to screen dailies now."

Meyer looked at him quizzically as he lit a Chesterfield. "What's going on, Gene?"

"I'm trying to manage our time. We can't afford to stay here an additional night, you know that. We check out tomorrow at noon. Then we pick up the last scene at the warehouse. Wrap by midnight, hopefully no later, load up and get the hell out of here."

"Hold on," Meyer said, lifting both hands to ward off what he was hearing. "This is insane. We need to see what's in the can."

"What good will that do?" Hoffman asked, his voice rising to a half-yell. "We can't grab any reshoots, no matter how bad the footage is."

Meyer wasn't sure what was bugging Gene, but he didn't feel like picking a fight with his producer on the penultimate day of production. The dailies could wait.

"Fine," he said coolly. "We'll do it on Monday. You're the big cheese."

He tossed his still burning cigarette over the railing and started to walk away.

"Where you going?" Gene asked.

"I want to at least get the cans inside. I'm allowed to do that, right?"

"What are you talking about?"

Meyer smiled sheepishly. "I left the film in the van last night."

"Look," Hoffman said, making an active effort to control his voice. "Don't kid me now."

"I just forgot, OK? Don't worry, they're all sealed."

The color of Gene's sunburnt face went from red to purple.

"You're fucking kidding me, right?"

"No. I'm not kidding."

"Goddamnit!" Hoffman roared. He slammed a fist down on the railing, making it vibrate like a giant guitar string. "How could you be so careless?"

"Back off, Gene! I'll take care of it."

"The hell you will! Cliff's gone, and he took the van."

A dumb pause from Meyer. "Where'd he take it?"

"That's an incisive question, Shel. Just what I'd expect from a razor-sharp mind like yours."

Meyer's lips started flapping in a reply but there wasn't much coming forth. Hoffman looked at him with disgust, an emotion he'd never quite let himself feel for his business partner.

Through all the crazy nonsense they'd dealt with making pictures together, Shel had always been dependable on a certain core level. No matter how much he'd bitch and carp, no matter how acutely his insecurities would take hold, the man was a professional. He had some sort of fail-safe mode that could be counted on to kick in and handle the essential functions of his job.

That mode completely evaporated on this project. Hoffman was sick of trying to figure out the source of his director's collapse, and he was no longer willing to fool himself into thinking that somehow Shel would pull it all together. This latest fuckup was the last straw, and it was unforgivable.

On a micro-budgeted shoot like *Crimson Orgy*, exposed film is the one asset that can never be compromised. There's absolutely no way to go back and reshoot something when working with such a tight margin of error. Equipment could break, crew members could quit, sets could be destroyed; all of these were surmountable crises. But to lose a day's worth of canned footage was a crushing, devastating blow.

For this exact reason, Stupendous Pictures had an ironclad process for dealing with exposed film. As soon as each roll was removed from the camera, it was loaded into a canvas bag that was to be handled by Shel Meyer and no one else. When the crew returned to production HQ, Meyer put the bag in a foot locker to which he had the only key. When it was time to make a run to the lab, Meyer would open the locker and hand the cans over to a runner. At that point, it was up to fate to make sure the film got to the lab and the processing instructions were followed correctly.

Yesterday, in the confusion of getting to safe lodgings before Estelle broke, Meyer just forgot about the film. Simple as that. He carried the Mitchell and its lenses up to his room, leaving the canvas film bag in the back of the van.

He didn't remember it until ten minutes ago, when he awoke with a jolt.

It was huge gaffe, one he'd never made. Dressing quickly, he hoped to sneak out and grab the film before running into Gene. So much for that plan.

He probably shouldn't have admitted the truth just now. He could have come up with some other excuse for stepping out to the van, but something about Gene's pissy mood made him not care too much about riling him.

Shelly's lost his grip, that's all there is to it, Hoffman thought to himself. Realizing his unintentional pun, he laughed hoarsely. Christ, what else was there to do?

"He'll be back," Meyer was saying in a jittery tone. "Cliff would never screw us so badly."

"I'm glad you're so sure about that. Really puts my mind at ease."

"Come on. Why would he just disappear?"

"I don't have the slightest interest in figuring out anyone's motivation at this point. All I care about is what they do or don't do. Right now, my gut tells me he's not coming back."

"We'll track him down in Miami."

"Sure, assuming his hasn't already destroyed the film. You know how crazy he's been, talking about a curse."

Meyer allowed the possibilities to sink in. After a few seconds of grim visualizations, his head was clutched in his hands.

"Oh, my God."

"How much footage was in the van?" Hoffman demanded to know.

"Everything we shot yesterday," Meyer said, his voice muffled. "Plus the wet scene from the church, on the front end of roll 14."

Hoffman's grip on the railing tightened until his knuckles looked like eight huge alabaster shells. The situation was even worse than he thought.

All of the sudden, an undeniable truth dawned on him. *Crimson Orgy* was the last movie he'd make with Meyer. It was over. Roll the closing credits on Stupendous Pictures. They'd had a good run, longer than most. Maybe it was destined to go sour eventually. Maybe they should have stuck to the nudie format, and left this gore business to Herschell Gordon Lewis and others who had the stomach for it.

In any event, Gene Hoffman wrote off Shel Meyer in his mind at that very instant. They'd finish this picture and part ways. Hopefully it could all be handled in a friendly spirit.

Unable to look at him, Hoffman turned his back on Shel.

"How was I to know he'd go AWOL?" Meyer asked weakly.

The timidity in his voice only enraged Hoffman. Turning abruptly, he grabbed the director and started pushing him toward the stairs, just as Meyer had done with the late Julie Baylor a few nights ago.

"Let's talk to the manager. Maybe he saw Cliff leave."

As soon as these words had left his mouth, Hoffman stopped in his tracks.

He spun Shel around like a rag doll and shoved him in the opposite direction.

"On second thought, I'll deal with that. Wake her up and get her out. She'll have plenty of time to sleep soon enough."

With a push hard enough to send Meyer to the floor, Hoffman wheeled away and lumbered down the stairs.

Ernest's office was totaled. The launched umbrella hung off the side of his desk among hundreds of glass shards. Two cabinets had been overturned, spilling masses of paper onto the floor. Miraculously, the television had been spared but the phone line was still down, which was driving Ernest into a frenzy as he tried to contact his insurance agent.

The moment Hoffman stepped inside, Ernest dropped the dead phone and started raving about the damage done to the Sand Palace, as if Gene were either responsible or somehow able to fix it. Hoffman had to literally drag him out of the office just to get his attention. After a few pointed questions, it was clear the distraught manager wasn't able to offer any information regarding Cliff's whereabouts.

Hoffman was about to ask if they could expect a partial refund on the rooms when a woman's shrill scream tore into the air. Both men froze. The scream died abruptly, as if by force.

Then it broke free again, louder and more desperate.

Despite himself, Hoffman couldn't help thinking, *I wonder if that scream would satisfy Shelly. Sounds real enough to me.*

"That's Rosa," the manager said with alarm.

"Who?"

"My cleaning lady."

The urgency in his voice made it sound like she did more than just clean for him. Another cry rang out, closer to a moan than a scream, and Ernest started running. Following him, Hoffman knew this was not going to be a good scene. He knew, somehow, where they were headed. Some spasm in his gut told him the source was room 111.

Jerry Cooke's room.

111's door was ajar. Deranged cursing could be heard from inside, drowning out broken pleas for mercy in

Spanish. Ernest charged through the door, Hoffman close behind.

Jerry was on his knees, pinning the plump Cuban cleaning lady to the floor. His hands were on her throat, muffling her desperate wails.

"Give it back, give it back!" Jerry howled into the woman's face.

Hoffman brushed Ernest aside and laid two heavy hands on Jerry's shoulders. Ripping him off the cleaning lady, he slung the diminutive actor clear across the room with a swift lateral heave.

Jerry landed in a chair that tipped backward with the momentum, sending his head into a plaster-spraying collision with the far wall.

Ernest tenderly helped Rosa to her feet. She was babbling in semi-hysterical Spanish.

"What the hell's the idea, Jerry?" Hoffman demanded to know.

An indignant scowl was his only reply.

"I'm not gonna ask again, *Ace*!"

"She broke in and was stealing my valuables," Jerry screeched. "I caught her red-handed!"

The manager took umbrage. "Rosa's worked here for nine years and she's the best cleaning lady I ever had. She never stole nothing."

"Just hold on a minute," Hoffman replied calmly. "How can you be so sure?"

"Because I know her."

"Well, I know him," Hoffman said, pointing to Jerry. He started to explain what a perfectly normal and upstanding citizen his actor was, but didn't trust himself to get the words out in a believable fashion.

Instead, he turned to Rosa and said, "Let's back up and find out exactly what happened."

He offered her a chair. She sat with trepidation, as if expecting a tack to be hidden in the cushion.

"Start from the beginning, *señora*," Hoffman said. "*Por favor.*"

With much weeping and sputtering, Rosa's version came into focus. She was making her morning rounds, starting on the ground floor as she always did. The door to 111 was open. She knocked but got no answer. Stepping inside, she began to make up the bed. Then the little man in the black suit came lunging out of the bathroom, grabbed her by the throat and threw her to the floor. He was like a wild animal, *un lobo loco*. She tried to explain herself but there was no chance in the face of his mad attack. It was terrifying.

Hoffman listened to Ernest's labored translation of Rosa's account, knowing in his heart every word was true.

"Well," he said after a pause, "I don't mean to question this woman's honesty, but that doesn't sound like the Jerry Cooke I know. The boy wouldn't harm an ant."

Ernest pointed a shaking finger to the wall behind Hoffman. "What about that?"

Hoffman turned, seeing something he hadn't noticed before. It didn't help his case.

Tacked to the wall above the bed was a poster from the 1960 exploitation classic, *Sex Kittens Go To College*. Hoffman had seen the movie when it opened at the Rialto. He recalled feeling a bit envious, as it was made with an obviously bigger budget than he could ever muster and featured real stars such as Mamie van Doren, Tuesday Weld, Conway Twitty, and Vampira.

The poster, which showcased the smiling faces of Mamie and Tuesday, was spattered with red paint that dripped from the starlets' four eyes. Looking closer, Hoffman noted with a small shiver the eyes had been cut out.

"Jesus, Jerry," he wheezed under his breath. The kid was really taking this thing a bit far.

172

Of course he didn't say that. Instead, he turned back to face Ernest and broke out his most magnanimous diction.

"I'm afraid we've had a little misunderstanding. You see, Jerry's an actor. This is how he prepares for his role. It's a certain style of performance that helps him get into character. What's it called again, Ace?"

"The Method," Jerry muttered sullenly.

"Right," Hoffman said, nodding. "The Method. I understand even Marlon Brando approaches his work this way. Rosa here can be excused for not comprehending."

"Well," Ernest said, "I'm not excusing the little shit for strangling her."

"There's no harm done. She appears to be of robust stock."

"What are you saying?"

"I'm saying the lady seems understandably shaken but otherwise unharmed. Look at how puny this boy is. I doubt he could hurt her if he tried."

"Hey!" Jerry whined, offended.

"Shut up!" Hoffman barked.

"He did try to hurt her," Ernest said. "That's the point."

"Sir," Hoffman intoned, stepping forward and lowering his voice another octave, "did it ever occur to you he may have felt he was protecting your establishment? For all he knew, Rosa here was a thief who'd broken in to pillage some towels. I'd say the lad deserves your thanks."

It was unclear if Hoffman's syrupy, vaguely legalistic tone succeeded in pacifying the manager. He seemed confused more than anything. Rosa had regained her breath and stared silently at her orthopedic shoes.

Hoffman was just about ready to continue his oration when he glanced down and noticed the collection of severed Barbie heads neatly lined up along the edge of the night stand. They had been glued in place with puddles of the same red paint congealed around their necks. Trickles of it ran from their little plastic eyes.

Repositioning himself to block the heads from Ernest's view, he soldiered on.

"Are we all willing to put this misunderstanding behind us?"

"I think I want you people to leave," Ernest finally said.

"Beg pardon?"

"You heard me."

"Wait just a minute. The whole week's been paid in advance."

"Don't care. I'll refund the difference, just get out."

"Let's not overreact here," Gene said, his voice not quite as solicitous. "Do you really want to turn away paying customers after the tremendous hit you've just taken? Do you expect anyone to check in *now*?"

"I'm not telling you again, mister. Leave."

Hoffman tried to read him for a sign of weakness, but Ernest appeared resolute.

"There's nothing I can do to change your mind?"

"No."

"Very well," Hoffman said, letting his shoulders slump in defeat. He turned toward the door. "Better get packed, Ace."

Jerry looked up at him in mute discomposure. He couldn't believe his producer was folding so easily.

Ernest helped Rosa to her feet, pausing to glance at the bloodied doll heads. He shot a look of revulsion at Jerry, who recoiled even more deeply into the chair.

Just as Hoffman reached the door, he turned with an animated expression, as if some wonderful idea had just occurred to him.

"Say, Ernest," he drawled at a perfectly measured pace. "Have you ever considered an acting career?"

SATURDAY (P.M.)

It was the most achingly beautiful sunset they'd had all week. The sky was brilliantly lit, almost Hollywood in its wanton flashiness. A sweet-scented breeze kicked up from the shoreline. The gulls were out in full force, reclaiming the air after being forced to seek shelter from Estelle's rampage.

Shel and Barbara sat in the cooling sand up by the high dunes, looking at the ocean. They had the whole beach to themselves as far as they could see in either direction. The tide had just rolled in, generating frothy breakers that roared softly against the wet sand.

Barbara leaned back on her palms as Shel balled himself up in a nervous hunch.

"This wasn't part of the deal, Sheldon. It's not fair for you to spring it on me now."

"I know. I hate to do it, but we're in a real bind."

Barbara didn't say anything else, just let her fingers sink deeper into the sand.

Meyer asked her to take a walk after they wrapped two quick scenes near the motel in the early afternoon. The first of these had been unusually challenging, since Shel was told about six minutes before the cameras rolled that he had to write in a small part for Ernest. At first he thought Hoffman was joking but it soon became clear that, unless the manager was given some lines, the whole crew would be booted from the Sand Palace immediately.

Grinding his teeth hard enough to loosen the fillings, Meyer quickly penned a conversation between Kelly and an eyewitness to one of the murders. Amazingly, the potbellied manager did a halfway decent job with no rehearsal, and they were able to briskly move forward.

The only hassle was keeping the actors dry. Meyer couldn't afford them any kind of shelter from the sweat-spawning sun; there just wasn't enough time to create a lighting scheme that would bounce shadows off their faces. So they shot the entire scene out in the open. Barbara was spritzed with a light sheen by the end of the first take, while Ernest looked like he'd just waddled out of the Atlantic in a tank-top and soiled dungarees. It couldn't be helped.

Cliff still hadn't resurfaced and it was asinine to harbor any hope at this point. Still, Meyer had shown amazing resilience in the face of this most recent debacle.

There was one crucial silver lining: for reasons not entirely clear, Ricky had unloaded the entire grip package from the van last night and stored it in the maintenance shed behind the pool. When pressed why he made such an unusual move, Ricky said with his customary vacant stare that it just seemed convenient, since their first setup today took place near the shed.

Possibly there was nothing more to it than that. Yet Meyer couldn't help thinking Ricky'd had some sort of premonition.

Whatever the case, he didn't question this bit of good fortune. He just accepted it gratefully and promoted Ricky to Key Grip. Without that equipment, the production would have been sunk.

There was still the issue of the stolen film to deal with. Rather than pull out the remnants of his thinning hair, as Hoffman contemptuously expected him to do, the director devised a plan.

Of the three scenes they had lost, only one was essential: the murder at the church. The other two scenes were dialogue-heavy and frankly not all that interesting. Losing them would reduce the movie's running time by seven or eight minutes, but Meyer was confident he could pad that gap with random filler: tossing in a few extra shots of Barbara by the pool... extending the car chase by recycling each angle four times instead of the customary three... prolonging the opening credits. These and other means of creative cutting would probably get the job done.

Meyer knew the paying customer wanted to see blood, and wasn't too concerned with what happened in between the murders. The gore needed to be absolutely intense, that's all that mattered. That's what the poster and the trailer would promise, and that's what the movie had to deliver. So when Shel realized they'd lost the scene where Ace Spade extracts a beating heart from the preacher's daughter, he knew there was only one solution.

They needed to add another, even more gruesome murder. Only problem was, they didn't have anyone left to kill.

The prospect of casting a new victim at this late hour was out of the question. Driving to Miami, running over to the Cottontail Club, finding another girl and getting her down to Hillsboro (all by tomorrow night) clearly was too tall an order even for the Herculean Hoffman.

There was only one girl who could realistically be slaughtered.

And she was already right here.

As the crew broke for a late afternoon meal, Shel asked Barbara if she'd take a stroll. He didn't relish the impending conversation but it was unavoidable.

"I can't believe he just vanished," Barbara said after Meyer told her about Cliff. "He'll be back."

"No, he's gone."

"Even so, I'm sure you'll get your film back."

"Eventually, maybe. Gene's not apt to just let this go. But we can't bank on it."

"You really need another gore scene?"

"Absolutely. After we shoot the throat-cutting tonight we'll only have four murders. That's not enough to carry a feature."

"Sounds like plenty to me."

"That's because you never saw *Blood Feast*. The scene we lost was going to be the highlight of the whole damn picture."

"So now Kelly needs to die. Are you sure the audience will accept that?"

"She only dies in her dreams. I'm thinking it could actually be more powerful than anything we'd planned on doing."

"Walk me through it," Barbara said warily.

Meyer turned to face her, framing the shots with his hands as he always did when pitching an idea.

"It takes place right after the love scene in the park. We cut to a scene of Kelly lying by the pool where Frank works. She's been going through her notes but decides to close her eyes and soak up some sun for a few minutes. Ace Spade appears from behind the lounge chair and attacks her, brutally. She wakes up with a scream."

"So the audience doesn't know it's a dream until it's over."

"Exactly!" Meyer said, pounding a fist into his palm. "It'll scare the bejesus out of 'em."

"How does he attack her?"

Meyer's brow furrowed. He cupped some sand in his hands and let the grains fall through his fingers.

"I haven't figured that out yet. It'll depend on what kind of effects I can put together on such short notice."

"When do you want to shoot it?"

"Tomorrow morning, first thing. Get it out of the way and the rest of the day should be a breeze. We'll wrap at the warehouse sometime in the evening. That's our last location, then we can all go home."

Barbara wrapped her arms around herself as the falling sun ushered in a chilly breeze. It occurred to her the weather had grown utterly schizophrenic, careening from one extreme to another.

"I'm not too comfortable with this, Sheldon."

"To be honest, I don't see the problem. You already took your clothes off."

"That's completely different. I'm not ashamed of my body."

"But you're ashamed to put a little red goop on it?"

"It's what the goop signifies," she said, her temper rising sharply. "I don't want to help you turn pain into entertainment."

"I'd say you're doing that already."

"Exactly. Enough's enough."

"Look, it's only a dream sequence. After about two seconds of violence you wake up safely in Frank's arms. Kelly survives, but it's important to show the psychological impact of all the death. That's why Ace Spade does it. He's killing these girls to exact a toll on the entire town, and no one escapes completely unharmed. You told me to give the story more context, remember?"

179

"Your pitch is pretty smooth, but I'm still not happy about this."

"It's just make believe, Barbara. Like dressing up for Halloween."

She couldn't stand being pressured, especially by him. She stood up, grabbing her sandals. Meyer rose as well.

"I feel like the ground keeps moving under my feet," she said. "Every day there's a new surprise, something I hadn't bargained for."

"Remember the first conversation we had? On the phone?"

"Yeah," she said with a faint smile. "You were so nervous, it was ridiculous."

"I'd seen those photos you did for *Cheesecake*. I admit, I'm a subscriber."

"So you saw me in the raw and you figured, there's a girl who can be talked into anything."

"No, no," Meyer said, laughing. "I thought, there's a girl who's absolutely impossible to photograph badly. I mean, it was obvious whoever took those shots didn't know what the hell he was doing."

"I guess not," Barbara said. "He had one hand on his crotch the whole time he was shooting. Poor old guy, I think he was lonely more than anything else."

Meyer stopped laughing and looked at her seriously. "That's what I like about you so much."

"Oh God, *what*?"

"You always find something sympathetic in people. Even when it's not there, I suspect."

She didn't have anything to say to that. Shel checked his watch. Almost 6:30. It was time to get back to the motel and prepare for tonight's shoot.

"Will you do the scene? You said you'd do whatever it takes to help me finish."

Barbara took a few more steps, her face betraying nothing.

"Why do I have the feeling I'm going to regret those words?" she eventually asked.

They walked along silently after that. Meyer had gotten the concession he was looking for and he didn't want to push his luck.

* * * * * * *

Frannie Johnstone was clutched in a spasm of terror. Her lacy nightgown shimmied with tremors that wracked her frail eighty-two-year-old body. Eyes wider than silver dollars, her mind reeled with fright. Though this condition was not exactly new to her, tonight it was far worse than she'd ever experienced. Her heart might not be able to withstand it.

Frannie clutched the old fashioned rotary phone by her bed in one liver-spotted hand, while the fingers of her other hand tried to remain still long enough to dial her daughter Lucille.

After six rings, Frannie got an answer. Lucille's sleepy voice first asked her mother if she was OK, then asked if she knew what time it was. These late night calls were becoming a problem. Lucille knew her mother craved company and she did her best to make the old woman feel loved, but this was getting out of hand. It was time to set some boundaries.

Frannie wouldn't listen to any of that. She frantically implored Lucille to hand the phone over to her husband Bill. Lucille was reluctant to comply, but after a minute or so of tearful begging she caved. Bill covered the phone for a moment so he could voice his extreme dissatisfaction with being awoken at 11:40 P.M. for what he knew was no good reason at all.

181

Going on a year now, Frannie had taken to phoning three or four times a month with some life-threatening emergency, which usually ranged in urgency from a burnt-out fuse to a runaway cat. As a dutiful husband and son-in-law, Bill had shown admirable forbearance with these disruptions of his sleep. But tonight was the last straw, and he intended to let Frannie know that if he could slip a spare word into the midst of her nonsensical babbling.

A simple man who'd never traveled further than Tallahassee, Bill had been in love with Lucille since the third grade and he'd proposed the night of their senior prom. Their marriage, thirty-three years and counting, had been on balance one marked by happiness. Inheriting Frannie as part of the package was, Bill felt, a small if taxing price to pay for the privilege of sharing a bed every night with her only child.

Frannie lived on Islip Drive, on the southern border of Hillsboro Beach. Less than fifteen miles from Bill and Lucille's modest bayside residence in Pompano. Sometimes Bill wished he'd pushed harder to relocate in the city, but Lucille wouldn't hear of it. Her mother was all alone out there on that lonely stretch of the highway. She needed family nearby in case of an emergency.

Lucille's father Clarence was torn in half by a land mine on Guadalcanal in '42. A grief-ravaged Frannie had never for a moment considered remarrying. Her ramshackle woodframe house sat on the northern border of a desolate graveyard. She'd lived there since her marriage and it made sense to stay put after Clarence's death, as he was planted less than a hundred paces from her front door and could be visited daily with ease, even with her acute arthritis.

Fairview Cemetery was a grim place, despite its pleasant name. It was a flat, grassless rectangle comprising four square acres and dotted with a depressingly dilapidated collection of headstones. Most of the souls underneath had been killed in the two great wars. Nowadays few local residents chose to deposit their dearly departed within Fairview's iron-fenced perimeter.

Living so close to such a bleak storehouse of death could play on anyone's mind, and Frannie Johnstone had always been slightly unhinged to begin with. In her dotage she'd acquired a superstitious bent that flirted with outright lunacy. She was always hearing mysterious noises coming from the graveyard in the short hours of the night. She saw innumerable spectral forms dancing outside her bedroom window. With growing frequency, she was calling Bill to report these sighting.

It usually took a minimum of fifteen minutes to convince Frannie that whatever phantasm she'd seen presented no threat. "Sure, you saw a spirit," he would patiently tell her. "Go on and leave the poor soul be, and I'm sure you'll be shown the same courtesy in return. Good night, Ma."

That's how it usually went down, but on one or two occasions she was so hysterical Bill felt obligated to run over just to make sure she wasn't suffering a heart attack. Lucille never asked him to do it, not directly. She would just toss restlessly next to him, sighing with fervor in the darkness of their bedroom. He got the hint eventually and would lumber out to his car to make the drive to Frannie's house. By the time he arrived, his mother-in-law could usually be counted on to answer the door with a snarl, asking why he was bothering a poor old lady in the middle of the night.

Tonight was different. After listening for a minute or two, Bill sensed there may be some factual basis to Frannie's panic.

She'd been disturbed from a lovely dream (her brave Clarence standing in uniform on the the deck of an aircraft carrier) by an unholy din coming from the graveyard. Sounded like the final judgment was unfolding just outside her window. Barely gathering the courage to peer through her drapes, Frannie saw a terrible sight. Not just one ghost but a whole *platoon* of phantom soldiers. The army of the dead had finally grown too restless to be contained underneath Fairview and were walking above ground!

They were trooping through the tombstones, backlit by an eerie white glow that seemed to rise from nowhere. They carried strange looking weapons and cursed in the foulest language. It was horrifying.

Frannie put the drapes back and returned to her bed, praying these dreadful visitors would return to whatever hellhole had sprung them. But they didn't go away, only grew louder as the night went on. She heard angry voices issuing terse commands in the distance. Then a bloodcurdling scream of a young girl split the still air.

Frannie crawled back to the window and drew the drapes aside an inch. Just as she was telling herself it was only her imagination, she saw something that would have turned her hair white if it hadn't already been that color for twenty years.

A shapely teenage girl ran screaming through the cemetery. Even at such a distance, Frannie could make her out clearly in the strange fluorescent light.

The girl's throat was slashed.

Ghastly dark blood covered the front of her dress. A man wielding a butcher knife ran close at her heels. As the girl frantically tried to climb the fence and escape from the graveyard, he grabbed her ankle and pulled her to the ground.

It was right about then that Frannie lunged for the phone.

Bill listened to this account with the weary realization that he was going to have to drive up to Hillsboro again. Was it possible the old shrew actually saw something

184

this time? He instructed her to hang tight and said he'd be right over.

Pushing the sheets aside, Bill told Lucille this was the last time. Tomorrow morning, they would have a serious conversation about finding a more appropriate living situation for Frannie. Fumbling into his clothes, he trudged down the stairs.

As he passed the hall closet, a thought occurred to him. Suppose there *were* trespassers out there? They might not be too keen on having their party disturbed.

For the hell of it, Bill opened the closet and pulled down his grandfather's Winchester Model 1894 from the top shelf. The closest thing he owned to a family heirloom, the rifle had been handed down to his father and later presented to Bill for his fortieth birthday.

Though a certified antique, the rifle was still in prime working condition, thanks to the superb craftsmanship that defined the Winchester label. Or so Bill's father had said when handing it over. He'd never had the slightest desire or opportunity to test that claim, and he certainly didn't plan on doing so tonight. But Bill decided to bring it along just the same.

If there really were vandals loose within the morbid confines of Fairview Cemetery, they were almost certainly kids. The mere sight of the rifle should be more than enough to scare them off.

* * * * * * *

It was closing in on midnight and they'd been shooting for less than an hour. No one knew who to blame, and what difference did it make? For any number of reasons, it took way too long to get started tonight. Meyer seemed to be on the verge of angry tears and Hoffman was lighting fresh cigarettes from the burning tips of others. He'd already left a dozen butts scattered among the graves.

It was a skeleton crew. Just the director and producer, plus Vance, Ricky, and a young woman named Faye Dwight who was playing the role of "DIANE" (a.k.a. "VICTIM #4"). She'd arrived from Miami this afternoon with the expectation that she'd be able to drive home at a reasonable hour. That clearly wasn't going to happen. Faye was already starting to manifest signs of her displeasure.

Vance wasn't needed in front of the camera for the cemetery scene. He'd been recruited to fill in as a grip for the superstitious Juan, who was back at the motel praying for the souls of his blasphemous colleagues.

On the drive out to Fairview, Vance came clean with Hoffman about the altercation with Cliff. They were riding alone in the Fairlane, and he felt he could afford to tell the whole story as long as Meyer wasn't within earshot. He stressed he was only defending himself.

The Key Grip went insane out there in the middle of the storm. He would have killed Vance if he succeeded in dropping him over the railing. They were better off without Cliff, even if the big lunatic did make off with some valuable footage.

Keeping his eyes on the road, Hoffman listened to Vance's account passively. He was beyond anger at this point. And he knew Cliff was probably to blame for whatever happened. The guy had gone haywire, there was no denying it. So rather than berate the actor, Hoffman told him to forget about it.

Vance was so relieved not to get reamed out, he decided to drop the other topic on his mind. Specifically, whatever happened to the contents of that metal box? They still hadn't shot any scene involving an Easter basket, at least not one requiring his participation. So what gives? If Vance was correct in assuming there was no prop mannequin to be found on the set (and he didn't have any reason to believe otherwise) then everything

186

Gene told him about the box had to be taken as utter bullshit.

Nothing sinister, necessarily. But damn strange.

Where did that arm and pair of eyes really come from? Hoffman's story about having a buddy at some morgue seemed a little too easy, in retrospect. As the Fairlane sped through the darkness, Vance found himself wondering about that chick who'd driven down from Tampa the other night, the one who practically had a nervous breakdown when they strung her up to film the crucifixion scene. What was her name again?

Julie. Did anyone actually *see* her leave?

In one piece?

He couldn't remember, not for sure. Of course, if Vance had read Julie's obituary in the *Ledger*, he needn't have bothered himself with morbid speculations. But Hoffman made sure no one other than Cliff and Meyer learned about the poor girl's watery demise, so the wheels of suspicion kept spinning.

Despite his unease, Vance decided to let the matter of the metal case slide without further investigation. It just didn't seem worth going into at this point. They were rounding third on the whole miserable shoot. If everyone concentrated on the job, Gene assured him with one flabby arm resting on the wheel, the next twenty-four hours should be relatively painless.

That optimistic assumption was put to the test as soon as they arrived at the gloomy gates of Fairview. The first hurdle to arise was simply getting into the cemetery. Ricky scaled the fence only to find the gate could not be opened from the inside any easier than from the outside. A rusted padlock kept watch over the dead.

Not to be daunted, Hoffman grabbed a pair of bolt cutters. His face grew red with the strain but he won the battle. The severed lock fell from sight into some unkempt shrubbery surrounding the entrance.

It was not an ideal night for shooting. The afternoon's cool breeze had abruptly died, leaving the air entirely windless. Thick, heavy clouds now blanketed the sky. Visibility was at a minimum. Every so often a clear patch would break through, revealing a fat yellow moon. During these short intervals, the entire cemetery could be seen clearly. Row after row of crumbling, moss-covered headstones highlighted in the lunar glow. The most talented Hollywood artisans could not design an eerier setting.

Once "The Jenny" started purring, they were able to create enough light to see what they were doing. After setting up the camera and 1Ks in front of a particularly embattled tombstone, the next crisis reared its head. Tonight's wet scene called for Ace Spade to attack a young woman as she lays a bouquet on her mother's grave. (Why she chooses to pay her respects in the middle of the night was a question no one had the nerve to ask Meyer. Put in context with all the other absurd plot holes, it didn't make all that much difference.)

The scene was to be captured in four shots, all of which were carefully mapped out. In terms of running time, this would be the longest murder in the film, and Meyer had actually gone to the trouble of sketching out some rough storyboards in a half-baked homage to Hitchcock.

All his planning was scrapped when Faye Dwight decided not to play along.

Faye was decidedly uncomfortable with the requirements of the role. She'd been briefed on the blood, but no one got around to mentioning the final shot of the night called for her to pose dead, sprawled across an actual grave. She balked. Meyer tried cajoling, then shouting, then brought in Hoffman for extra artillery.

No dice. Unlike the unfortunate Julie, Faye did not back down in the face of heavy two-pronged pressure.

She absolutely refused to participate in the scene as scripted.

Shel was livid. He understood filmmaking was a creative endeavor rooted in compromise, but how much more could he forfeit and still maintain a shred of integrity? The dramatic punch of tonight's scene mandated the girl's corpse be left on her mother's grave. It was a subtle but potent reference to the fact that Ace is doing his messy work as a way of avenging the deaths of his own parents.

Meyer tried explaining this concept to Faye, who stood with supple arms crossed in a posture of impatience. She wasn't phased by his liberal use of forty-cent terms like *dramatic subtext* and *thematic undercurrents*. He had reason to hope she'd be swayed by such a scholarly argument; Faye mentioned during her audition that she was enrolled in a creative writing class at Miami-Dade Community College.

It wasn't happening. Faye cut him off mid-sentence and told him he could either come up with another idea for the final shot, or find another girl to do it.

So he came up with another idea.

Instead of draping Diane across the headstone, Ace would leave her body hanging from the lowest limb of a magnificent oak in the southeast corner of the cemetery. After some haggling, Faye agreed to this compromise.

The first two setups came off without a hitch. The attack itself was probably the simplest gore effect of the entire picture. Ace Spade approaches Diane from behind as she kneels at the grave, covers her mouth with one hand and uses the other to slit her throat. Meyer had conceived the effects rig himself. He took a steak knife from his own kitchen cupboard and dulled the blade against a cinderblock. He then attached a plastic tube, one-eighth of an inch in diameter, along the blunted edge. The tube was inserted into the sleeve of Jerry

Cooke's jacket, and was attached to a hot water bottle at the other end which was filled with stage blood.

As the camera rolled, Jerry tucked the hot water bottle under his arm and squeezed, causing the blood to squirt out from the edge of the blade as he ran it across the girl's throat. It worked beautifully. They nailed the effects shot in two takes, which was a good thing because they expended almost their entire supply of blood on the second one. It was a truly grisly effect, the most realistic bit of butchery they'd captured so far.

Still, Meyer wasn't happy.

As good as the image looked, the audio was lacking. Once again, he found himself disappointed with the scream. What did he have to do to make these girls understand? Had they never felt pain or fear? Were those such difficult emotions to fabricate?

Faye was less tolerant of his constructive criticism than the other actresses had been.

"What exactly do you want?" she demanded.

"I want to believe what I'm hearing."

"I screamed, didn't I?"

"You made a noise of some kind."

"Listen to my voice. It's raw after two takes."

"Faye, please. You sounded like you saw a mouse. That's not quite the level of terror we want to communicate here."

"How much terror can I communicate after my throat's supposedly been slashed? Did you even stop to think about that?"

Wow. This pert little saucepot was drawing upon her impressive background of two weeks at a junior college to openly disparage Meyer's storytelling abilities. He never in a million years envisioned such impudence. He cleared his throat in preparation of itemizing all the girl's deficiencies, both as an actress and a human being, but was cut short by Hoffman.

190

Gene reminded Shel once again that a more convincing scream could be added in post. They should be happy with what they'd gotten and move on. This was an absolutely miserable place to spend the night. With any luck, they could wrap well before the sun came up.

Squawking his frustration, Meyer tromped away to set up the next camera angle.

After the attack, Diane manages to scramble free. Although badly wounded, her panic gives her speed. Ace chases the girl through the graveyard and pulls her to the ground just as she's trying to escape over a fence. Meyer planned on fading out over a long shot of Ace repeatedly driving the knife into Faye's chest. Then opening up again on her corpse hanging from the tree.

As the camera was being repositioned, Vance snuck off to a darkened patch of ground to take a leak. At least that was the plan. Standing there with his knees locked, he cursed his uncooperative dick for freezing up on him. It wasn't like he didn't have to go, desperately. He'd been dancing around on one foot for the past half-hour, twisting himself into a corkscrew to find momentary relief for his engorged bladder.

His inability to let fly was due to the fact that he felt pretty guilty about pissing on consecrated soil. Almost as bad as he felt while shooting the wet scene in the church. But he had no choice tonight. A man can't keep ninety-six ounces of beer inside his body forever.

A few hours before, as the crew was preparing to depart for the cemetery, Vance knocked on the door of 113. He hadn't spoken with Ricky and Juan since Cliff faded to black, and he wanted to set the record straight. The last thing he needed to worry about was being ambushed in an act of misguided retribution on behalf of the former Key Grip.

Ricky had let him in guardedly. Juan barely looked up from the floor as he packed his grubby clothes into a paper suitcase. Vance explained his version of events, pulling everything he had out of the bag in terms of charisma.

As Vance kept talking, he noticed an unopened twelve-pack of Hamm's gathering heat on the dresser. He licked his lips. The last alcohol he'd tasted had been regurgitated just minutes after being swallowed on Tuesday night. The beer looked damn good to him.

After a few minutes, Ricky seemed to come around. He had no reason to be angry with Vance. If anything, he should thank him for playing a role in Cliff's meltdown, the direct upshot of which was his promotion to Key Grip. Juan, however, remained aloof, apparently unwilling to let bygones be bygones.

Tough shit, Vance thought. *One out of two ain't bad, and the spic wouldn't dare make a move without Ricky's backup.*

Feeling much better about life in general, Vance proposed they seal their truce by shotgunning a few frosties before leaving for the cemetery. Under normal circumstances he would have considered Hamm's beneath contempt, but these were not normal circumstances. The back of his throat was pining for a taste of that brew.

Ricky eagerly consented to the idea and together they ended up killing all twelve beers in short order. It was an eight/four spit in Vance's favor. Their swilling didn't do much to improve Juan's mood, as he'd been looking forward to a few cold sips himself. Vance and Ricky could sense his displeasure. They found it hilarious.

As they left the room, laughing and grab-assing, Juan grimly warned them they were putting their immortal souls in jeopardy by participating in tonight's blasphemous shoot. He said he'd pray for them. That heartfelt pledge only served to further break them up.

Now, feeling the humid night air against his skin as he urinated onto a rectangular divot of dry mud, Vance

192

felt a little bad about tearing through all the beer like that. He should have left at least one for the pious little Cuban. God knows he'd worked hard this week, even if he was a dicey fella to warm to.

Whack!

Someone slapped Vance on the back of the head, hard enough to throw off his balance. Badly startled, it was a minor miracle he'd already finished zipping up. Three seconds earlier and he could have easily made himself a eunuch.

Whirling around, Vance saw Ricky standing behind him with a dopey grin.

"Jesus," he growled. "What's the idea?"

"Sorry," Ricky said, not sounding sorry at all. "We need you to help move the 'The Jenny.'"

"Fine."

The clouds separated for a moment, allowing the moon to shine through. From his peripheral vision, Vance saw something that made him jump.

"Hey," he whispered, grabbing Ricky by the collar. "Look over there."

"Where?"

"Shut up. There."

Vance pointed to the southwest corner of the cemetery, some fifty paces from where they stood. A small cluster of trees gave some form to an otherwise empty piece of ground where no tombstones were planted. Ricky squinted hard enough to cross his eyes but couldn't discern much in the blackness. The clouds had blotted out the moon once again, limiting visibility beyond a few feet.

"I don't see anything."

Vance remained silent for almost a minute as he looked intently across the barren ground.

"There's someone standing behind those trees," he finally said.

"Come on."

"I'm serious. Looks like he's holding a gun."

"Bullshit, Vance."

Ricky hoped he sounded tough, because what Vance just said unsettled him deeply. He instantly thought of Juan's ominous warning and wondered if they should have taken it more seriously.

"Don't you see him?" Vance whispered.

Ricky squinted some more. He couldn't tell if Vance was fucking with him, trying to get back for being startled a minute ago. He wanted to believe that was the case.

"All I see's a shadow."

"I'm telling you, that's a person."

Another sliver of moonlight opened up and Ricky's eyes beheld what his mind didn't want to accept. A tall figure stood in silent silhouette near the cluster of trees. He appeared to be holding a rifle.

"Fuck," Ricky squeaked, feeling his bowels chime in by sealing up tight. "What's he doing?"

"It's probably the night watchman."

"Why doesn't he say something? Why's he just stand there?"

Vance laid a hand on Ricky's shoulder and turned him around.

"Let's walk away. Slowly."

"Good idea."

"Quiet. Just walk."

Vance didn't trust Ricky not to do something stupid. The kid (and that's all he was, "Key Grip" or not) was obviously feeling twitchy.

Vance was pretty spooked himself, though he wasn't sure why. What did it matter if someone was standing alone in the trees? No reason to think he meant any harm. After all, they weren't doing anything wrong, just trespassing in an abandoned graveyard in the middle of the night.

Ricky had little choice but to follow along as Vance dragged him back to the camera and the lights.

"You fellas hold it right there!"

It was a deep baritone, and it did not speak with hesitation.

"Keep walking," Vance said under his breath.

"I said hold it!" the voice called again. "I'm warning you, I'm armed!"

Trading a glance, they both froze. Turning around slowly, Vance and Ricky saw the shape of a man emerge from the shadows. The barrel of his weapon glinted in the moonlight.

The armed figure, still just a blur, was an ominous sight to Vance and Ricky. But they had no way of knowing just how scared *he* was.

Bill held the rifle out in front of him, pointed downward. He really didn't feel comfortable with a firearm in his hand, having never discharged once since he was a boy. At the same time, he was glad to have it on him.

When he pulled his car up to the gates of Fairview Cemetery several minutes before, he'd been surprised to see a small group of vehicles parked nearby. Further surprised to see the creaking gate wide open. He considered going to check on Frannie, then figured he'd better get a handle on what was happening in here.

It didn't take long to hear the voices echoing across the patchy ground. Even from many yards off, he could make out the strange white glow Frannie had mentioned. It didn't look supernatural; it was clearly manmade. But that didn't go very far in explaining the situation.

Bill was working up the courage to move in closer when he saw Vance approach out of the darkness and stop to take a whizz. Getting a good look at him, Bill was even more perplexed. He was expecting to find a bunch of teenagers pulling some idiotic prank, like he'd done more than a few times while growing up around here.

But the guy he saw was clearly in his twenties. Then another guy showed up and they started talking. That's when Bill decided he'd hung back in the shadows long enough.

"You fellas realize you're trespassing on private property?"

"We were just leaving," Vance said, still taking small steps backward.

"Not so fast." Bill jerked the barrel of his gun in the direction of the electric glow. "What in the Sam Hill's going on over there?"

"None of your business," Ricky ventured with false belligerence that fooled no one.

"Shut up," Vance hissed. "We're shooting a movie, mister. Just about finished and we'll be on our way."

Bill couldn't process that bit of information. It was too implausible. He felt his initial trepidation receding and a rush of anger replacing it. Whatever he'd stumbled upon made no sense at all.

"You're doing *what*, now?"

"Making a motion picture, just like in Hollywood. How's about you put the carbine down?"

"I don't think so. I came out here to look into a disturbance." Bill nodded vaguely in the direction of Frannie's house. "The old gal yonder heard you fellas loud as thunder. Damn near scared her to death."

"Oh. We're real sorry about that," Vance said as sincerely as he could. "Didn't know anyone was in that house."

"Hell, yes. My mother-in-law, to be precise about it."

Vance was starting to feel genuine concern about where this was heading. The Winchester was now aimed more or less directly at his chest.

"Like I said, we didn't know. I really think you ought to put the gun down."

"You guys have some kind of permit to be here?"

"What's a permit?" Ricky asked.

"Shut up!" Vance said. He turned back to the man with the rifle. "Look, why don't you talk to the producer, Mr. Hoffman. He'll be glad to answer any questions."

"Well now, that sounds like a good idea. Where would I find him?"

"Right over by those lights. Come on, I'll introduce you."

Careful to take measured steps, Vance moved forward. Bill followed directly behind, so close Vance couldn't keep track of him out of the corner of his eye. He tried slowing down just a bit to see if Bill would catch up, but apparently the guy was too smart for that.

Ricky was walking in lock step to Vance's left. He was fidgeting like a hamster in a cage, obviously on the verge of a freakout. Vance made a small gesture with his hand telling him to keep cool.

What Vance did *not* want was for them to surprise anyone on the crew, inciting some rash reaction that might cause the gun to go off. If that happened, he'd be the first sorry sucker to take a bullet.

The camera and lights had been moved to the far corner of the graveyard, where the oak stood. As they got closer, Vance could see that Meyer and Hoffman were involved in a tense debate and had no awareness of their approach. Faye and Jerry were nowhere to be seen.

"Gene? Someone here wants to talk to you."

Hoffman looked up. It took him less than three seconds to assess the situation. He put a hand on Shel's chest, indicating that the director stay put, and stepped forward.

"This gentleman..." Vance began, turning to Bill, "Sorry, I didn't get your name."

"Bill Henderson."

"Mr. Henderson was wondering if we had a permit to shoot here."

Hoffman gave Vance a quick look that said, *Relax, I'll handle this.*

"Gene Hoffman," he boomed, extending his hand to Bill, who made no move to accept it. "I'm the cofounder of Stupendous Pictures and the producer of this project."

"That's what this fella told me. I couldn't quite believe it myself."

"I realize we may not appear all that impressive for a motion picture company, but you'd be surprised what happens behind the scenes. It's not nearly as grand as most people assume. Why, *Casablanca* was shot in less than ten days, with barely more people than you see here tonight."

Hoffman's tone was reassuring in its professionalism. Bill shouldered the rifle, figuring that, whatever bizarre operation he'd found, it almost surely posed no danger to his safety.

"This is private property you're on," he said.

"I'm well aware," Hoffman agreed briskly. "Rest assured all necessary protocol has been followed. I personally contacted the proprietor of this fine cemetery and he granted my crew every permission to film here."

Bill blinked a few times, unable to keep up with Gene's motormouthed barrage.

"You mean Mr. Tomlinson?"

"The very man," Hoffman said with a broad grin, as if speaking of an old friend. "He seemed quite excited about the prospects of having his establishment featured in a high-quality cinematic entertainment."

Listening to Gene's dulcet tones, Bill started to relax a bit. It all seemed rather dubious, given the lateness of the hour and the ragtag appearance of the people assembled. But who knew how motion pictures got made? Never much of a moviegoer, Bill had not once in his life stopped to wonder about the inner workings of show business.

"OK," Bill said, scratching his head and inadvertently moving the barrel of the gun so it pointed at an alarmed Shel Meyer. "Here's the problem. My mother-in-law lives right there, all by herself. You people gave her a terrible fright. I could hear you clear from the gates."

"For that, I apologize. Sometimes things get a bit noisy in the heat of battle. I assure you we'll be finished in no time at all. You'll never see us again, except on the big screen."

That sounded reasonable enough.

"Well, I suppose if you got permission from Mr. Tomlinson..."

"Allow me to send an autographed photo of Myrna Loy to your mother-in-law just as soon as I return to California," Hoffman said, really selling everything he had to make this yokel disappear. "She's an old pal and I'm sure she'd be happy to oblige. Just a token, but I hope it will make up for our disturbance in some small way."

"That's awful nice of you, Mr. Hoffman."

Gene's really good, Vance thought to himself. The producer just had a natural ability to put people at ease and come across as everyone's favorite uncle, no matter how old they were.

With his quick mind and quicker lips, Hoffman had just extinguished a potentially hazardous situation. This guy Bill had been completely fleeced and he'd loved every second of it.

Hoffman grabbed a pen from his pocket so he could jot down Frannie's name and address. Bill was starting to take an interested look at the Mitchell, to Meyer's chagrin.

Then Faye Dwight appeared from the darkness, Jerry Cooke close behind. She was a ghastly vision. Anyone would think her throat had really been slashed.

"Dear Lord," Bill gasped.

Hoffman tried to redirect Bill's gaze from where Faye stood, but the damage was already done.

"Very realistic makeup, isn't it?" he said with a smile that suddenly looked more predatory than avuncular.

Jerry Cooke noted Bill's wide-eyed reaction and mistook it for appreciation. Thinking he could impress the man with some impromptu theatrics, Jerry grabbed Faye by the shoulder and jabbed the knife into her ear, squirting out what remained of the blood.

The rifle fell from Bill's hands. His eyes swam and his stomach capsized.

Turning on one heel like a weathervane in a high wind, he started running away at top speed before the Winchester even hit the ground. It landed on a jagged rock at just the right angle, pushing the trigger against the bolt and discharging a round with an ear-shattering boom.

Ricky screeched as a bullet tore into the flabby pale flesh of his right thigh. He dropped to a crouch, clutching his leg and howling in pain.

"Stop him!" Hoffman cried to Vance as Bill tore across the graveyard with greater speed than Gene would have granted him. Athletic ability had nothing to do with the fleetness of Bill's feet. It was blind horror that propelled him.

Vance gave chase, halfheartedly. Bill was still within his sights, darting among the graves as if he knew every inch of the cemetery by heart.

Vance didn't dare follow full-tilt since the footing was so treacherous and the lighting so bad. He wanted to catch the guy, but he had no intention of twisting an ankle on one of the hundreds of collapsed headstones sprinkled all about. This was not really his problem, after all.

Just as Vance was thinking those thoughts, he heard a strangled cry ahead of him. Rapidly followed by a dull thud. It sounded like Bill had done exactly what Vance was afraid of doing.

Advancing a few more yards, Vance saw this was indeed the case. Bill lay prone on the ground, face-down. He'd obviously tripped on a stone. His head was wedged right up against the sharp corner of a large grave. Vance kneeled down and turned him over. A large gash running across his forehead was visible in the moonlight. It looked bad, but he was still breathing.

"Over here!" Vance called out. He hadn't chased Bill more than a few dozen yards from where the crew was stationed. But no one came to the sound of his voice right away. Meyer was busy talking Faye out of bolting and Hoffman was tending to Ricky.

Forcing the wounded Key Grip to remove his pants over cries of protest even louder than his exclamations of pain, Hoffman determined Ricky had merely been grazed. Jerry Cooke stood a few feet away, chewing on his knuckles so his entire being would not explode with delight. He was absolutely thrilled to finally see some *real blood*.

"Just a flesh wound, kid," Hoffman said with a firm slap to Ricky's back. "Wear it like a badge of honor."

Ricky didn't seem noticeably soothed by Gene's diagnosis. He thought maybe a doctor ought to take a look, but Hoffman squelched that idea pronto. It was just a nick. Probably wouldn't require stitches, and even if it did none were available out here in the middle of the night, so why worry about it?

Gene grabbed a few bandages from the first aid kit and told Jerry to apply them. Clocking the look on the actor's face, he changed his mind and gave the bandages to Meyer. Then he went lumbering after the sound of Vance's voice.

Standing over Bill's inert form, Hoffman shook his head sadly.

"The fool. Why'd he run?"

"He thought he'd just seen someone get killed."

"Bah. A child would know it was a gag."

"Then how's it gonna work onscreen?" Vance asked, instantly mad at Hoffman's lack of sympathy.

"Don't get tart with me, kid. The old lady in the house must have heard that shot. Let's wrap and roll."

He started to turn away. Vance grabbed the sleeve of Gene's shirt, an aggressive move that surprised them both.

"What about him?"

"What *about* him?"

"We can't just leave him here."

Hoffman was nonplussed. "Oh, really? What do you suggest?"

"He needs to go to a hospital. Look at him."

"I see him, Vance. He's made a big problem for himself by acting like a dunce."

"Maybe so, but we can still act like human beings."

"I'm not prepared to answer a lot of questions about how this poor sap split his head open. Are you?"

"We can say we found him on the side of the road."

Hoffman took a handkerchief out of his pocket and mopped his sweaty brow. He seemed to give the matter serious consideration.

"You know what, kid? If you hadn't managed to get yourself in so much trouble this week, I might agree with you. But I don't think we can risk drawing any more attention to ourselves."

"That's horseshit, Gene. You can't pin this on me."

"I'm not trying to. I'm just telling you how it is."

A final glance at the fallen man cemented the matter in Hoffman's mind.

"He'll be fine. Wake up tomorrow with a monster headache and maybe learn a lesson about minding his own business."

Without waiting for agreement, Hoffman trudged off to join the crew. Vance looked down at Bill, feeling queasy with a sense of powerlessness. There was nothing to be done, was there?

Turning away, Vance couldn't help wondering, for about the hundredth time this week, what exactly he'd gotten himself into.

SUNDAY
(WRAP DAY)

9:05 A.M.

The mirror frightened her. It was a liar, reflecting an image of death that was no less terrible for being a fabrication. Though she didn't want to see it, she had little choice.

The image staring back at her did not look real. It looked worse than real. It was a nightmare, but she was awake.

Barbara stood in her bathroom, hands planted on the sink and eyes welded onto the mirror that was gradually fogging as the shower piped out hot water. A moist curtain of ultra-bright red poured from the top of her forehead, down her face and onto her chest.

She'd been standing here for quite some time, as the rest of the crew waited downstairs for her to rejoin them. Barbara had forgotten all about them. She was naked, with a crimson-soaked bikini lying in a sticky heap at her feet. It was her favorite one, a frilly pink and blue number with a white flower riding over the left breast. She was sick to lose it, knowing the blood would never wash out. Hoffman promised to buy her a new one of equal or greater value, for whatever that pledge was worth.

She wanted to move. She wanted to wash off the sickening mask, even as she could feel it drying on her skin. But she found herself inexplicably frozen. Her own distorted reflection was transfixing.

The shower kept running. Steam continued to dim the mirror and the red contours of her face blurred until they were no longer visible. Finally the image was gone, and Barbara remembered what she had to do. She stepped into the shower and started scrubbing.

She'd awoken this morning earlier than usual. Last night was the most peaceful of the whole week. While the rest of the crew was at the graveyard, she enjoyed an evening of solitude. She took advantage of it to write her grandmother a letter. It was the first attempt at communication since leaving Mobile three years ago.

More than anything, Barbara wanted to get an address where she could reach her mother, who was still living in a sanitarium in upstate Alabama as far as she knew. Beginning the letter with apologies for being out of touch, she tried to inject a tone of casual assurance that everything was just fine.

Halfway down the second page, she balled the letter up and dropped it in the wastepaper basket. It was too indirect a form of communication to bridge the gap time had created. She needed to reestablish contact in person, and that's exactly what she decided to do. Dozing off early, Barbara dreamed of the bus trip she would make to Mobile as soon as she got her hands on a ticket.

Waking up fresh and energized, she wanted to get rolling as soon as possible. Meyer still hadn't told her exactly what the unscripted wet scene would entail, so she knocked on his door a little before 7:00. He was already awake. After some hemming and hawing, he told her how it was going to play.

It would be a simple setup, requiring no dialogue and only one camera angle. Barbara wouldn't even have to move very much. All she had to do was lie in a lounge chair as if tanning herself.

"OK," she said impatiently. "Then what?"

"Remember, this is a dream. Kelly imagines herself lying in the sun. Then, with no warning, Ace pops up from behind the chair and scalps her."

A pause filled the cluttered room.

"He scalps her," Barbara repeated.

"Yup," Shel said proudly, mistaking her incredulity for admiration. "Not bad for a last-minute idea, huh?"

"How are you going to pull that off?"

"Simple. We tie your hair back and put a wig on you. Jerry takes a straight razor, the blade has already been dulled, don't worry, and he runs it across your forehead as he pulls back the wig. Underneath the wig we have a little bag of stage blood. All he has to do is puncture it with the blade and out it comes."

"Are you sure about this?"

"Absolutely. We're only gonna see it for a few seconds before we cut to Kelly waking up. It'll look fantastic."

"It'll look awful," Barbara said. "I guess that's the idea."

"I knew you'd understand."

Forty-five minutes later, the crew was gathered at the pool. Barbara found it ironic they were shooting this particular scene in the one spot where she'd felt most comfortable over the course of the week. Meyer wanted her to lie in her favorite chair as the attack happens. She wasn't sure if there was any specific reason for that or not.

The crew was tired, sluggish. They spoke little and Hoffman declined to provide any sort of breakfast. Not even coffee. Barbara had no idea what happened last night in the cemetery. She wasn't even curious enough to ask why Ricky was skulking around with a bandaged leg and a limp.

The wounded Key Grip got down on his good knee and stirred up a drum full of fake blood. It looked like much more than they would need, but maybe they were planning on using the rest for the final scene tonight. Ricky filled a small plastic bag with about a pint's worth and sealed it.

Meyer took over from there. He instructed Barbara to lie back in the chair and remain still. Placing the bag on top of her head, he held it there with one hand while using the other to pull on a wig of long blonde tresses. It was a good match of Barbara's own hair, just a tiny bit darker. Once the wig had been secured around her ears, it stayed firm and held the bag in place underneath.

The wig felt hot and oppressive on her head, the rough fibers bothering her ears and cheeks. But she didn't move a muscle, just concentrated on breathing slowly and telling herself this would all be over in less than ten minutes. Meyer had promised her that timeframe.

It didn't occur to her to ask Shel why he happened to have a blonde wig handy, one so close to her hairstyle. If he hadn't originally planned to shoot this scene, why would the wig be necessary? She didn't think of this until later in the day, and by that point it didn't seem like an inquiry worthy of pursuit.

She lay there quietly in the sun chair, waiting for the scene to start so that it could end. Out of the corner of her eye, she saw Jerry walk past to position himself behind her. The morning sun flashed off the side of the straight razor in his hand.

"OK, Barbara," she heard Shel saying from several feet away. "Close your eyes and try to relax. You're lying out in the sun, feeling the warmth cover you. It's a beautiful morning and you don't have a single worry."

Her eyes closed. The world didn't go black but dark red as the sun burned through her eyelids.

She heard the camera begin to roll. For a moment, Vance appeared in her mind. She wondered what he was doing. Probably sleeping off whatever he'd poured back last night. They hadn't spoken since their heated encounter in his room during the storm. Barbara thought it would be nice to have Vance around. Even if he was a jerk, his presence would be welcome right now.

The Mitchell purred. Barbara lay there sightless, waiting to hear Shel say "action." She wanted to hear that, because then she would know the attack was about to happen. As long as she could give herself a moment to brace for it, she would be all right.

Looking through the viewfinder, Meyer anticipated the thought process of his untrained leading lady. He knew it would be impossible for her not to tense up a bit if she realized Jerry was about to strike. It would ruin the spontaneity of the effect. So instead of verbally signaling for the action to begin, he gave Jerry a hand signal they had privately worked out earlier.

Another endless second ticked by in Barbara's head. Then it happened.

Without warning, she felt Jerry's clammy hand close over her throat. She opened her mouth in genuine shock as she felt the cold, dulled edge of the razor land on her forehead.

"Scream, Barbara!" she heard Meyer yelling from behind the camera. "Scream like he's killing you!"

She couldn't do it. Her mouth opened but no sound came out. She felt the razor being dragged across her skin and the wig being pulled back. The fake blood came gushing down from the punctured bag. Splattering across her face. Stinging her eyes and poisoning her mouth. It was a terrible feeling, but she could not scream. Her throat constricted, blocking any sound from escaping.

Then she heard Meyer yell, "Cut!" And it was all over. The whole thing hadn't lasted more than a few seconds.

Barbara heard the crew applauding. She tried to open her eyes but they felt pasted shut by the blood. Then someone was gently dabbing a wet towel across her face. Looking up, she saw Vance standing above her. He seemed to be taking the utmost caution in wiping off the makeup. The look he wore was pained.

She grabbed the towel and vigorously ran it across her face. Vance offered a hand to help her up and she allowed him, surprised to feel her knees wobble a bit. Pulling the wig off her head, she threw it to the ground.

Meyer walked over. He smiled, but it didn't fool her.

"You did great. A little quiet, but great."

"I'm sorry, Sheldon," she said, not knowing why she actually felt apologetic. "I tried. I don't know what happened."

"That's OK. We can loop something in later. Go get cleaned up."

His tone was soft but there was no denying the disappointment on his face. He still hadn't gotten the scream he felt was so important to this movie. Barbara had let him down.

"Let's hear it for our fearless leading lady!" Hoffman roared, initiating another round of applause. The rest of the crew followed suit, without much commitment. Vance, in particular, looked embarrassed. He'd come down from his room just as they were starting to roll. Still plagued with residual guilt about the other night, he figured maybe he could offer some moral support. They'd never spoken directly about her decision to shoot the wet scene, but based on their conversations about *Crimson Orgy* in general he was pretty sure she wasn't thrilled about it.

She didn't seem especially pleased to see him, barely registering eye contact as she took the towel. He mistook her numbness for contempt aimed at solely at him. So he slunk off to the background and bided his time. The last day on a shoot is always the longest, or so Hoffman had told him.

Barbara started to walk up to her room, determined to take assured strides. The makeup hadn't been removed by the towel, simply smeared across her face in wide streaks.

Meyer told her to take a nice long break. The rest of the crew would shoot the Easter basket scene in the front parking lot while she got cleaned up. After she rejoined them, it would be time to move on with the rest of her scenes.

Barbara barely heard the words coming from Shel's mouth as she crossed the courtyard. Vaguely, she seemed to notice a look of relief on Vance's face at the mention of the basket scene which had caused him so much pointless wondering. It occurred to her that she'd never gotten around to telling him about the mannequin in Meyer's room. But that passed from her thoughts quickly as she climbed the stairway to her room.

Almost an hour had passed by the time she stepped out of the shower and wrapped a towel around herself. She'd hoped to feel much better after cleansing her skin. She didn't.

One thought kept spinning around her head. It wouldn't go away.

The idea that she'd willingly decorated herself as a bloodied victim of violence made her feel sick. And she couldn't find any form of rationalization to relieve that feeling.

Meyer was full of shit. This wasn't like dressing up for Halloween. It was intentionally simulating the most depraved sort of behavior, which had far too many counterparts in real life, and shipping it across the country as entertainment. Barbara's stomach clutched with shame as she imagined all the people, kids especially, who would go to the local drive-in and pay to see her get scalped. Worst of all, they would think it was just good fun, unless they knew from experience that worse things happen every day. Like she did.

Sitting on her bed, she couldn't stop trembling. A soft knock at the door got her attention.

"Barbara? It's Shel. You about ready?"

"Almost," she said, embarrassed by the quiver in her voice. "I need a few more minutes."

He didn't hear her, so he knocked again. She got up to let him in, then returned to the bed.

Meyer tried to smile. "Look at you," he said. "Good as new. Not too much of a chore, was it?"

"No," she lied.

"Something wrong, sweetheart?"

"I'm fine."

"Good. We're about ready to move on, if you are."

She nodded, but didn't rise.

"I'll give you another minute," Meyer said, quickly withdrawing.

He was almost out the door when she called his name. A crack in her voice revealed plenty.

"OK, something is wrong. Tell me."

"It's nothing. I just..."

"Hey, it's all right. I'm your hurricane buddy, remember? Tell me what's bothering you."

"I know we're in a rush, and I know we're not allowed to make long-distance calls..."

211

"Who do you need to call?"

"I really want to talk to my grandmother. Just for a minute."

Shel appeared to consider the matter, biting his lip.

"Can it wait? We're really up against the wall here."

"I'll pay the expense myself when we get home."

"It's not that, it's just the time."

"Please?"

For a moment, it looked like he was about to cave. Then Barbara saw his jaw tense, an expression she'd come to recognize.

"Christ, I hate to be the bad guy here..."

"Don't blame yourself," she said, cutting him off. "I must have been out of my mind to make such a wild request."

"OK, you're pissed. But think about it for a second. This doesn't sound like a quick conversation. You wouldn't want to feel rushed speaking to her, would you?"

Barbara's head shook slightly. She wasn't answering his question, but marveling at his facile command of manipulation. Though transparent, it was also much more formidable than she would have given him credit for at first glance. He'd obviously learned how to get his way when making a picture.

"Fine," she eventually said. "Forget it."

Meyer took a step back. "We'll see you outside. OK?"

"Yeah."

He left, closing the door behind him.

"Go to hell," Barbara said after he was out of earshot. She slid down the bed to the night stand and picked up the phone. Punching 0, she gave a long distance operator the number in Mobile that she hadn't been able to dial for so long.

The phone rang. Barbara sat on the bed, listening, trying to control her breath as she waited for someone to answer.

212

* * * * * * *

9:20 A.M.

Lucille was in a state of high panic. She really didn't know what to do with herself. One thing she'd *never* do was forgive herself for not waiting up last night. She tried, but yesterday was a long day and by the time she crawled into bed she was dog-tired.

She didn't expect Bill to be gone long. Usually it took no more than a half-hour to drive up to Hillsboro, assure Frannie everything was fine, hop back in the car and return home. Lucille usually woke up to the creak of the bed as Bill lay down. Last night no creak came, and she slept like a baby all night.

Waking up was awful. It was a jolt to roll over and see Bill's side of the bed empty. Lucille almost couldn't convince herself it was real. She must be dreaming.

After pinching herself hard enough to generate tears, Lucille flew out of bed and ran downstairs. Maybe Bill had gotten up early and gone to the fishery without bothering to wake her for breakfast. He'd never done it in three decades of marriage, but there's a first time for everything. Lucille held onto that dim possibility as she dialed his work number.

The phone was still ringing when she glanced over and noticed his lunch pail sitting next to the kitchen table. The truth hit her without pity. He never came home.

Telling herself to be calm, she hung up and started to dial her mother's number. A fumbling sound at the front door caught her attention. She dropped the phone and ran out of the kitchen into the front hallway, calling out her husband's name.

There he was, leaning in the doorway. Lucille suppressed a scream. Bill's shirt was covered in blood that ran down from the left side of his head. His eyes were

213

glassy. Reddish drool fell from his slack mouth and he struggled to stay upright as he staggered into the house. Lucille rushed to catch his fall just as consciousness left him.

He fell forward into her arms, dragging her down. He landed on top, pinning Lucille to the hardwood floor. She cried out repeatedly and tried to squirm free but her husband's deadweight was too much for her.

* * * * * * *

12:10 P.M.

Hoffman pulled the Fairlane into the dusty parking lot of the Angler's Rest. This was a questionable move. He should be back at the motel right now, making sure some other unexpected crisis didn't pop up out of nowhere. He'd already been gone a good twenty minutes or so, handling the first of two tasks on his mind.

Finding a place to ditch the decomposed arm wasn't a challenge. Not in these depopulated parts. Still, Gene wanted to make damn sure it never got found, by accident or intent. It'd been a pain in the ass from start to finish; they ended up using the mannequin's arm for the scene this morning, just as he'd predicted. But screwy Shel Meyer insisted they have a real arm on standby, he was fucking obsessed with making this movie *real*. So his faithful producer had made some calls and procured a human limb, because that's what producers do. And now he had to get rid of the awful thing.

Gene parked the car on an appropriately empty stretch of A1A, kicked off his size 13 canvas shoes, and waded about a thirty yards into a thick marsh with the metal box clutched in his right hand. All the while thinking maybe he'd sit in the director's chair from now on, instead of seeking a replacement for Meyer. Stream-

214

line the process, impose final say over any harebrained "creative" ideas, and save some money. Why not, he was up to the job.

It pained him to lose the sleek metal case, which hadn't been a cheap purchase, but keeping the arm contained within was the surest way to prevent discovery. It would conceal any stench that might attract birds or a stray dog, and was more than heavy enough to sink below sight.

Except it didn't. The case just sat improbably on the soupy, grassy surface, even though Hoffman himself was shin-deep in the muck. He pushed down on it with one heel, almost losing his balance. Tipping to the side, the case slid neatly from view, sending up a few brown bubbles in parting.

Good riddance to another artifact of a very weird week.

Now, ten minutes later, Hoffman's wet feet trudged through the front door of the Angler's Rest. Time to take care of his second task and hustle on back to the set.

When he came here on Tuesday night to pick up those two bottles of Jameson's, he'd been pleasantly surprised with the price. A good twenty percent cheaper than you'd expect in Miami. Apparently there was one advantage to be found out here in the wilds. Since the crew was on lunch break, Gene figured he might as well swing by and stock up.

Crossing the uneven panels of the floor, Hoffman saw those two old fishermen planted at the corner. Exactly where they were five nights ago.

Must not be allowed to leave the joint, he thought. *Maybe they're paid to sit around and add local color.*

Hoffman stood at the bar, drumming his fingers on the deeply grooved wood. Sherry was at the register with her back to him. When Gene came in the other night she'd been friendly enough. They'd made some small talk about the movie and she asked a few innocuous questions about Vance. Hoffman had no idea, of course, what role she had played in his arrest.

Today she seemed to be doing her best to ignore him, if she heard him come in at all. He cleared his throat loudly and she turned.

Though she had undone her ponytail so her hair hung down low in front, there was no hiding the mottled purple bruise on her left cheek. It stuck out from the side of her face like a baseball, giving her head a disturbingly asymmetrical appearance. A pretty woven shawl concealed the scratch marks on her neck.

Sherry tried to keep her body half-turned away from Hoffman as she walked over to him.

"You're back," she said as if talking to a recurrent toothache.

"Soak it up. This is the last you'll be seeing of me."

"I'll try to get over it."

Hoffman smiled. He dug broads with spunk, especially if they could find a way to keep that kind of edge while sporting such a gruesome shiner.

"How many bottles of Jameson's you got?"

Sherry took a perfunctory look over her shoulder. "I can only part with two right now. Unless I go rooting around in the back."

"Would you mind? I'll take whatever you can spare."

She nodded and walked to the storeroom behind the bar. Waiting for her to return, Gene pondered whether he should say anything about the bruise. What good could come of it? She was essentially a stranger, and if she didn't have better sense than to tolerate getting knocked around there wasn't much he could do for her.

She reappeared with three bottles.

"It's your lucky day," she said, laying them on the bar. She gave him the total.

Hoffman peeled off some bills and handed them over.

"Keep it."

It was a huge tip, well beyond the twenty percent he was saving.

"Thanks."

"I hope we haven't caused too much of a disturbance around here."

Sherry didn't say anything as she put the bottles in a paper sack. Hoffman waited a moment to see if he got a reply, then just grabbed the sack with a smile.

"Well, good luck," he said.

Nodding cordially to the fisherman, he strode to the front door.

"Hey," Sherry said.

He turned.

"Tell Vance not to come back this way. Ever."

I don't think he's planning to, Gene thought. But all he said was, "I'll pass it along."

Hoffman stepped outside. Sherry listened to the door slam shut. The creak of the rusty hinges made her face hurt even more than it already did.

She didn't know why she just said that, any more than she knew why she called out Vance's name at the least appropriate time Friday night. There was absolutely nothing between her and the blow-dried actor. It was a ridiculous notion. She hadn't laid eyes on him since that first time, and wasn't even sure she remembered his name until it had escaped her lips.

Sex is irrational, as she'd tried to explain to Sonny in the tense aftermath of her blunder. At the peak of pleasure, all kinds of nonsensical thoughts and images flooded her mind. They didn't mean anything. One time, when he was going down on her, she shut her eyes tight and the image of Alexander Hamilton on the ten-dollar

217

bill materialized. What the hell did *that* mean? Was Sonny going to get jealous of the currency in his wallet?

In truth, she had been thinking about Vance over the past few days, but not in a sexual way. She was feeling vaguely guilty about turning him in. The kid may be obnoxious, but he was harmless. She was just in a bad mood that morning and his relentless flirtation rubbed her the wrong way. He probably didn't deserve to be arrested, and she knew all too well what a prick Sonny could be when he was feeling his law enforcement oats.

The other night on the couch she'd paid a heavy price for allowing Vance to invade her thoughts. Despite her best efforts, Sonny's wounded ego would not be assuaged.

He only struck her once but it was a good one. His knuckles landed with sinister heft. His bitten nails had already dug deeply into the flesh of her neck. Pushing her off him, he stalked to his bedroom and slammed the door shut. She spent the rest of the night curled up on the living room floor, shivering as the storm got louder and more frightening.

He was gone when she woke. Sherry tried to make herself look presentable and drove to open up the bar at 9:00. She'd spent two days wanting to call the station and say hello but felt he should call her first. *He* was the one who needed to apologize.

Gingerly exploring the contours of her bruise as she listened to Hoffman's car roar out of the parking lot, Sherry realized the warning she'd asked him to give Vance was almost certainly unnecessary. And a little embarrassing as well.

She was glad to have made the effort, just the same. She didn't expect to see the kid again, but she wanted to make absolutely sure. The sooner those wretched movie people got out of Hillsboro Beach, the better off everyone would be.

* * * * * * *

4:40 P.M.

They drove away from the Pompano Beach Medical Clinic, Lucille at the wheel. Bill slumped in the passenger seat, his head heavily bandaged. They didn't speak much until she turned north on A1A.

She'd finally been able to revive him this morning, enough to get him into the car anyway. He tried to tell her what happened on the drive to the clinic but she instructed him to remain still and preserve his strength.

After testing Bill's balance, coordination, and reflexes, the doctor concluded he'd received a fairly serious concussion but there was no apparent skull fracture. Bill was given a mouthful of anti-inflammatories and his head was wrapped tight. He was kept under observation throughout the afternoon but allowed to leave after the swelling appeared to recede and coherent speech returned. Though the doctor also encouraged him not to strain himself trying to remember what happened, Bill wouldn't let it go. As Lucille wheeled him to the car, the story came together in uneven fragments.

He remembered arriving at the cemetery and being amazed to see such strange goings-on. A cluster of lights in one corner and a small group of people walking around, making a hell of a racket. He remembered confronting two men and asking them what in God's name they were doing. Some nonsense about making a movie. He remembered getting very angry with the situation.

Then everything was a blank until he awoke this morning flat on his back in the tall prickly grass. His head was pushed up next to a tombstone.

The pain could not be described with mere words. It was mixed with a nauseous feeling that stole his equilibrium and made the world spin. It took what seemed like an hour simply to sit up without vomiting. How he drove home was almost inexplicable. He'd had to cover one eye just to stay within the lane.

In her panic to get him a doctor's attention, Lucille forgot all about her mother. But on the drive home from the clinic, hearing his account of violent trespassers, Lucille began to seriously fear for Frannie's wellbeing.

She wanted to drive directly up to Hillsboro but she knew she'd better drop him off first. Helping him into their bed and pulling up the covers, she picked up the phone and dialed Frannie's number. There was no answer, it just rang and rang.

Now Lucille was really worried. She kissed Bill's bandaged forehead and told him she needed to go check on her mom. He tried to protest, saying it still might not be safe, but she shushed him. It was time for him to just relax and let her take charge of the situation.

Flooring it up the highway, Lucille felt her concern turning to rage. What kind of awful people would break into a cemetery and attack someone who was only trying to look after an old woman? As soon as she made sure Frannie was OK, Lucille was going to call that nice deputy in Hillsboro Beach. He'd been agreeable enough to drop in on Frannie once or twice when Bill was out of town on business. He needed to know about what happened last night and, with any luck, track down the perpetrators.

Pulling her car to an abrupt stop in her mother's driveway, Lucille hopped out and started pounding on the front door. No one stirred inside the house, and no lights were on even though the sun had started to fade. Circling around to the back, she called out her mother's name through the open kitchen window, then climbed up and pulled herself through.

The kitchen was silent and empty. A ceramic bowl was on the table, half-filled with oatmeal that had hardened to cement. The TV in the living room was not on at a deafening level, which was unusual for this time of day. Frannie loved her stories.

Lucille mounted the stairs to the second floor, feeling a widening hole fill the pit of her stomach. The door to her mother's room was just slightly ajar. Stillness on the other side.

Lucille pushed the door open gently, wincing at the abrasive creak.

She wasn't at all prepared for what she saw.

There was her mother, kneeling by the open window that looked out onto Fairview. Her bent posture was highly unnatural, as if she'd been stuffed by a sadistic taxidermist. The afternoon glow came in through the window, tinting her white hair a faint gold. Her chin rested on the dusty sill, supporting her entire upper body. The phone was still clutched in one shriveled hand.

Stepping closer, unable to stifle a despairing moan, Lucille took a long look at her mother's dead face. It was frozen in a rictus of terror, eyes wide and dry puckered mouth agape. She was staring sightlessly at the grave-yard that had been such a source of fright for so long.

Whatever she'd seen last night had killed her, just as surely as a bullet. Lucille knew that beyond doubt. The chimeral horrors that haunted Frannie's mind finally became real somehow. It was more than the old gal's heart could stand.

* * * * * * *

6:20 P.M.

Barbara was standing in the courtyard as night fell, waiting for the rest of the crew to arrive so they could all leave together. She'd already loaded her bags into the Fairlane and was ready to go. Unable to reach her grandmother on the phone after three covert attempts throughout the day, she tried to ignore the feeling it was a bad omen of some sort.

Hoffman was in the manager's office, settling the bill in a highly contentious debate with Ernest. The crew was supposed to have checked out hours ago and now Ernest was trying to stick Hoffman for another night. Gene couldn't believe the manager would show such avarice after being granted a part in the movie. There was no way he was going to cough up the dough but Ernest had his credit card number on file, which complicated the possibility of a quick getaway.

Ricky and Juan were loading the equipment into their vehicles. Meyer was in his room, gathering his scant personal possessions. He seemed almost resistant about the idea of leaving the Sand Palace, which struck Barbara as ludicrous. She was counting the seconds until she could put this dump behind her. There were too many unpleasant associations held within its cracked and crumbling walls.

As soon as everyone was ready, they were all going to drive back to the abandoned warehouse to put a permanent wrap on this production. All except Vance, who was headed home right away. He wrapped his last lines an hour ago and would not be needed any more.

Meyer had unexpectedly written him out of the final scene. Rather than have Frank and Kelly vanquish Ace Spade together, Shel changed it so that Kelly perseveres by herself. When asked by Vance why he rewrote it, he gave some hazy answer about "the power of economic storytelling."

God, what a nasty week this had been. Moviemaking was an occupation for lonely freaks and desperate losers, Barbara determined. She should have followed her initial instinct and turned Meyer down when he first offered her the role.

Trust your gut, just like she'd heard Hoffman say a dozen times throughout the shoot.

Next time, she'd be wiser.

Those were Barbara's thoughts as she stood alone in the courtyard while the last traces of sunlight faded to shadow. The sound of Hoffman arguing with Ernest rippled out through the demolished window of the manager's office. Barbara tried to block it out. Hadn't there already been enough conflict? Could anyone really afford to expend more capital, emotional or monetary, in the name of *Crimson Orgy*?

She saw Vance walking down the stairs, a traveling bag in each hand. She still felt some warmth for him, against all odds. Their impromptu fuck the other morning was one of the few bright spots of the whole experience. Vance was selfish and immature, but there was nothing vicious about him. His motivations were as clear to himself as they were to anyone who laid eyes on him. He was essentially an overgrown kid who liked to walk on the sunny side of the street. Egocentric? Sure. Shallow? OK. Maybe he even had a little drinking problem, but at least that was a *normal* affliction.

He approached her across the courtyard, almost tentatively. Barbara smiled to let him know it was alright to come closer.

"Hey there, handsome," she said in a tired voice.

"Hey. Guess it's time to wave goodbye to this pleasure palace."

"Thank God."

"You know, I never got a chance to apologize for the other night."

"You don't have to."

"I want to. I was an asshole and I'm sorry."

"Agreed, and accepted."

"I tried to find you later but you weren't in your room."

"Good thing, too. The storm blew my door right off the hinges."

Vance paused for a moment, almost telling her about his fight with Cliff. Then decided she had nothing to gain by hearing about it.

Another loud curse from Hoffman echoed across the courtyard, with Ernest's insistent voice overlapping it. They were really going at it in there. Vance listened to the argument for a few seconds, then faced Barbara with an expression she could have sworn was sadness.

"Maybe I'll see you around," he said.

"Maybe, but I doubt it. If I don't show up at the premiere I hope you'll understand."

"I'm sure you'll have much better things to do."

"Actually, I'm thinking about moving back to Mobile," she said, testing the idea to see how it sounded coming out of her mouth. "Nothing there can hurt me now. I'd like to spend some time with my grandmother while she's still around."

"Sounds like a good plan."

Vance stepped forward and gave her a hug. She let him, then returned it. They almost kissed but backed away at the same moment.

"Know what I think?" he asked.

"What?"

"I think you should come with me. Right now."

"Yeah, OK."

"I mean it. My car's right out front. Get in, I'll take you home or wherever you want to go."

"I can't do that, Vance."

"Sure you can," he said, slapping a mosquito that landed on his neck. "You don't owe these people anything."

"I've been paid to do the whole movie."

"What, a few hundred bucks? Who gives a shit? Mail it to them if you want. Just leave with me."

"What's gotten into you?"

Vance swallowed dryly. He hadn't expected to make this move. It surprised him, but he didn't feel like he could walk away without making some sort of gesture.

"I don't trust these guys, OK? They don't care about anything but finishing this stupid movie, and they'll run over anyone who gets in the way."

"That's probably true, but I think I can handle it for another few hours."

"Look, I've heard some strange things."

"About what?"

"About you. I'm worried about what they've got planned for tonight."

Barbara laughed, weakly.

"You want to explain that?"

"I can't, really. It's just a feeling. Hoffman said something to me a few days ago. I should have told you before, but I..."

"You what?"

"I was too much of a coward. I was scared he'd take me apart. Now I could care less."

"Vance, if you're trying to get laid again..."

"I'm not," he said quickly. "I mean, that's not what this is about."

"Then tell me what it *is* about, because you're not making any sense."

Across the courtyard, Hoffman's monstrous head poked out the office door and yelled to Barbara that everything was settled and they'd be ready to leave in a few minutes.

Then the head disappeared again.

Vance looked up at Shel Meyer's door.

"I don't think they're happy with what they're getting," he said, his voice lowered to a whisper. "The gore looks fake, anyone can see that."

"What's that got to do with me?"

"How did you land this role? Let's face it, you couldn't act your way out of a parking ticket."

"Thanks a lot." She wasn't angry because it was so obviously true. It was refreshing to hear someone say it to her face, and Vance's honesty moved her.

"Haven't you ever wondered," he asked, "why you got the lead in a movie you don't even want to be in?"

"Shel says I have an intangible quality he was looking for."

"Shit," Vance snorted. "How many times do you think he's used that line?"

"He hasn't tried to get in my pants, if that's what you're worried about."

"Barbara, listen to me. The reason you got hired is because you don't have any ties in Miami."

She was stunned to hear that, coming from Vance. How would he know?

"That's true, isn't it?" he asked.

"So what?"

"And you told that to Meyer, didn't you?" Vance said, pressing her. "The first time you met him."

"Did he tell you about our conversation?" Barbara asked, feeling ill that Shel would have passed along anything personal from that boozy first meeting at the Coconut Grove.

"In fact," Vance persisted, "no one even knows you're living in Miami. You've only been here a little while. You don't have a steady job and you haven't been in touch with your family for years."

"What are you trying to prove, Vance?" she asked, getting angry and feeling tears rise at same time.

"Being so unattached makes you kind of vulnerable, don't you think? Why would you share so much information with someone you just met?"

"I'm not unattached and I'm not vulnerable, OK? Please mind your own business."

"Listen to me!" he said, grabbing her. "I'm telling you I think you're in danger."

She shook her head, mainly so she could wipe away an errant tear without drawing attention to it. "You don't really believe that."

Vance let her go, feeling a kick in his gut as he looked into her shimmering eyes. Why couldn't he keep his mouth shut and just get the hell out of here?

"Well, *do* you?" she asked.

"No," he said, looking away. "Not really. I just don't think you belong here, and it's not too late to walk away."

Barbara exhaled deeply. She had no idea what he was trying to accomplish. She wanted to write off his motives as entirely self-centered, but his level of urgency wouldn't let her.

Something inside told her to trust him.

Vance decided he couldn't wait around for her to make up her mind. He was lucky enough to be getting clear himself.

He picked up his bags, holding one under his arm and grabbing the other with his hand. He extended his free hand in a gesture of invitation.

"Forget what I said," he said softly. "Come with me, anyway. You don't need a reason."

"My bags..."

"Leave 'em."

Barbara felt her hand moved to meet his, almost involuntarily. It was crazy, but it made sense. She *did* want to leave, to take off without looking back. She'd been wanting that ever since she got here.

Just as their fingers locked, they heard a door squeak open and slam shut. Looking up, they saw Meyer trudging along the walkway at a fevered pace, carrying his luggage. He looked down over the railing and called out, "OK, let's get rolling!"

His shrill voice seemed to snap Barbara out of whatever trance Vance had put her in. She withdrew her hand and gave him a friendly smile in its place.

"Have a safe drive," she said. "I want to finish this."

"You sure?"

"Yeah. I don't like loose ends."

Her composure had returned and her voice was firm. Vance looked at her for a moment, then nodded.

"Good luck."

He blew her a kiss and turned away. Meyer had just gotten to the bottom of the stairway and stood with his hand extended in a gentlemanly pose. Vance shook it tersely, then kept walking.

Continuing past the manager's office from which Hoffman had just emerged, Vance didn't even turn his head, just advanced until he disappeared under the arched entrance of the motel.

He was gone.

Barbara watched him disappear, feeling Shel place a cold hand on her shoulder. He was grinning broadly, almost maniacally.

"Well, well," he preened. "Only one star left on the set now."

She really didn't like being touched by him at this particular moment. Hearing heavy footsteps, she turned her head to see Hoffman lumbering over, his strides broad and swift.

"That's right," he boomed, picking up where Shel left off. He also took the liberty to wrap a huge arm around her waist. "The spotlight's on you now, kid."

Barbara stood there, encased within the arms of the two men, all exits blocked. She looked up at Hoffman, then over at Meyer. They both had unnaturally wide smiles glued onto their faces, lips stretched tight across rows of teeth flashing in the light reflected off the pool.

They look insane, both of them.

The gleeful lunatic's countenance of Jerry Cooke popped into her mind and she shuddered.

Neither Meyer nor Hoffman released his grip, just squeezed in tighter. Sandwiching her. Barbara couldn't think of anything to say. Her mind was a blank and there was nowhere for her to move.

* * * * * * *

7:00 P.M.

Deputy Sonny Platt smashed the phone down onto the cradle, hard enough to send a stack of unfiled speeding tickets perched on the edge of his desk fluttering to the floor. He was sorely tempted to let rip with a throaty, "Yee haw!"

Over at dispatch, Officer Harrison lifted his head from his own desk to see what the fuss was about. Then he set it back down.

It was a slow shift. The station had been virtually silent for most of the night, other than the hum of an oscillating fan and one or two incoming calls. Harrison should have fielded these but he was too busy napping. Typical. Sonny decided to let him doze and answer the phone himself, mainly to ward off his own boredom.

Apparently this last call had really gotten his blood worked up.

"Look alive, Larry," he shouted as he rose from his chair. "We got some roughnecking to do."

Harrison, unwilling to abandon his comfortable position, just blinked a few times and waited for a more detailed explanation. He'd really been hoping to stay at his desk for the rest of the shift, like he did most nights. In all the years Harrison had worked under Deputy Platt, he'd never made more than two or three night patrols in a single week, and he was thinking this might be the very first time he'd get through five full shifts without having to leave the station once.

"What's the ruckus, Sonny?"

"I'll tell you in the car. Call Lineweaver and tell him to double-time it over to the Sand Palace Motel."

Sonny stuffed a handful of .38 shells into his shirt pocket. He grabbed his nightstick. Somebody was going to get his head broken tonight. Maybe a few folks, but there was no question in Platt's mind who'd be the first to taste wood.

"Hey," he called out to Harrison, who still hadn't achieved full verticality. "I mean do it now!"

Harrison lurched to his feet and went for the CB so he could call in Officer Lineweaver, who was out paroling the highway. Linewaver was the most junior of the three officers who comprised the Hillsboro Beach Police Department. Apparently, the deputy figured he needed as much muscle as he could muster tonight.

Throwing his holster around his fleshy waist, Sonny thought about Sherry. She popped into his consciousness without warning or invitation, wearing a black eye and a brokenhearted scowl. It was not a welcome image. He'd managed to put her out of his mind for most of the past two days. Leaving his house early yesterday morning after checking for storm damage, he couldn't bring himself to wake her as she pretended to sleep on his living room floor. He hadn't yet seen the harm he'd inflicted upon her lovely face but knew it had to be ugly. Just picturing it sunk him into a pit of guilt more treacherous than quicksand.

Still, he could not bring himself to apologize. At least a dozen times he'd picked up the phone and dialed six of the Anger's Rest's seven digits before changing his mind. *No way*, he thought indignantly. He would *not* be the first to make amends. She'd brought this unpleasantness on herself.

And yet she was not truly the guilty party, which left Sonny in a terrible bind. He'd been wronged but he'd lashed out at the wrong person. This was an unacceptable situation and only one solution was possible. There could be no closure until the real culprit was punished with terrible alacrity for invading their lives.

Vance needed to pay, dearly.

And, like another miracle from providence, Sonny Platt had now been given a chance to make that happen.

The call he just took came from a frantic Lucille Henderson. Sonny remembered her from the few times she'd phoned to ask if he'd run over to her crazy mother's house in the dead of night. Something about the old crone seeing hobgoblins at her window or similar nonsense. Sonny had obliged her in the past, mainly because he didn't have anything better to do at the time.

He expected Lucille to make the same request tonight, but it soon became clear she had more urgent matters to discuss. Her husband had been savagely attacked and her mother was dead. Breaking and entering was involved. Desecration of sanctified ground. It didn't make much sense, and she was babbling at a frenetic rate. Sonny initially thought she must be drunk.

As he pressed Lucille for more details, a little tingle began to appear somewhere inside his belly. It was too good to be true but every word she said only further validated his suspicion. Even before she got to the part about the motion picture camera, he'd put the pieces together.

A group of strangers, loud voices, strange equipment, odd glowing lights. It all added up.

Those fucking movie people broke into Fairview Cemetery. Thank you, Jesus.

Sonny's excitement was so extreme he almost hung up before telling Lucille he knew who the intruders were and where to find them. She was still uttering tearful thanks as he slammed the phone down.

This is what I've been waiting on, Platt thought to himself. *I got me a wide open shot.*

It was all too predictable, really. Maybe that producer thought he'd bought himself a blank check when he paid for the pretty boy's release. Figured he and his whole outfit could raise as much hell as they felt like around here, just use Hillsboro Beach as their own personal toilet and then blow back to Hollywood when they'd had their share of grins. Well, they'd gone too far this time. Desecrating a cemetery was no minor offense.

It was time for a lesson in small town justice.

Harrison got through to Lineweaver on the CB and told him what to do. Two minutes later he was riding shotgun in the deputy's cruiser as it roared onto the highway. Sonny filled Harrison in as they drew closer to the motel.

"We're looking at a gang of six, tops. That'll include a woman. I want to cuff the men straight off. One or two might cause headaches. This producer fella's a goddamn land whale. If he gets squirrely, crack him a good one in the knees. I think that'll discourage any mischief from the others."

"All right, then."

"One more thing," Platt said. "You see a kid looks real pretty? Skinny, with an Elvis 'do? He's mine. Otherwise, have at it."

The cruiser sped on for another few minutes until they could see the glow of the Sand Palace's sign. Lineweaver's patrol car was just approaching the motel's driveway from the opposite direction. Sonny grabbed the CB and called him.

"Kill your lights and wait for us. No sirens."

Thirty seconds later they pulled in behind Lineweaver. The first thing Platt noticed was that the parking lot was empty except for one car he knew belonged to Ernest. His teeth began to grind.

There was no way he would be deprived of this opportunity. He would not allow it.

Telling Lineweaver to sit tight, Sonny and Harrison charged over to the manager's office. Ernest was dozing in front of the TV as usual. The office was still in a state of semi-shambles, though the shattered window had been taped up and most of the paper gathered from the floor.

With a firm prod of his nightstick, Sonny got Ernest's attention. Their conversation was brief and fruitless. All the manager could say was that the movie crew checked out less than a half-hour ago, and good riddance to them. They were a troublesome bunch, bringing nothing but bad luck with them.

Sonny pressed for any clues as to their next stop. Ernest said Hell would be his recommendation.

That wasn't quite specific enough for the deputy, and he was quickly losing his patience.

* * * * * * *

7:45 P.M.

It was a desolate, doomstruck place. The abandoned warehouse rose from the horizon like a crumbling ruin from a forsaken age. A stark essence of decay emanated from the ground and swirled about in the air. Even the insects seemed smart enough to keep away.

"It's spookier than the graveyard," Ricky said as they unloaded the equipment from his truck.

"In other words," Shel replied, "it's perfect."

They'd shot two scenes at this same location earlier in the week, but that had been during the day. At night, it was a completely different environment.

The warehouse had not been in use for a number of years. Originally built to store heavy machinery during World War II, it had fallen idle in the early '50s and now occupied an overgrown plot of sandy ground right off the beach. The entrance to the unpaved driveway had long been obscured by tall dry sawgrass. It was as remote a location as any exploitation filmmaker could ask for. You could raise hell all night long and no one but the gulls would ever be the wiser.

The warehouse was not located within Hillsboro Beach proper. It sat just outside the city limits, on the northern perimeter of the town. If Hillsboro could be called no man's land, then this stretch of the coast might be designated as a place where not even disembodied souls dared to tread. The landscape was not so much lunar as paleolithic.

Meyer shouted out directions to the crew as they unloaded the gear. An aura of heightened, manic energy seemed to overtake the operation. They were almost home and everyone was moving in quick bursts to facilitate that goal. No one had slept more than twelve hours total over the past three nights but right now that was actually serving as an advantage, giving the group a quivery collective edge.

After a while, continual stress combined with sleep deprivation can act as a weird kind of stimulus. The body starts pumping emergency doses of adrenaline into the bloodstream just to maintain basic motor functioning. What suffers in the bargain is clarity of thought, but Meyer didn't need anyone to think tonight. He just needed them to react, without hesitation.

He was pleased to note that just about everyone seemed as wired on a glandular basis as he was. It was destined to be a short ride, with an inevitable crash waiting at the other end, but Shel was hopeful it would last long enough for them to stay on target until the final shot was captured. They could worry about the long drive to Miami after that.

The tide came in powerfully with the night. Waves smashed against jagged rock outcroppings that jutted up from the shoreline like the bottom half of a crooked smile. The wind held a mean edge.

The warehouse was in pretty bad shape a few days ago and fresh damage suffered at Estelle's hands only furthered its downfall. Many windows had been blown out and large filthy puddles were everywhere. A gaping hole in the roof made a popular nest for gulls who shit through the opening onto the dusty floor far below.

It didn't take long to get the equipment moved inside once Meyer determined the best area to set up the scene. Using a flashlight for guidance, he explored the enormity of the warehouse before finding a relatively dry space he thought would work, about thirty feet in diameter. Within minutes all the camera and lighting gear was in place, and "The Jenny" was milking out enough juice to create a small umbrella of illumination in the stale musty air.

Only one piece of equipment required special care. It was the key prop to be used in tonight's scene, one Meyer had almost squealed with jubilation upon finding.

It was an antique 36" buzz saw, the kind that had either been outlawed or simply driven off the market due to a delayed onset of basic common sense. Shel found it at a farm auction several years ago, long before he'd begun planning *Crimson Orgy*. Something about the contraption grabbed his imagination. It was such a frightful looking device, so glaringly devoid of even the most basic safety features, he just had to buy it on the spot. Somehow he knew he'd find a use for the damn thing.

The gap-toothed old farm worker who collected his money said the saw had been the culprit in no less than fifteen bad accidents. It had claimed six hands, a foot, and untold digits before being retired. Meyer couldn't help noticing how the man smiled when tallying the saw's grim history, revealing broad swaths of purple recessed gum and two stubborn choppers stained a dark tobacco brown.

It even had a name, painted in fading letters on its creaky wooden base: "The Dismemberer."

God, how wonderful, Shel thought as he forked over fifty bucks. The clunkiness of the name, no doubt devised by some awestruck hick in the aftermath of a particularly dreadful accident, was a perfect match for the ungainly nature of the saw itself.

The Dismemberer weighed at least a hundred pounds and had to be gingerly transported into the warehouse due to its rickety, worm-eaten state. The meager base looked woefully inadequate to hold the enormous vertical blade in place but somehow managed to keep the serrated cutting edge suspended about four feet from the floor. The blade itself was badly rusted, with many of its curved fangs either broken or missing.

Nonetheless, the thing worked. Meyer had tested it himself, just once, shortly after purchasing it. He'd been mesmerized by the sight of the circular blade spinning at a terrible speed, rendered to a metallic blur.

While they figured out the composition of the first shot Barbara walked around the massive empty floor, straying as far from the camera as possible while remaining within the curtain of thin light provided by the 1Ks. This was her first time in the warehouse, since she hadn't been present for the Wednesday shoot.

She immediately hated the place. It was impossibly big and empty. The ceiling was so high she could only make it out by a thatch of moonlight lighting up the chasmal hole where the gulls roosted.

Stay calm, she told herself. *This is almost over.*

Tonight would mark not only the final scene of the shoot but the final scene of the movie itself, which takes place after Kelly tracks down Ace at his secret lair. A struggle ensues. Kelly almost succumbs but manages to push him off at the last second. Ace loses his footing and ends up getting cut in half by the buzz saw.

Meyer hadn't devised any way to simulate a man being severed into two pieces, so he intended to accomplish the effect strictly through editing. There would be a shot of Ace stumbling back toward the saw. A quick close-up of the spinning blade. Another close-up of Ace's panicked eyes. Then a cutaway of some blood splattering on the wall. Then Kelly's horrified reaction.

That was it. No lingering shots of internal organs, no gore and guts spattering the lens. Barbara asked Shel if he wasn't worried it would be a bit anticlimactic. He dismissed the question, saying that there's only so much bloodshed an audience can withstand before becoming desensitized.

Barbara found it odd, and fairly disturbing, that the deaths of the female victims were all shown in sickening detail while the male killer's demise was largely suggestive. She could have raised this point to Meyer, but by the time it occurred to her she didn't have the energy to get into it. Who cared, anyway? This trashy little movie was his personal obsession, not hers. She was ready to wash her hands of it, assuming the noxious fake blood would ever come off. Her neck and forehead were still lightly rouged despite intense scrubbing.

Meyer intended to shoot all seven setups in chronological order. They added up to quite a complicated little sequence, and he had less than 1,000 feet of film to capture it all. Tonight's shooting ratio would essentially have to be 1:1, which meant that they had to get all seven shots on the first take.

Do or die. Or both.

After they nailed the first four shots, Meyer gave the crew a short break. He asked Barbara to step outside for a moment. She was glad to do it. The unventilated warehouse felt oppressive from the moment they entered. Over the course of the past hour, with the blazing lights and rising tensions, it had become an inferno.

They sat down on a mound of sandy grass near the entrance, looking up at the star-addled sky. Barbara felt the sweat cooling on her forehead.

She was surprised to see Meyer take his wallet out of his back pocket. It was about as thick as a dictionary, and not with money. He opened the billfold and out spilled all kinds of random junk: receipts, cocktail napkins, business cards. It was the kind of thing only a compulsive packrat would carry around.

For a moment, she had the delirious thought he might produce a condom and attempt some inept bit of seduction here on the sand.

Instead, he fished out a small black and white photograph and held it intently before his eyes. It was badly creased in a dozen places so that it resembled a patch of alligator skin. Meyer handed it over to her.

"My parents."

The picture, almost sepia-toned with age, showed a primly dressed couple sitting on a cement stoop in front of a brownstone. The man wore a business suit, bow tie, and grim expression. The woman was a plump but pretty brunette, dandling an infant on her knee. Barbara had to smile at what an undeniably cute baby Shel had been.

It's amazing what happens to us along the way, she thought. *We all start out so sweet.*

"There's the real Estelle," Meyer said.

"She was very pretty."

"Yes. I've been thinking about what you asked the other night. Whether she'd be proud of me."

"What do you think the answer is?"

Meyer finished his cigarette.

"You know the answer."

"Why are you showing me this, Sheldon?"

"Something occurred to me this morning, when we were shooting by the pool. You had your hair pulled back as we were fitting the wig on you. I'd never seen you wear it like that."

He took the photo from her and placed his thumb over the image so that it covered his mother's dark mane, leaving only her face visible.

Barbara looked, not sure what she was supposed to say.

"Don't you see it?" Meyer asked.

"I guess," she said uncertainly. "No. What?"

"Look at her face. The resemblance is striking."

Barbara took another cursory look, then glanced away as his intention dawned on her.

"What, she looks like me?"

"Of course. Her face is a bit fuller, but look at the shape of her mouth. And her eyes. It's uncanny."

"I really don't see it. At all."

"You can't be serious. It hit me this morning and damn near knocked me over when I made the connection."

"Look, you're giving me the creeps, OK?"

"Sorry," he said, quickly returning the photo to his wallet. "I thought you'd be interested."

Barbara was feeling uncomfortable with this conversation, and with the weird glow that seemed to be lighting Meyer's eyes from behind. Was this really why he dragged her out here, or was he just trying to prolong the shoot in any absurd way he could think of?

"Well," she said, "I think our break is up. Let's finish this thing."

"Hold on a sec," Shel replied. "There's something else I'd like to discuss."

As she folded her arms with an impatient sigh, he began to tell her what was really on his mind. A new idea for the climax had occurred to him just a few minutes ago. Only a minor change, but one that would leave a powerful impression on the audience. It wasn't quite the unambiguously upbeat finale he'd originally planned on. For some reason, that just didn't work for him anymore.

Rather than show Ace's blood splattering on a wall, it would be much more effective to see it covering Kelly as she watched him get torn in half by the saw. She would exit the warehouse drenched in the killer's gore, a powerful metaphor for Meyer's concept that no one, least of all our heroine, can walk away from Ace's carnage without bearing some kind of scar.

Fade to black. Cue the music. Roll credits.

Barbara couldn't believe what she was hearing. There was no end to the man's presumption. First Meyer concealed from her what kind of movie this was. Then he told her she wouldn't have to be directly involved with the gore, a promise he later broke. Now he was asking her to do it again.

"Absolutely not," she said calmly.

"I thought you might react that way, so let me just explain..."

"I'm not listening to you."

"Look, filmmaking is a team sport. Everyone needs to make sacrifices, do things they might not want to do."

"I've already made sacrifices. That's all you're getting out of me."

"Barbara..."

"Forget it, OK? This conversation's over."

She stood up, unintentionally kicking some sand into Meyer's face. He scrambled to his feet and grabbed her just a bit harder than he meant to. All he wanted was to hold her attention for a few more moments but it came across much more hostile than that. And it was uncomfortably reminiscent of the way he'd handled her in the courtyard on Tuesday night.

In a virtual replay of that moment, she spun around to hit him but he was ready for it this time. His hand caught hers at the wrist and squeezed firmly enough to make her yelp.

"Listen to me," he said in a low voice. "We're going to go back in there and finish this the right way. Just cooperate and I promise, it'll all be over before you know it."

"Let go!" she cried, trying to wrest her arm from his grip.

They struggled for a moment, Meyer trying to subdue her while at the same time thinking, *This is crazy, what am I doing?*

The two figures stood there locked in a violent embrace, silhouetted by the dim glow of the stage lights coming through the open door. It looked like someone was being murdered, but it wasn't clear who the victim was.

* * * * * * *

8:10 P.M.

Vance's Impala bolted due south. It was eating up the road as rapidly as the speed limit would allow. The white dashed lines disappeared under his hood. He was tempted to count each one of them. Every time a new dash was sucked from view, Vance knew he was that much closer to Miami. And that much further from whatever was happening behind him.

Eager as he was to put maximum distance between himself and Hillsboro Beach, Vance was careful to keep an eye on the speedometer. The last thing he needed was another run-in with some gun-toting country mutant, badged or otherwise, out here on this lonesome night. Having no further entanglements was Vance's number one goal. So he let the Chevy purr along at 55 and tried to enjoy the sensation of liberation that flooded through every cell in his body.

Four days ago, it almost seemed impossible to envision this moment. It was all over. No more sweat-soaked nights in that moldy fleabag. No more raging dawns met with white knuckles and a dry throat. No more hick cops. No more crazy Jerry and blowhard Gene. Best of all, no more Shel Meyer.

This had been the longest week of Vance's life. He'd entered into it with a sense of total confidence that was rudely shattered with his arrest Tuesday morning. From that moment on, pretty much everything that happened knocked him off his guard in some way, making him doubt his ability to handle himself.

From the severed arm to his romp with Barbara to the brawls with Cliff and the hurricane and the scene in the graveyard...

All of it seemed to lack a certain grounding essence of reality.

Vance felt as if he'd spent a week trapped within the kind of hackneyed melodrama Shel Meyer and his ilk were so proficient at producing. Maybe that's how movie folk were able to come up with new stories, by intentionally inviting that kind of weird chaos into their real lives.

Who needs it? he thought.

The first mileage sign for Miami hove into view. In less than an hour Vance would be back at his pad, the scene of so many good nights. The wet bar and waterbed awaited. The Hi-Fi was begging to be cranked up after a week of sad silence. And his little black book bulged with numbers. Hell, he'd be home early enough to hit the bars, maybe wash down this incredibly strange week with about a dozen cocktails and some fresh poon.

As much as he tried to cheer himself up with this line of thinking, Vance couldn't fully relax. He still felt terrible about leaving that guy in the graveyard. And a bit foolish about the heavy rap he'd laid on Barbara. Why had he said those things? He didn't really believe she was in danger, not in any concrete sense.

There was just some ill-defined fear eating at the back of his mind. Something didn't add up.

As Vance took his foot off the accelerator to bring the car's speed back down to 55, the source of his unease came to him.

Cliff's disappearance. Nothing about it made sense.

There was no logical explanation for why the burly Key Grip would vanish so suddenly. Especially when you considered the loyalty he obviously felt for Stupendous Pictures. Cliff had genuine history with Hoffman and Meyer. It just didn't figure that he would decide, out of the blue, to shaft his two employers in such a major way.

Even more puzzling was Shel Meyer's reaction to the situation. This was a man who virtually fell apart when the slightest thing went wrong. Yet when presented with a genuine catastrophe like the Key Grip disappearing with a day's worth of celluloid, Meyer hardly reacted at all.

It was almost as if Shel expected Cliff to do what he did. The more Vance thought about this, the more the scenario bothered him.

Let it go, man, his inner voice calmly intoned. *You got out clean and you gave her a chance to do the same. She can handle herself.*

Those thoughts just couldn't find a toehold. To ease the tension, Vance tried to trace a sequence of cause and effect. In what way would it be advantageous for Cliff to disappear with all that footage? What was the immediate result of his action?

Vance could only think of one: the last-minute addition of the dream murder. The one scene not written into the original script.

Suddenly, it seemed to him that maybe it had been planned all along. Why else would Meyer happen to have a blonde wig ready to use, a wig that matched Barbara perfectly?

Yes. There was no other reasonable explanation. Cliff's bug-out had been staged.

This conclusion started to gel in Vance's mind.

Then his tire blew out.

The explosion was jarring. The Impala veered madly to the left, crossing over the double yellow line and missing an oncoming truck by inches. The truck's horn blared and its headlights flooded the inside of Vance's car as he struggled to bring it back into the right lane.

He slowed down and guided the Impala onto the shoulder. Another car passed him from behind, honking angrily.

"Fuck you!!!" Vance hollered. Then he just sat there for a moment, regaining his composure.

Stepping out, he saw the front left tire was the one that blew. It was completely shredded, wrapped around the rim like an old rubber bag.

Jesus H. Christ. There seemed to be no end to the shit luck this week had in store for him. Vance wondered if the curse of *Crimson Orgy* would ever let him be, or if he'd damned himself to a lifetime of foul fortune by signing up with Stupendous Pictures.

At least he had a spare in the trunk. He retrieved it and started to jack up the front end. The lug nuts were slightly stripped and didn't turn easily. Pulling with all his might, the jack slipped loose and he skinned his knuckles on the gravel.

Hissing at the sting, Vance decided he was moving too fast for his own good. He set the jack down and stood up, allowing himself some long slow breaths.

A small white glow appeared in the distance, headed from the south. After a few seconds it separated into a pair of headlights. Vance watched as the vehicle drew closer. It was barreling toward Hillsboro Beach at top speed.

Several moments later, Vance could make out the shape of the vehicle within the glare of its headlights. It was a van, seeming to decelerate a bit as it approached.

By the time it was a few car length's away, the van had slowed to no more than fifteen miles per hour. Before he even had a chance to look, Vance knew who he would see in the driver's seat.

Cliff's moony face glared out at him through the window, eyes expanding with recognition. The bruises and gashes Vance had inflicted upon him were clearly visible through the glass.

Cliff brought the van almost to a complete stop as he pulled even with the Impala. They shared a loaded moment of dual identification across two lanes of highway.

Then Cliff hit the gas and the van rattled off.

Vance watched its fiery tail lights recede until they were no more than a blurred crimson dot.

Every wild hypothesis he'd been indulging just before the tire blew out suddenly came washing over his mind with the power of not just logic, but inevitability.

He was right. Cliff didn't simply disappear of his own volition. The dumb ox wasn't smart enough to do something like that on his own. He'd been ordered to leave, apparently for as long as it took to get Vance off the set. Meyer had conveniently decided to write Vance's character out of the last scene for reasons that made no sense whatsoever. The director couldn't even think of a decent lie to explain the decision.

And Hoffman let Vance off way too easily when he told him about his brawl with Cliff during the storm. Gene had made it explicitly clear that one fuckup was all it would take to personally rip him apart, yet he didn't seem the least bit peeved that Vance may have played a role in Cliff's decision to go AWOL.

None of it made sense. He'd been set up, that much was clear. Except he couldn't see any reason for it.

In another instant, he knew why. Because Barbara was the one who had really been set up. Vance was just an impediment to whatever they wanted to do with her, so he'd been sent packing.

Forget it, man. It's none of your business.

That thought really wanted to stick. Vance allowed it to float in his head for a few agonized moments before permanently kicking it out.

The hell it isn't!

Reaching for the jack, Vance started cranking at the lug nuts as fast as his hands would move.

* * * * * * *

8:25 P.M.

The welts on Ernest's face were rising. They would be the size of golf balls by morning. His round shoulders shook lightly and a small whimper escaped his lips as he waited for Sonny to bring the hammer down again.

The deputy was just about ready to do it. He'd given Ernest a thirty-second break to scour his memory and make absolutely sure the movie crew gave him no indication where they were going.

Ernest had proclaimed his ignorance a dozen times but Platt wasn't buying it. He thought he could jar loose some tiny but significant clue if he just hit the man hard enough in precisely the right spot.

246

Tired of waiting, the deputy cocked a fist and prepared to drive it into Ernest's kidneys. He was halted by a firm tug on the shoulder from Officer Harrison.

"That's enough, Sonny!"

Platt wheeled around, ready to unload on his junior officer the same way he'd been been doing on the manager. But he only waited for Harrison to explain himself.

"He doesn't know where they went," Harrison said softly. "He doesn't know, OK?"

Platt looked from the junior officer to the manager, then back again. His right upper eyelid was twitching like a hummingbird's wing, though he was not aware of it. He knew what Harrison said was the truth. Had known it all along but just couldn't accept it.

Ernest, at heart a gentle soul despite his gruff exterior, began silently weeping. He hadn't taken a beating like this since he was a teenager, when he was often picked on for being so chubby. He didn't understand why the deputy was hitting him. He'd given all the information he had.

It wasn't his fault the movie people had caused so much trouble. If he'd had any idea, he never would have let them stay here to begin with. For God's sake, he was just trying to bring in some sorely needed business.

A small moan grabbed everyone's attention in the passing silence. Rosa was standing in the doorway, her face ashen. How long she'd been there no one could say, but she'd obviously seen plenty.

Platt seemed to take her appearance as his cue to suspend the interrogation.

"Call the station if you happen to remember anything. Anything at all."

Ernest nodded vigorously.

"And remember, boy," Platt said with a chuck on the shoulder that made the manager flinch. "This is a police matter. Nothing personal."

With that, he left, brushing past the cleaning lady. Harrison cast an apologetic look at Ernest, then followed the deputy outside. Rosa ran to comfort her boss and lover. The two rotund figures clutched each other in the dingy light of the storm-ravaged office.

Lineweaver was leaning against his patrol car in the driveway. Nervously. He'd heard Sonny walloping Ernest and wondered just what the hell was going on in there. He'd been tempted to sneak a peek but was glad he decided to stay where he was told.

"Get back to the station," Platt commanded him. "We need someone on dispatch."

"OK, Sonny."

"It's *Deputy Platt*, goddamnit!" Sonny spat in his face, rearing back as if to launch a blow but stopping short.

Lineweaver practically dove into his cruiser and eased it out of the driveway. He was immensely relieved to be getting away from here.

Platt whistled to Harrison. "Give me the keys, Larry. I got an idea where we might find these sumbitches."

Harrison hesitated for just a moment. "Maybe I ought to take the wheel, Sonny. You got your dander up pretty good right now."

Harrison regretted saying it before he'd even finished. The look in the deputy's eyes was more than enough of a rebuke. Harrison dug the keys out of his pocket and tossed them over.

* * * * * * *

8:30 P.M.

The warehouse was still. The lights were killed to preserve juice. All action ground to a halt. The Dismemberer, which had been spinning furiously for the camera minutes ago, stood dormant.

248

Ricky and Juan were impatiently killing time outside the entrance of the warehouse, chain-smoking. They could hardly believe Hoffman had called a time-out so close to the wrap. It was as if they were deliberately finding ways to stretch out this process, just to allow maximum time for something else to go wrong.

Meyer had walked off onto the beach by himself. He wanted to stay but Hoffman ordered him to disappear for a while. No one had seen him since.

Barbara was still livid. Her contempt for Meyer, which fluctuated in degree over the course of the week, had now bubbled up to a level from which it could never recede. She'd actually begun to feel close to him that night during the storm. Now the mere thought of any emotional intimacy with the man revolted her.

She was standing next to the Fairlane, waiting to get in and be driven from here. Hoffman stood next to her. The keys were in his pocket. She would have snatched them if she thought she had a prayer of getting away with it.

Barbara told Gene not to bother with any of his vaunted powers of persuasion. She wanted to leave, right now. He could hardly deny her after what just went down.

Hoffman heard her out. To her great surprise, he didn't try to change her mind.

Barbara never felt she was in any true danger during the brief altercation with Meyer. His presumption was what upset her so acutely. The notion that he could lay hands on her like that. It made her entire body go hot with anger, mixed with a kind of cerebral nausea that swam around her head rather than her stomach. She felt dizzy with rage.

Images leapt before her eyes during their ridiculous tussle and she could not dismiss them... her father lurching across the moldy carpet of their living room floor in Mobile, chasing her mother as she fled for the flimsy sanctuary of a locked bathroom door... never quite getting there, his hands catching her at the last second... and then the screams, pleas for help, and thuds of fist against bone that took over Barbara's young world.

That's what burst into her mind as Meyer tried to physically force her to do his bidding. A fury inside her broke free. She was ready to scratch his eyes clean out of his head before Hoffman broke them up. Intervening in Shel Meyer's many confrontations at the last possible moment seemed to be Hoffman's primary talent.

Now, still shaking, Barbara laid it on the line for him.

"I won't do it, Gene. He's a fucking madman and I won't work for him anymore."

"You're right. You're absolutely right. He's lost it."

She didn't have a quick response to those words.

"Are you surprised to hear me say that?" Hoffman asked. "Well, don't be. I've made sixteen pictures with Shel. I know him about as well as two straight guys can know each other and I'm done with him. He's out, as far as I'm concerned, and for good. So don't worry, you won't have to listen to another word from him, I swear."

"OK," Barbara said, her voice calmer. "Thank you."

"No. Thank you, for putting up with so much crap."

Barbara didn't say anything. She couldn't quite believe he wasn't fighting her.

"Now listen, we're gonna be finished here in about twenty minutes. That's *it*, I promise. You'll never have to see this rotten place or any of us kooks again."

"Good." She couldn't help smiling just a bit.

"Just one thing," he added, almost as an afterthought. "We do need you for the last shot."

Barbara started to back away, her anger surging again. Hoffman saw it happening and raised his hands in a conciliatory gesture.

250

"You don't have to deal with Shel, I told you that. I'll direct the scene myself. It's a piece of cake. No lines, just a reaction shot. We need to see your face as you watch Jerry fall into the blade."

"No. I'm sure you can do without that."

"If I thought we could, I'd drive you home this minute. But we need to have that shot, otherwise the scene won't cut together. It's the closer of the whole flick. We can't afford to have a big piece missing from it. You understand what I'm saying?"

Barbara looked into his eyes for a long moment, seeking something she could trust.

"No blood."

Hoffman nodded vigorously. "No blood, just the way we talked about doing it before."

"I don't want him anywhere near me."

"You have my word."

"Not even in the building. If he stays outside, I'll do it. Just one shot, that's it."

"You got it."

"Let's get it over with."

He grinned proudly but refrained from touching her. "That's my star."

"Don't call me that, Gene."

* * * * * * *

8:45 P.M

The speedometer read 85. Vance wanted to push harder on the gas even though the pedal was already mashed against the floorboard. He had trouble steadying the wheel. The Impala really wasn't in a condition to be safely handled at this speed. Cursing, he eased off the gas and brought it down to 75.

251

Vance was brimming with self-reproach for taking so long to change the tire. If he'd accomplished the task a bit faster he would have certainly overtaken Cliff by now. He was fully prepared to force the van off the road, pull Cliff from behind the wheel, and beat the truth out of him.

Now it seemed like he wouldn't be able to catch up with the van before it arrived at the warehouse. Vance had no doubt that was Cliff's destination. He was coming back from wherever he'd been hiding to help Meyer and Hoffman (and Jerry Cooke, probably) execute whatever perverse plan they had in mind for the final scene.

Vance couldn't completely allow himself to think they were going to kill her. It strained credulity, at least as far as Hoffman was concerned. The producer was too much of a savvy businessman to take such a risk. And what would be the point, from Gene's perspective?

Shel Meyer was a different proposition altogether. He was clearly driven by compulsions he didn't seem interested in examining too closely. A man who spent so much time in a flurry of physical and verbal motion probably had little awareness of who or what was standing behind the curtain, pulling his strings. The motion itself became a defense mechanism from troubling thoughts, a way of keeping all attention focused outward.

Fear the man who knows not himself.

That's what Vance's churchgoing father told him once when he was just a boy. The words stuck, even though he wasn't sure what they meant. Tonight, thinking about Meyer, Vance felt like he understood his old man's intent for the first time.

Vance knew exactly what he would do when he arrived at the warehouse. Walk in calmly, grab Barbara by the hand, and take her out of there. Whether she wanted to go or not. Hoffman wouldn't stop him. Neither would Meyer, or Cliff. Nothing would.

He barely noticed the road sign telling him he had re-entered Hillsboro Beach. By his calculation, he figured the warehouse was another fifteen minutes north.

Vance suddenly remembered the way Hoffman assaulted him after he'd been arrested, throwing him up against the vending machine. There was definitely a current of lunatic rage running underneath Gene's hepcat coolness. He was probably capable of anything, Vance concluded. Pretty much everyone is, under the right circumstances.

And then, appearing in the courtroom of his mind as Exhibit Z, slamming the case closed beyond a reasonable doubt on some sort of malevolent intent, was the matter of the metal box. The fact that they did eventually shoot the Easter basket scene as scripted (with a mannequin's arm, as Vance sheepishly noted at the time) did nothing to alleviate the grossly improper existence of the box's contents. It went beyond mere unprofessionalism, which Vance saw as standard operating procedure for Stupendous Pictures. Hoffman's box was proof positive that something very wrong was afoot.

Vance knew he should have acted sooner. With a little luck, it still wasn't too late.

Up ahead on his right, he saw the neon sign of the Sand Palace fade into focus. The speedometer read 80. He floored it, ignoring the way the steering wheel jumped around in his grip like a lizard trying to squirm free.

The entrance to the motel was less than a hundred feet away, flying toward him in the windshield. Vance only had a heartbeat to see the rear fender of the patrol car as it barreled recklessly out of the driveway.

His foot sought the brake but there was no chance.

In the few seconds before impact, time didn't slow to a crawl for Vance, as he'd read about. Nor did his life flash before him. But as the futile screeching of the Impala's brakes tore into his eardrums, he was afforded a crystal clear view of Officer Harrison's terrified face in the passenger side window.

And somehow, Vance knew beyond a doubt that the detested deputy was in the driver's seat.

Then the collision came, with a violence beyond comprehension, and Vance didn't know anything at all.

* * * * * * *

9:05 P.M.

The final setup was in place. The Mitchell was positioned just a few feet from Barbara's face. Hoffman framed the shot himself, something he'd secretly wanted to do for years but never had the gumption to ask of Meyer.

The Dismemberer would not be seen within the frame but Hoffman wanted it running so they could capture the audio clean. Ricky stood next to it, waiting to flick the power switch on Hoffman's command.

"OK, Barbara," Gene said, trying to parrot Meyer's directorial tone. "You're watching Ace Spade die on that huge blade. You know he deserves it. He's taken a half-dozen lives and he just tried to kill you. But you're still horrified to see him buy the farm like this. Got it?"

"*Yes*," she hissed with overt exasperation. "Let's roll."

Under different circumstances, Barbara would have found it comical to watch Hoffman try to crouch his mass behind the flimsy little tripod. He groaned with the effort.

"Cue the saw, Ricky!"

Pulling at the rusty switch, Ricky set the blade into motion. The Dismemberer began its rotation at a torturously slow pace. Like a miniature ferris wheel designed for the Inquisition, each serrated edge moved forward, spinning slowly upward. Then it gathered speed and its

254

harsh mechanical whine penetrated the air. In another moment the blade was a quivering blur, with the wooden base rocking underneath.

Hoffman had to shout to be heard. "Action!"

Just outside the warehouse, Meyer stood leaning against the front door. He'd wandered back from his lonely walk on the beach after he thought it was safe to do so. Peering into the darkness, he could barely make out what was happening under the umbrella of light.

Shel expected to feel sick about not being a part of this final shot. To have come so far only to be exiled at the last minute should have tormented him. Instead, he felt liberated.

A lot of things suddenly made sense. Primarily, his own preposterous conduct.

His fight with Barbara, unpleasant as it was, freed him somehow. In a flash of clarity, he realized he'd been taking this project *way* too seriously.

It was a crummy little exploitation picture, for God's sake. Shel's whispered hope of exorcising his past through the creation of simulated bloodshed appeared to him now as ridiculously adolescent. Worse than that, infantile.

Leaning against the doorway as his movie wrapped without him, Meyer felt a sense of buoyancy filling him like helium in a balloon. He began grinning. Then chuckling out loud. The mental burden he'd been carrying all this time like a chain on his back, which he himself had forged, now revealed itself as the biggest joke of all time. And it didn't even have a punch line.

He really wanted to thank Barbara, if she ever allowed him to speak to her again. She was the only person to call his bluff. During all the nights Meyer sat up with Hoffman trying to communicate what he thought *Crimson Orgy* could accomplish, Gene never once questioned Shel about the validity of his motivations.

255

Barbara had taken the time to listen, and she was clearly repulsed by what she heard. She asked Meyer all those pointed questions that he found irritating, even offensive at the time. Now he realized she was doing him a tremendous favor. She forced him to examine the workings his own mind. And when he took a serious look, what he saw disgusted him just as much as it did her.

It's amazing how much your perspective can shift in a single moment, he thought.

Sure, they would complete *Crimson Orgy* and release it onto the drive-in circuit. Maybe it would make a mint and maybe it would be totally ignored. Didn't matter. Shel would never attempt another gore movie, regardless of how profitable this one turned out to be. He would go back to making harmless nudies that celebrated life rather than death. Maybe someday, if he ever worked himself up to it, he would write that optimistic little story held dearly in the back of his mind. If he couldn't find anyone who thought it would make a successful film, he'd tackle it as a novel. It's never too late to create something pure.

Just as Shel Meyer made this transformational leap in his mind and his heart, Cliff the Grip smashed him over the head with a heavy rock.

Meyer dropped to his knees, then face-planted onto the ground. Cliff let the rock fall from his hand. He stepped over Meyer and into the warehouse, toward the dim glow and the whine of the Dismemberer.

No one heard him coming. They were all absorbed in capturing the final shot. Ricky stood behind the Dismemberer with two fingers plugging his ears. Juan and Jerry crouched off to the side, waiting to hear the final "Cut!"

Barbara was stuck in the glare of the 1Ks. Hoffman squinted through the Mitchell's viewfinder, trying to get the right reaction before running out of film.

"Give me more horror!" he cried over the saw. "You're looking at a man getting cut in half! It's terrible, the worst thing you've ever seen!"

Barbara tried to comply. She raised her eyebrows, opened her mouth, covered her face with the back of her hand. She even gave an honest shot at a scream.

It wasn't working. She knew it and didn't care.

Hoffman was losing patience. Her reaction was totally phony. No one would buy it. Then, seemingly from nowhere, he saw Barbara evince the exact look of wide-eyed shock he was seeking.

This was because she'd just seen Cliff grab Ricky by the waist, lift him into the air, and slam his face into the cement floor. The jawbreaking impact was immense, knocking him out.

"Good!" Hoffman shouted encouragingly. "Keep it up!"

Barbara tried to warn him but her voice was swallowed by the din. In another second it was too late.

Gene felt Cliff's hand fall heavily on his shoulder. He turned around just in time to take a fist in the face like a battering ram.

It knocked him into the camera, tipping the tripod. The Mitchell rocked back, then steadied itself as Cliff landed an elbow on Hoffman's nose, shattering it.

Gene was more stunned than injured but his fractional pause gave Cliff an opening to drag him to the floor.

Watching it unfold from behind the lights, Juan took a moment to check on Ricky, just long enough to determine he was still breathing. Then Juan decided he'd had more than enough. Making the sign of the cross, he turned and ran out of the warehouse. He hopped into his pickup truck and threw it in gear.

Cliff was hammering Hoffman hard enough to loosen teeth.

Jerry Cooke stood hypnotized by the fierce struggle. He was frozen like a bug under glass, totally conflicted. The character he'd become named Ace was thrilled by the opportunity to see real violence, maybe some actual death.

The ultimate expression of The Method!

Another side of Jerry's identity, one he'd been suppressing ever since he accepted the role, told him this shoot had finally gotten too weird to handle. The line separating fantasy from reality may have been wafer-thin, but it was there.

Finally, Jerry recognized it.

Following Juan's example, he fled out the front door. He almost tripped over the bleeding Shel Meyer, who was struggling to raise himself from the ground.

Emerging outside, Jerry cried out to Juan to wait but the pickup was already barreling out of the driveway. Barely breaking stride, Jerry kept chasing after it and was soon lost within the tall curtains of sawgrass.

Meyer managed to pull himself to his feet by leaning against a work bench. The rock had opened up a large gash behind his left ear. He could feel the blood pouring down the back of his collar. He was dizzy. Remaining vertical was a mammoth task. Taking a cautious step forward, his legs betrayed him and he fell again.

Hoffman and Cliff were on the floor, thrashing and clawing like two bears in a gypsy circus cage. Cliff gained supremacy and wrapped his fingers around Hoffman's throat.

"This is wrong!" he bellowed, pounding the back of Hoffman's head against the concrete. "I tried to tell you this is wrong!"

"Get... off!" Hoffman attempted to yell but could not produce sufficient oxygen to get it out.

Hiding behind a stack of empty crates, Barbara was torn by indecision about what to do.

She saw Jerry run out. She wanted to do the same, without hesitation. Just go.

Then go! her brain cried.

In a delayed reaction, her feet obeyed, one after the other. Her pace quickened after a few steps. She decided she could run all the way back to Miami if necessary.

She stopped halfway to the door, not even noticing Meyer as he tried once more to lift himself from the ground. Even at this distance, it looked clear that Cliff was intent on strangling Hoffman to death. Barbara could see the producer's face as it went dark from the pressure on his throat. His eyes bulged from the sockets.

Gene had been the only person who was straight with her throughout the shoot. He always listened to what she had to say and seemed genuinely interested in protecting her.

If she left him like this, she would never be truly free of *Crimson Orgy*. That certainty hit her hard, and she responded.

Remembering how she'd managed to pacify Cliff when he attacked Vance, Barbara ran back into the light and grabbed his shoulder with both hands.

"Let go, Cliff! Let him *go!*"

Keeping one hand on Hoffman's throat, Cliff swung the other over his shoulder to loosen her grip. The back of his hand struck Barbara like a shovel, squarely in the mouth. It knocked her senseless.

Meyer had crawled within the umbrella of light and saw it happen. He watched Barbara stagger back, seemingly unconscious from the blow yet still on her feet.

Meyer found some tiny untapped reservoir of strength and pulled himself upright.

He lunged at her, trying to catch her fall. Landing on his stomach, he barely grazed the hem of her dress. He felt the fibers of fabric run across his fingertips.

Then felt them disappear as Barbara tumbled away from him, into the Dismemberer.

This is not happening, Meyer's brain signaled in denial of what he was seeing.

The blade caught her between her neck and left shoulder. Her eyes jumped open reflexively. They did not close as the saw took hold.

It's not happening!

A sound that wanted to be a scream escaped Barbara's lips but came out as a gurgle. Tearing into her with horrific dispatch, the blade sent a geyser of blood and bone fragments arcing outward as her subclavian artery was severed like a gossamer thread. Her right hand flailed spasmodically, clutching at air. The machine's centrifugal force pulled her in hard enough to yank both feet off the floor. Her eyes stretched wide with sheer animal panic, seeing nothing.

It's not happening it's not happening it's not happening... Meyer's head was a needle stuck in a groove. *It's not happening...*

The blade dug deeper, opening her up like a huge zipper. Reaching Barbara's ribcage, the base coughed and shuddered in a frenzy. The blood that gushed out grew darker, more glutinous. It looked nothing like the red paint they'd been using all week. Then ropy, glistening bits of viscera started to seep through. Rattling crazily, the machine would not stop.

Already crumbling into catatonia, Meyer crawled behind the Dismemberer, grabbed the power cord and yanked it from the outlet on the generator's side.

The diminishment of the saw's rotation took forever. A churning sound replaced the whine, slowing down to a series of moist *thunk-thunk-thunks*. Barbara's twitching grew more sporadic. She was still by the time it finally creaked to a stop. Her body, cleaved almost to the naval, hung from the blade in two widening pieces.

Meyer lay balled up on the floor behind the saw, clutching his knees to his chest and babbling out the same delusional mantra. "It's not happening it's not happening it's not happening..."

He didn't hear Cliff walk over. Didn't know how long he'd been standing there, but at some point Shel realized a large shadow had fallen over him. He looked up.

Cliff loomed above, a monolith completely drained of the fury that mobilized him just minutes ago. There seemed to be nothing inside him as he looked down at Meyer. No rage, no shock, not even simple surprise.

"I tried to tell you," he said dully.

"It's not happening, Cliff," Meyer said in a voice that didn't belong in a grown man.

"I tried to tell you," Cliff repeated. Then he stepped away.

He walked out of the warehouse. Meyer could vaguely hear him climbing into the van, starting the engine, and peeling out of the driveway.

Slowly dragging himself to his feet, no longer aware of any pain or dizziness, Meyer surveyed the scene. He nodded briskly, running his hands through his hair firmly enough to pull out thick hanks and reminding himself that everything was all right because this wasn't happening. The Mitchell was still purring, running down the final feet in its 800' load.

Good, the camera's still working.

Ricky still lay silently on the floor.

Good, he'll wake up any minute.

Hearing a weak groan, Meyer turned and saw Hoffman roll over on his side. He'd taken a pretty good beating and was barely holding on. The wheezes that came out of his damaged windpipe sounded asthmatic.

Good, there's Gene. He's fine. Everything's fine.

Then, though he didn't want to, Meyer turned to look at Barbara. Her eyes, sightless but still open, stared right at him. He tried to think of something to tell himself but nothing was there. The calming voice of denial just wouldn't come this time.

In its place came a veil of merciful blackness, brought on by the gash in the back of his head and some kind of internal tripwire designed to preserve his unraveling sanity.

Just as Meyer succumbed to a complete shutdown of his faculties, he became aware of a high keening noise splitting his ears, digging in like an electric needle. It was the sound of a thousand souls buried underneath Fairview Cemetery, moaning in eternal unrest... of a young woman struggling for air in a bottomless natural spring, feeling her life slip away one panicked second at a time... of a six-year-old boy trapped in the lap of his dying mother on a bitter cold Illinois evening... of nightmares made real.

In the last split-second before losing touch with consciousness, Shel Meyer realized he finally found that perfect scream he'd been seeking all along. And it was his own.

The camera stopped rolling.

EPILOGUE

From the *Miami Ledger*, page 2
Tuesday, August 10th, 1965

BIZARRE DEATH IN HILLSBORO BEACH; LOCAL OF-
FICERS INJURED IN RELATED ACCIDENT

A woman died in unexplained circumstances at an
abandoned warehouse north of Hillsboro Beach Sunday
night. Barbara Cheston, 22, was killed in what's been
described as a "freak accident" during the production
of a low-budget motion picture. Miss Cheston was pro-
nounced dead at approximately 10:30 P.M. when she
was delivered to the Pompano Beach Emergency Clinic
by Gene Hoffman, later named as the motion picture's
producer.

Doctors declined to describe the cause of death in detail, other than to say that Miss Cheston suffered massive trauma to the neck and upper body. Hoffman was also treated for minor injuries he said were sustained in attempting to prevent the accident that took Miss Cheston's life.

Earlier in the evening, two officers of the Hillsboro Beach Police Department, Deputy Sonny Platt and Lawrence Harrison, were badly hurt in an auto accident less than ten miles from the warehouse. According to Platt, who spoke to reporters from his hospital bed, the officers were on their way to the warehouse to question Hoffman and company about suspected criminal activity related to the production.

Their patrol car was struck by another vehicle while backing out onto Highway A1A in front of the Sand Palace Motel. Officer Harrison was on the side of impact and suffered the most serious injuries, but this morning doctors placed him in stable condition.

In a further bizarre twist, the other vehicle involved in the accident was driven by a member of the same motion picture company, Vance Cogburn. The driver, whose identity was known to Deputy Platt from a traffic stop earlier in the week, was nowhere to be found when an ambulance called by the Sand Palace's manager arrived to extricate the two policemen from their demolished cruiser. A warrant is out for Cogburn's arrest on charges that include hit and run, reckless driving, and endangerment of a peace officer.

It is not known how many people other than Hoffman were present at the time of Miss Cheston's demise. The producer claimed only he and director Sheldon Meyer were on hand at the warehouse, as the other members of the production team had been sent home earlier. Hoffman said he and Meyer were filming the last shot of the movie when the accident occurred.

"It happened so quickly, there was no way to save her," Hoffman said. "She just lost her footing and that was it."

Hoffman had no further comments. It is not known if any charges will be filed in connection with Miss Cheston's death, though both Hoffman and Meyer have been told by investigators to stay in the area should they be needed for further questioning. The two men may still face charges for the alleged misconduct Deputy Platt is investigating...

* * * * * * *

From the *Chicago Tribune*, METRO Section, pg. 3
Monday, August 9th, 1980

SUICIDE IN LAKEVIEW HEIGHTS

The body of a man was discovered in an apartment on the thirteenth floor of the Lakeview Heights apartment building late Sunday night, apparently the victim of a self-inflicted gunshot wound. Police were called to the building after neighbors reported hearing the shot.

The victim, Sheldon Meyer, lay on a rollout bed with the killing instrument, a twelve-gauge shotgun, at his side.

Meyer had been living by himself in Lakeview Heights for over a decade, seldom socializing with neighbors. He worked a number of odd jobs over the past few years, including driving a cab and selling papers at an all-night newsstand.

Meyer achieved some minor notoriety in the world of show business as a film director in the late 1950s. Working in the Miami area along with a handful of other "exploitation" filmmakers, he directed dozens of so-called nature films that featured frontal nudity at a time when censorship prevented such material in mainstream Hollywood productions.

Meyer is best remembered for directing an obscure "lost" film that was never released in theaters but nonetheless garnered an avowed cult following among horror enthusiasts. *Crimson Orgy*, shot in 1965, is famous for the tragedy involved with its production. Barbara Cheston, an unknown actress in the lead role, perished on the final night of shooting in an accident many felt was never fully explained.

Alicia Colver, who lives across the hall from Meyer's apartment, said he never spoke about his moviemaking past and that he grew sullen and even hostile when asked about it. Mrs. Colver's husband, Victor, is a film professor at Northwestern University with an interest in horror movies, who approached Meyer on numerous occasions about speaking to his students. Meyer always declined, and relations between the two men grew strained.

"He didn't want to talk about it," Colver said. "He threatened to knock me out if I asked him again."

Colver noted that Sunday night marked the fifteenth anniversary of Miss Cheston's death...

* * * * * * *

Excerpted from *Cahiers du Splatter*
Ed. Henri Coyne
Vol. XXIII, September 1990, Paris

(Taken from the article, "From Meyer to Romero: Ballets of Blood" by Claude Rouche. Translated from the French.)

We know for certain, based upon an interview he gave to this publication in 1971, that Gene Hoffman was the driving force behind the completion of *Crimson Orgy*, insisting the film be edited despite the events of August 8th, 1965. Sheldon Meyer, who was still in a state of shock, complied, apparently under duress, but the precise length of the cut he delivered is not known.

And this is what vexes students of the film so terribly, because we are unable to definitely ascertain that the 76-minute version first appearing three years ago (which remains the only version available at this point) is in fact the director's cut. Not knowing this, we must content ourselves with what we have, and pray that a longer, or at least cleaner, version comes to light in the future.

It is well known what transpired after Meyer completed his edit. Distraught with grief (and guilt?) over Barbara's death, his mind apparently snapped. Taking the negative and leaving only a few hundred feet of outtakes behind, he disappeared.

Gene Hoffman claimed he explored every possible avenue for locating his runaway director but eventually gave up and moved out to California, where he pursued a career producing softcore porn films before his untimely death by cardiac arrest in 1973. Meyer's suicide in 1980 has, of course, become the stuff of infinite speculation among fans of the film.

So what should we make of the rumor that the "accident" was in fact deliberately manufactured in order to record an actual death on film?

Faced with no definitive evidence, I must draw upon personal experience to reach my conclusion. Having interviewed Hoffman in '71 and finding him to be a most reasonable man, I cannot accept the notion that he would have been involved with such a scheme. In his own words, Miss Cheston's fate was "an unintended accident of criminal proportions." His contrition struck me as genuine.

I should note that, during my interview, Hoffman revealed certain facts off the record he insisted not be printed. I feel a sufficient amount of time has passed, and in light of the fact that the three main participants are deceased, I can now share them with you.

The primary revelation was that, contrary to the statement he gave to investigators at the time, Hoffman and Meyer were *not* the only two people present at the time of Barbara's death. In fact, the entire crew was on hand for the filming of the last shot, though most of them (Hoffman was unclear on the exact number) fled as things began to spiral out of control.

In an attempt to verify this, I personally managed to track down Jerry Cooke at his unlisted number in Miami, but when the intention of my phone call became apparent he hung up and refused to answer my subsequent calls.

Who then was to blame for Barbara Cheston's death?

Hoffman declined to place responsibility on any one person, cryptically saying, "In a sense, the movie killed her." When pressed, he intimated the most liable party was one Clifford Schepps, who had served as Key Grip on all of Stupendous's earlier films.

Schepps allegedly underwent some sort of severe mental collapse during the production of *Crimson Orgy*. Hoffman was reluctant to speculate about the cause, but suggested Schepps was disturbed by the content of the film (truly radical for the era) and that he went so far as to steal and destroy several cans of exposed footage.

When I asked Hoffman why he had not named Schepps in the police report, he said he felt at the time that the simplest way to handle the matter was to treat it as an accident.

"She was already gone," he told me, "and a misguided murder investigation wouldn't do her any good." I suggested perhaps Hoffman himself was the one who would not benefit from such an investigation, at which point he abruptly ended the interview and told me he'd sue if I printed any of the preceding conversation.

Regardless of how it happened, I do not believe Hoffman would have taken the risk of inserting footage of Barbara's death into the film, even if the camera did capture it.

Of course, others hold different opinions. Some even claim to have frozen the tape and dissected it one frame at a time, insisting that several shots clearly show Barbara in the last agonized seconds of her life.

One particularly obsessed fan from Bamberg, Germany, claims to own an eight-track cassette recording in which Meyer and Hoffman are heard plotting the murder. (When asked to produce this mystery recording, the man said his mother threw it away while cleaning out his closet.)

Having watched *Crimson Orgy* no less than seventeen times, I am convinced that what we are seeing in the final scene is *not* the death of Barbara Cheston. When Ace Spade falls back into the saw, it is perversely tempting to assume that contained within those rapid-fire cuts is footage of Barbara's body being severed in two. But one can only arrive at this conclusion by liberal use of the imagination. The pace of the editing is so quick (well ahead of its time) it's almost impossible to say for sure what is taking place, at least from the low-resolution VHS copies currently available.

Should a fresh print ever surface, perhaps more definitive proof will be evident. Nothing I have seen so far changes my feeling that all this adds up to little more than an unsubstantiated urban legend. And yet the speculation continues, only seeming to gain force over time.

Of all the unanswered questions surrounding *Crimson Orgy*, the one I find most fascinating is the fate of Vance Cogburn. His performance indicates a nascent leading man whose career may have enjoyed some mainstream success if circumstances had conspired differently. Cogburn radiates a hip casualness with a tinge of machismo that calls to mind a mix of Dean Martin and Robert Mitchum, with Ricky Nelson's matinee idol looks thrown in. We can only wonder what he may have accomplished working with other directors and material.

What happened to Vance Cogburn? Did he wander away from that terrible auto wreck, fatally wounded, only to die somewhere amidst the acres of sawgrass and leave his corpse to be consumed by indigenous fauna? Or did he hitch a ride back to Miami and pack his bags, returning to his native Kentucky or some other locale where he could hope to put his experiences with Stupendous Pictures behind him?

No one can say, but at Splatterfest VI last month in San Diego (which your author was fortunate enough to attend) Vance Cogburn reared his head after so many years of obscurity, in a manner of speaking.

As the Master of Ceremonies was introducing a midnight screening of a pristine 1/2" tape of *Crimson Orgy* recently found at a garage sale in Denver, he called for silence in the packed auditorium and held up a letter he had received that morning by certified mail. The return address was marked "V. Cogburn" and, underneath, a post office box in New Orleans.

By the time the M.C. had finished reading the letter to a stunned crowd, a pin could be heard to hit the floor in the 300-seat theater. The subsequent screening of the film was rendered even more cathartic in the wake of this bombshell (I can assure you Meyer's masterpiece has never affected me as powerfully as it did that evening).

I have reprinted the letter in its entirety and will allow the reader to determine whether it is authentic, or the work of a mischievous prankster.

To all attendees of
Splatterfest VI:

It has recently come to my attention that the cursed motion
picture of which I was a part for
that hellish week of 1965 has, in
recent years, attained something
of a cult status. Having never seen
Crimson Orgy myself but having a
pretty good idea of how dreadfully
amateurish it must surely appear
(especially to modern audiences)
I can only conclude that the fascination with this movie resides
solely in the tragic events surrounding its production.

While I can understand this kind
of morbid curiosity, the same
which compels motorists to slow
down whenever they see blood on
the road, I must tell you that I am
deeply offended and saddened.
Barbara Cheston's death was not
the stuff of cheap entertainment,
it was real. I attempted to prevent
what happened that night, but
my efforts were in vain and I'm
still paying the price for not acting sooner. I assume you all are
familiar enough with the background events of the movie not
to require further explanation on
this point.

Whatever you may think of me, Barbara's memory deserves than to be poked and prodded like a sideshow oddity. I ask you, out of respect for the dead, *not* to screen the film at your convention or on any other occasion in the future. Don't give *Crimson Orgy* any more life than it already has claimed.

Barbara, Meyer, Hoffman... they're all gone now. Please, let them rest in peace.

Respectfully,
Vance Cogburn

During the wine and cheese party following the screening, much lively debate held sway regarding the authenticity of the letter. One gentleman, a bar owner from San Antonio and self-proclaimed expert on *The Texas Chainsaw Massacre*, dismissed it outright.

I offer his direct quote, as best I can hear it on the miniature cassette with which I secretly recorded the more stimulating conversations of the party:

"Hell, I knew Vance Cogburn. He used to drink in my joint during the summer of '78, when he was living in Texas for a spell... (unintelligible). After a few beers, he'd start telling tales about *Crimson Orgy*. I must have listened to him two dozen times and I can tell you that (unintelligible) would never use fancy language like 'dreadfully amateurish.' That letter's nothing but a hoax from someone with a sick mind."

ACKNOWLEDGMENTS

I owe a debt of gratitude to many people for their contributions to the creation of this book. First and foremost, my father, mother, and brother for their unending support. Thomas Monteleone at Borderlands Press for his vision and leap of faith. My agent Svetlana Katz for her wise and tireless advocacy. And the following people, for reasons too numerous and varied to mention: Dorothy and James Williams, Forrest J. Ackerman, Richard Amadril, Drew Bourneuf, Michael Caulder, Shura Dvorine, Deb Elliot, Roslyn Fleischer, Eric Fulford, Jeff Gilbert, Todd Hallberg, Daniel Peacock, Susan Pettit, Erik Quisling, Maggie Roiphe, Jensen & Andrea Rufe, Mark Schwartz, James Otto Stack, Art Strawbridge, Stu Toben, John Trozak, and Stefanie Vishab.

The background image in the cover artwork is based on an illustration by H.J. Ward for *Spicy Mystery Stories*, V6, #5, March 1938. Cover design and author photo by Le Baron.

Finally, the following books offered valuable assistance in researching the history of exploitation filmmaking:
Splatter Movies: Breaking the Last Taboo of the Screen by John McCarty
Cult Movies, Volumes I, II & III by Danny Peary
RE/SEARCH: Incredibly Strange Films edited by V. Vale and Andrea Juno
Shock Value by John Waters